LEAD POISONING

KEVIN MARKINSON SERIES

BOOK 1

J.E. SEYMOUR

*To Connie
Thanks for your support!
JE Seymour*

BARKING RAIN PRESS

Lead Poisoning (Kevin Markinson Series, Book 1)

Edited by Brenda Morris

Barking Rain Press
PO Box 822674
Vancouver, WA 98682 USA
www.barkingrainpress.org

ISBN Trade Paperback: 1-941295-05-3
ISBN eBook: 1-941295-06-1

Library of Congress Control Number: 2014939102

First Edition: November 2010
Second Edition: June 2014

Printed in the United States of America

9 7 8 1 9 4 1 2 9 5 0 5 2

DEDICATION & ACKNOWLEDGEMENTS

This book is dedicated to John, who has tolerated and supported my writing and has always been my first reader.

There are many, many people who have helped out by reading my work, including members of various live writing groups. To all of you, thank you, most notably to the Salem Mystery Writers Group.

There have also been many online readers who have helped with critique who deserve thanks. Sean McCluskey, Deputy United States Marshal, has been invaluable in his technical assistance. Suzanne R., former DEA agent and online writing buddy, also gets a big thank you. Rae Francoeur was one of the first to read the completed manuscript. To one and all, thank you.

For this second edition, a big thank you to my longsuffering editor, Brenda Morris.

CHAPTER 1

Kevin Markinson liked his routine. Wake up at ten. Stretch out the kinks with some tai chi. Shower, shave, dress. Breakfast at his favorite Whitestone bakery.

"Morning." The black-haired man behind the counter handed over a black coffee and a plain doughnut.

Kevin nodded and paid. He grabbed a copy of the *Wall Street Journal* out of the rack and slid into a booth, facing the front door. Before he settled down with his paper, he opened his wallet to the pictures of his family and studied them. He put it away and scanned the store. The place was empty; it always was at this time of day. That was one of the reasons Kevin came here.

The morning crowd had long since gone to work, and Demetrios Mitropoulos, the owner of the bakery, didn't make lunch. Kevin had been coming here on and off for at least fifteen years. Demetrios's accent had pretty much disappeared through the years, but his hair remained as dark as it was the day Kevin had first wandered in, drawn by the smell of fresh coffee.

Today was Wednesday, which meant that Tony Masiello would be in to pick up the paper bag he came for every week. Two cream puffs on top of a certain amount of cash. Kevin wasn't sure of the amount, but he was sure the cash was there. It wasn't part of his responsibility to make sure that Demetrios paid the money or Tony collected the money, but he watched the transaction every week just the same. Tony knew him. Kevin knew that, but Tony never acknowledged him. Even if he had, Kevin would have ignored him. Kevin didn't want Demetrios to know that he knew what was going on.

Tony had been doing this same thing every Wednesday for as long as Kevin had been coming here. Tony was starting to show his age; he had to be over seventy, and he was slowing down. Kevin wondered why he didn't send somebody else on this errand, somebody younger.

Tony came through the door at eleven. Kevin glanced up from the paper, met his eyes for a moment, and saw something unusual there. He set the paper down to watch the interaction between Tony and Demetrios, wondering what was wrong with Tony. Tony turned away from the counter and met Kevin's gaze again, looking away in a hurry. There were beads of sweat on his face, unusual in the cold weather. Kevin watched as he turned and headed out the door.

Just outside the bakery were two large kids, maybe eighteen, nineteen years old. They were dressed in the popular gangsta style—baggy pants, huge jackets, and bandanas on their heads in a color that Kevin associated with a gang. He had no clue what gang; he was too old and out of the loop to have any knowledge of that sort of nonsense, but something in the back of his mind told him there was a connection there. *Two gang members, hanging around this neighborhood on the day when Tony just happened to be making his rounds? Did they know the old man would be carrying cash?*

Tony stepped away from the kids, Kevin watched them crowd him, and he got to his feet and pulled on his jacket and gloves.

"See ya around," Kevin said to Demetrios.

"Yes, sir," the man responded, craning his neck to look outside as well. The glass windows of the bakery were a bit foggy, but not so much as to block the view. Kevin zipped up his jacket, put on his sunglasses, and closed his right hand on his Colt 1911. Then he shouldered the door open and limped into the chill.

The two teens backed up as though joined at the hip. Kevin could read confusion in their eyes as he glanced from face to face. One kid was white with brown hair peeking out from under his rag, the other Hispanic with rough dreadlocks. The first kid had the paper bag in his hand, and the second kid had something hidden under his jacket.

Kevin saw the flash of a blade and had the Colt out in an instant, backpedaling as he drew the weapon, putting some distance between himself and the knife.

"Drop it."

The kid turned pale so fast that his tanned skin took on a grayish tinge and Kevin thought he might faint. The knife clanged to the ground. The other kid shifted his gaze from Kevin to Tony, hesitated, then turned and ran, still holding the money.

"Jesus, don't fucking shoot me, man."

The boy started to blubber and Kevin thought he was in danger of pissing all over his boots. This kid looked over at Tony, too, confusing Kevin for a moment. *Why were they acting as if they needed Tony's permission?*

Kevin put the safety on and tucked the gun away.

"Go on, get out of here. Don't let me catch you in my neighborhood again."

As the youngster scurried off as fast as his huge, untied shoes allowed, Kevin heard an exhalation of breath and realized he'd forgotten that Tony was even there.

"Thanks, Duke."

Kevin shot him an angry look. "You need to get someone to come with you or get someone else to do this. You could have been killed by those idiots, all for whatever little bit of cash was in that bag with your creampuffs."

Tony was staring at him with his mouth hanging open. Kevin could see the wheels turning in the old man's head and imagine what Tony wanted to say. But he also figured that Tony didn't have the balls to say it. Sure enough, Tony just closed his mouth and turned to his car. Kevin watched him drive off, shook his head, and glanced back at the bakery. Demetrios was staring at him like he'd grown an extra eye. Great.

His hands were shaking, and he shoved them in his pockets. He took deep breaths, wanting a cigarette, but he waited to get to his car first.

He lit a Camel. It wasn't easy, but he got it lit and sat there for a few minutes, breathing smoke.

Kevin parked in the lot down the street from his boss's place of business and picked his way along the icy sidewalk. Glancing up at the abandoned building across the street, he looked for something that would tell him if it was safe here. Nothing to be seen, no reflections off camera lenses, no fogged-up glass where there shouldn't be. He tugged open the heavy metal door marked "Aces Wild Social Club—Private—Members Only" and stepped out of the cold into the warm, smoky darkness.

The first floor had no windows at all, just a few lights along the walls above the small tables. The back of the room featured wooden stools in front of a long, wooden bar. The man behind the bar was polishing it with a soft, white rag, rubbing circles of wax into the surface. He looked up as Kevin came in, but didn't say anything.

Kevin settled himself on a stool. The bartender set a cup of coffee on a coaster in front of him just as Justin Stewart sat down beside him.

"Hey, Boss."

"Is the man up there?" Kevin lifted his chin towards the ceiling.

"Yeah."

"I need to talk to him."

"I'll see what I can do."

Justin came back in five minutes, just as Kevin was draining the last of the coffee from the mug.

"All set."

Kevin ground out the Camel, got to his feet, and followed Justin up the narrow stairs to the second floor.

"Kevin."

Charles got to his feet and came around the desk, right hand extended.

Kevin shook his hand and nodded, then turned to the heavy leather couch. He watched as Charles sat back down behind the desk and smoothed his black hair back into perfection. Then he leaned back into the deep couch cushions.

"What can I do for you?"

"Tony Masiello got himself into trouble today." Kevin relayed the story, emphasizing Tony's inability to deal with the threat.

"You think this is a real problem, or do you think the kids are gone?"

"I don't know. I just think Tony needs somebody watching him or needs to retire somewhere warm."

Charles nodded, rubbing his chin. "I'll look into it. Is there anything else?"

Kevin got to his feet. "No, sir."

Kevin sat at the bar again in front of the TV, which was playing some sort of special news bulletin. Forty-one shots fired at an unarmed man. He got the gist of it, that an African immigrant had been killed by four undercover police officers in the Bronx, and riots were breaking out all over the city. He wondered if it would be a problem out here in Queens. The cops would be on edge, which wouldn't be good for him.

He turned around as the door opened and Tony Masiello stepped into the dark room. The man stood for a moment, unbuttoning his long, wool coat. Tony stopped about three feet in front of Kevin, looking around the room. "You need to learn to mind your own business."

Kevin narrowed his eyes. "Last time I checked, we both worked for the same guy. That makes it my business."

Tony shook his head. "This had nothing to do with you, and now I get a phone call saying the boss wants to see me. Did you run straight to him, tell him what happened?" The old man took a step forward. "What are you, a rat?"

Kevin got off the stool, put his hand on his weapon. "What did you say?"

Tony blanched. "Mind your own fucking business." He turned and headed for the stairs.

Kevin eyed the bartender, who looked at the floor.

When Tony came back down, he left without even looking at Kevin. Close on his heels came Justin.

"He wants to talk to you."

Kevin sat on the couch, looking at a map of Europe that he wasn't sure was there the last time he was here.

"So Tony is a bit angry with you."

"Yes, sir."

"You know he's a made guy."

"Yes, sir." Kevin understood the implication. He could never be a made guy, he wasn't even Italian. Tony had been around a lot longer than he had and was higher in the pecking order, even if he was an old man.

"You need to lay low for a while."

"What?"

"Didn't your wife and kids move somewhere up north? New Hampshire, maybe?"

Kevin didn't have an answer for that. He looked over at Justin, who wouldn't look at him. Brought his attention back to his boss.

"You should go visit them for a while. Okay?" Charles got up and came around the desk. "Take a break, sort of a vacation. Just until Tony cools off. Let me talk to him, figure this out."

Kevin swallowed. "Understood."

CHAPTER 2

Kevin drove up the long driveway, staring at his wife's house for the first time. He was less than impressed with the place. It was a dumpy, ancient, clapboard-sided farmhouse, with white paint fading to gray. The driveway was lined with big old trees and snow piled high on both sides, obscuring the view into woods on the left and a large field on the right. Way too much territory to keep an eye on. Still, he liked that there were no other houses in view, not even any street lamps out here in the middle of nowhere.

The red barn loomed straight ahead as he pulled alongside the house. He looked around for a place to park and pulled to the left, sliding his Jaguar in next to a small Ford he didn't recognize. *Didn't Cindy have a big car, a four-wheel drive SUV?* He could picture a garage here, a place to put his car instead of leaving it out. He'd talk to her about that.

As he stepped out of the vehicle, he was surprised at how cold it was up here. When he'd left the city five hours earlier, it had been maybe thirty-four degrees and raining. In this state it had to be in the teens, but at least the sky was clear. It was after dark but bright with a full moon.

He dragged his old green duffel out of the trunk and headed for the house, his combat boots crunching on the chunks of snow in the driveway. As he stepped up onto the porch, he dropped his cigarette, ground it out, picked up the butt, and reached for the doorknob. It was locked. It surprised him that nobody had come out to greet him; they must have seen the car. He knocked on the heavy wood and bent over to look in through the panes of glass. A heavy-set woman he didn't recognize approached. He had a moment of doubt. Was this the right house? The number on the mailbox matched the address Justin had given him, but suppose this wasn't even the right town?

"Yes?" She raised her voice as she slid the curtains aside, but didn't open the door.

"Yeah. Look, you want to let me in? I'm Cindy's husband." He didn't know what else to say. He tried a smile.

She looked doubtful. "Mrs. Winterling didn't say anything about her husband coming." Her accent revealed small town New Hampshire roots. "She's not here right now." The unspoken message was, "I didn't even know she had a husband," and the suspicious glare reinforced the attitude.

At least this seemed to be the right place. He was pretty sure Winterling was the name Cindy was using now. Kevin was starting to get cold, and he didn't want to spend the night standing on the porch arguing with the housekeeper. He could see the flickering light of a television in another room, and he assumed that would be the boys. "Are the kids here?" The woman frowned and still didn't open the door.

"Why don't you go get them? They know me."

She turned and disappeared into the interior of the house. Kevin stomped his feet, dropped his duffel, and began rubbing his arms. He was cold in his leather jacket and feeling stupid for not calling first. When the woman reappeared, she turned on the porch light. Kevin blinked and looked through the glass again, trying to catch a glimpse of the boys. He could see his younger son Michael now, standing taller than the plump grandmother type. Michael nodded and said something to the woman; she turned a key in the lock and opened the door.

Kevin scooped up his duffel, ducked through the doorway, dropped his bag, and grinned at his son. "God, I thought I was going to freeze to death out there. She's quite the watchdog, this one."

The housekeeper gave him a dirty look and walked away.

"So how are you, Mike?" Kevin pulled off his gloves and reached a hand out to his boy, marveling at his height. Even though he'd seen him less than two months ago, it seemed the kid had grown six inches.

The boy ignored the offered hand. "I'm okay, I guess."

Kevin stuffed his hands into his pockets. "Where's Andy?"

"Watching TV."

"He doesn't know I'm here, right?"

"He knows."

Kevin frowned. He wondered if he should have brought the boys something. That had always worked before. Studying the kid in front of him, he tried to remember how old he was. Michael was born on the tenth of October in 1985. He knew that. What he wasn't sure of was what year this was. It took him a minute to remember it was 1999. The kid was thirteen. What do thirteen-year-old boys like to play with?

"Where's your mother?"

"At work."

He should have thought of that. She'd told him something about working rotating nights. She worked three twelve-hour shifts and got paid like she worked forty hours, full benefits and all. "Look, Michael, where should I put my bag?"

"I don't know."

Michael walked off while he was thinking about it. Kevin called after him. "I'm beat. Where's your mother's bedroom?"

The boy stopped and looked at him. Kevin almost thought the kid was going to make some kind of smart remark, but instead he pointed. "Top of the stairs, take a right, down the hall on the left." Kevin picked up his bag and started that way.

"Dad?"

"Yeah?"

"What happened to your face?"

Kevin let his fingers drift across the fresh scar on his forehead. "Car crash."

"Oh." The boy walked back towards the flickering light of the TV.

Kevin dragged his duffel upstairs into her room and dropped it in the middle of the floor. She'd gotten a new quilt, but it was the same pine headboard he remembered from however many years it had been since he'd last been in her bed. He walked to the windows, parted the curtains, and looked out over the front field. He could see any car coming up the driveway, which was a good thing.

He opened a couple of drawers—all her stuff. He didn't blame her; there wasn't anything of his that she should have kept, except for a few things in the safe. He hadn't found that yet. He opened the closet and studied more of her clothes—green scrubs, simple dresses, her sensible shoes on the floor.

The clock showed nine-thirty in bright red numbers. He could hear doors slamming in the hallway and assumed that was the kids. He thought about walking out to try again with them, but decided it wasn't worth it. He could talk to them tomorrow; use Cindy to run interference. She'd be happy to see him. He paced for another moment, trying to settle. It was cold in the house, nothing like his little apartment back in the city.

He stripped down to his boxers and A-shirt and wiggled his toes on the wood floor. Stepping onto the threadbare rug, he started evaluating muscles and tendons. Closing his eyes for a moment, he tried some tai chi, but he was just way too cold. Central heat seemed to be a foreign idea here. He climbed under the crumpled bedclothes. She'd never been one to bother making the bed. Settled on his side but grabbing her pillow, he curled himself into a ball, and thought about her, breathing in her scent.

CHAPTER 3

It was morning when he saw her; he'd dragged himself out of bed early to be downstairs when she got in. His routine was shot all to hell, but he didn't want the housekeeper telling her he was here. He sorted out the coffee maker, more accustomed to buying his brew ready-made than having to make it himself. He didn't see any doughnuts, and yearned to be back in the city.

Cindy let herself into the kitchen just before eight. He was sitting at the table, nursing a cup of horrible coffee, and smoking a Camel, using a saucer for an ashtray. He stood up as she walked in, and she looked up at him with surprise, then with that look she had—the angry one, the green-eyed glare—reaching into his soul.

"I thought that was your car." She pushed a stray strand of black hair out of her eyes. "Not a lot of seventy-four Jaguars around." Her gaze shifted to the cigarette. "Put that out."

He punched it out.

"Why didn't you tell me you were coming?" She hung her denim barn coat on the back of a chair.

"I wanted to surprise you." That wasn't technically true. He simply hadn't thought of calling first, but he didn't want to tell her that.

"You sure did. How'd you know where to find us?"

"Justin."

"When did you get here?"

"Last night."

"Where did you sleep last night?"

"Your bed."

She frowned. "Have you had breakfast?"

"No, I'm not really hungry."

"A steady diet of coffee and cigarettes will do that to you." She sat down and took off her bright plastic clogs. "Are you clean?"

He settled back into his chair and tried to figure out what she meant.

"I won't let you stay here if you're drinking, you understand that?"

That was what it was about. "I think it's four thousand and seventy-six days now."

"Just making sure." She poured herself a cup of coffee. "You planning on staying?"

"I don't know."

She sat down again, took a sip from the chipped stoneware mug and made a face. "You still working?"

"Sort of."

"Sort of?"

She looked at him, and he looked away, uncomfortable with the scrutiny. He didn't feel ready to jump into this conversation. He'd never told her any details. But he knew she knew more than she let on.

"Well, I'm going to get a bite to eat. You want anything?"

He shook his head.

"You look thin. How much do you weigh?"

"I don't know."

She looked him up and down and frowned. She popped a bagel into the toaster oven, poured herself a glass of orange juice, and sat down.

He took another sip of coffee and shuddered.

"So why are you here?"

"I wanted to be here." To say anything other than that would have been way too complicated. He wasn't sure if he was ready to go into the details with her. Didn't know if he wanted to explain about the mess with Tony and the police shooting and everybody being on edge that had somehow come together to send him up here.

She snorted. "Always thinking of yourself, aren't you?"

He didn't understand this way she had of attacking him when he came back to her. It was like she wanted to let him know up front how much he had hurt her before she could relax and let him know how much she had missed him. He decided to wait it out. He contemplated the cigarette in the saucer. He was trying to quit anyway, but it still bothered him to see the thing squashed there like that. The toaster oven dinged, and he jumped.

She laughed. "You sure you don't want anything to eat?" She carried the toasted bagel over to the table, spread butter on it.

He looked at the food on her plate. "I'll have a bite of yours, if you want."

She handed him half. "Have you seen the boys?"

He shook his head. "Not this morning."

She glanced at her watch. "They're probably still asleep. Did you see them last night?"

"Yes."

"So they know you're here?"

"Yep."

She opened her mouth to speak, and then closed it again as the housekeeper stepped into the room. Kevin jumped to his feet, nearly knocking over the chair.

"Good morning Mrs. Winterling," the lady said, not looking at Kevin.

"Morning, Mrs. O'Brien. I'm sorry if my husband disturbed you last night."

"No, ma'am, he didn't disturb me, I just wasn't expecting anyone. I'm afraid I left him standing on the porch for a bit." She was looking down at the coat in her arms.

"Well, it serves him right, showing up without calling." Cindy smiled. "This is Kevin, by the way. Kevin, Mrs. O'Brien."

Mrs. O'Brien cast a glance at Kevin, looking more at his chest than his face. He tried a smile. She continued. "If it's all right with you, ma'am, I'll be getting home now. Will you be needing me tonight?" She fiddled with the clasp on her pocketbook.

Cindy looked at her husband. "Kevin, how long are you going to be here?"

"I don't know."

"Well, I guess you'd better come then, just in case he decides to take off this afternoon."

"Yes, ma'am. Six-fifteen?"

"Yes. Thank you."

"Yes, ma'am." Mrs. O'Brien slipped into her coat and headed out.

Kevin flopped back into the chair, took another bite of bagel. "I can watch the kids."

"No, you can't. They hardly know you. I think they'd be more comfortable with her here. Besides, that way if you get it into your head to take off, I won't have to worry about them."

"How much does she cost?"

Cindy frowned at him. "I can afford it. She doesn't make as much as I do."

"I've got a little money. I could help you out."

"I don't want your money, Kevin."

"You don't seem to mind living in my house."

"This house wasn't paid for in blood."

"My blood, Cindy, this house was paid for with my blood." It was his turn to glare at her. He didn't think he needed to remind her that the money for this place came from a lawsuit over his getting beat up by a cop.

She rolled her eyes. "You want me to move out?"

"No. It's your house." He picked up the cigarette, got to his feet again. "I need a smoke."

"When are you going to quit?"

"Quit what?" He wasn't sure what she was referring to. Maybe the cigarettes, maybe his job.

"Anything."

"I don't know." He headed out onto the porch without thinking about the temperature. He was wearing a sleeveless undershirt and a pair of jeans, no shoes. The cold hit him like a sledgehammer to his chest, and he sucked in his breath. The sun was reflecting off the snow, sparkling like a million tiny jewels. He shaded his eyes, wishing he had his sunglasses, and then lit the cigarette as fast as possible. He only managed to smoke half of what was left before giving up and heading back inside. She was gone when he got in. Gone upstairs to sleep, he figured.

He glanced at his watch. Eight-thirty. He climbed the back stairs this time, just off the kitchen. He still hadn't figured out where the safe would be. He passed the boys' rooms and came to one last room at the end of the hall. This room was largely empty, a couch on one wall, a large oak desk with a computer, and a rolling office chair. He found a small closet, and that was where his safe was. He opened it without even thinking of the combination, it was just one of those things etched in his brain. There were more papers in here than he remembered. He glanced through the stuff—his discharge papers, his birth certificate, her important papers, the kids' birth certificates, both the real ones and the fakes. Extra copies of everything. It was okay; she was doing a good job. The last thing he checked was a packet he had requested from Justin a few years ago, a passport and other important papers in a new name—one he had never used. Justin had done a good job getting this stuff. Justin always did a good job. He tucked everything back in the safe and closed it.

He limped down the front stairs and into the living room. It was spacious, with windows on three sides, a fireplace, the same wide board floors and some comfortable furniture. She'd never been one to collect antiques. He prowled around, taking in the pictures on the walls, noting that there were only two with him in them—

e and an old photo of him in his dress blues. God, he must have
t one. No wait, seventeen. He narrowed his eyes for a second,
d almost remember when it was taken, his uniform stiff, his
:e set in that frown, that tough guy look. Why did she have
tter yet, where in hell did she get that picture? She didn't even
ybe he had given it to her, although he didn't recall doing it.

n the photo, he looked for something to take his mind off it.
ve grown up all of a sudden, but looking at the pictures on the
tages he had missed. It surprised him how much Andy looked
air, the cold blue eyes. Michael looked more like his mother,

came back down, Kevin had examined nearly every inch
't wanted to go outside again, but other than that he'd seen
tic. He was impressed now. This place would do.

CHAPTER 4

Kevin spent much of Saturday spread out on the couch, dozing. The kids appeared at one point, but when they saw him, they turned and left. It didn't matter; he wouldn't have known what to say to them anyway. It was like living with foreigners. Or space aliens.

She found him there. He was on his feet before she spoke. "How about some lunch?"

"Sure." He chewed on a ham sandwich, not noticing the taste. Washed it down with a glass of milk.

She was silent, as well, and he wondered if she was going to talk to him at all. "What happened to your face?"

"Car crash."

She took that with just a nod. "You bring any weapons with you?"

"Couple."

"They locked up?"

"No. One's in the trunk of my car, the other's in my jacket pocket."

"Where's your jacket?"

"In the hall closet."

"So you're telling me you left an unattended gun in this house?"

He could hear the anger in her voice. He'd already made a mistake. He started to get up. "I'll go get it."

"I'll make up your bed while you're doing that."

He stopped. "What are you talking about?"

"I'm not ready to sleep with you."

"What the hell does that mean?"

She sighed, looking past him now, staring at the doorway leading to the front hall. "I've been seeing a therapist. She thinks I need to assert myself more, that I need to have more control in this relationship."

"Relationship?" In all the time they'd been married, he'd never heard her use that word to describe their union.

"You've put me through a lot, you know. It's hard waiting to hear from you or having you pop in when I don't expect you. I feel like I have to jump every time you snap your fingers. I mean, look at last summer. I barely had time to settle in, and you dragged me into bed."

"You were a willing participant in that." He brought his left hand up to his face, scratching at the stubble. "Besides, we're married, for chrissake. Don't you want to sleep with me?"

"I hardly know you anymore."

A thought stuck in his brain. "You're not sleeping with someone else, are you?"

"No." She snorted. "I'm just not sure I'm ready to go to bed with you right away. Besides, there's the other thing."

"What other thing?"

"Your job. You told me last summer you were going to stay put in prison. You promised. You had us move up here, let us get settled, and then you break out and show up. Working again."

"That was the last one, I swear. I'm really out of it." He was walking now, wanting a cigarette but settling for pacing to work off the nerves.

"Then why the guns?" She was twisting her wedding ring on her finger.

"I have to be able to protect myself; you've got to give me that much."

"I don't think I can handle it anymore, Kevin." She cleared her throat. "Kayla thinks it's affecting my whole life, the kids, too."

He stopped in his tracks. "You told your therapist what I do for a living?"

"Yes." She paused. "Sort of."

"Good God." He sat down hard, the gun forgotten. "Why don't you just call the fucking FBI while you're at it?"

"Watch your language."

"Watch my language? Who are you kidding?"

She got to her feet. "I'll go fix you a bed in the spare room."

He watched her back as she walked away—watched her draw herself up taller. He felt at sea, as if the room was spinning. He sat there for a moment, his brain refusing to function. He was tired, but his first instinct was to grab his gear and get back in the car and just go. He rehearsed it in his brain then, getting it to work, and picking up steam as he considered his options. Grab the new paperwork from the safe and go somewhere. Leave her for good this time; quit messing up her life. Maybe that was what she wanted. Let her get out of this relationship thing.

He headed upstairs, got his bag from the bedroom, and crossed the hallway into the office. He was opening the safe when she came in. He gave her a quick look, and then reached in for his new passport.

"What, you're leaving already?" She had her hands on her hips. "Running again?" Kevin didn't pause, just kept putting the things into his duffel. "I'm sorry I was so hard on you." Her voice was softer now.

"It was stupid of me to come here. You were right." He stood up. "I shouldn't be bothering you, messing up your life. You've settled in here, the kids seem to be thriving. What I've seen of them anyway. There's no room for me."

"Kevin, you've been here, what, eighteen hours?" She walked across the room. "You've got to give it a chance."

He looked at her, confused again. *What was with her?* A few minutes ago she was ready to throw him out. Now she was asking him to stay. Everything was upside down. His whole life was a mess, and this was just one more aspect of it he had screwed up. Then, looking in her eyes, losing himself in those green pools, he hesitated. He dropped the bag and shrugged his shoulders, letting his eyes drift away from hers. "I'll give it some time, okay?"

She nodded. "That's all any of us need."

She cooked supper for him, spaghetti with her special sauce. He sat at the wooden table, close to the woodstove, soaking in the heat. He watched her cook, thinking about how many times he had watched her do this over the last, what, twenty-four years? He couldn't be that old. He remembered what had drawn him to her in the first place—the green eyes, her shape, her spunk. He got up and limped to her side, slipped an arm around her waist, which was still narrow after two kids. She poked him in the ribs with her elbow, laughing. "Come on, I'm working here."

He stepped back, landing wrong on his weak left leg. He managed to grab the counter to keep from falling, but she was staring at him.

"You okay?"

Stabbing pains were running up and down his leg. "I'm fine," he hissed through gritted teeth.

"Sit." He scooted back to the chair and sat. She put down her wooden spoon and crossed the room, knelt beside him, and wrapped her hands around his knee. He closed his eyes for a moment. It wasn't just the pain; it was her touch that burned. She made him melt, made him want to follow her to the ends of the earth. "Tell me about it," she said.

He had to swallow before he could speak. "Tore some ligaments in a car accident, couple weeks ago."

"Same one you mentioned earlier?"

"Yeah."

"Did you get any treatment for that?"

"Had a cast on it for a bit. Asked the doc to take it off; too hard to get around in it."

"Did he give you a brace or anything?"

"Yeah, he gave me this bulky sort of thing to wear for a few weeks."

"So how come you're not wearing it?"

"I can't bend my fu... uh, my leg with it on."

"There's a reason for that."

"Yeah, well, it makes it difficult to drive. That's my clutch foot."

She shook her head. "Why don't you just use a different car? Get rid of that old sports car."

"Why don't I just hire a freaking driver? I don't want to be an invalid."

"If you don't let it heal, you'll be an invalid a lot longer." She sighed and stood up again. "Why did you have a cast on it at all?"

"I told you, I got into a car accident. The doctor who treated me in the emergency room thought the cast was a good idea, because I had some torn ligaments and old damage to that leg already."

"Emergency room?" Cindy turned back to the stove. "How'd you get into a car crash?" Her voice had changed; it almost sounded as though she was worried about him.

Maybe she did still care. He needed her to. "I can't talk about that."

"You could at least use a cane."

Andy stepped into the room and snorted. "That'll be the day."

Cindy turned. "Oh, hi, Andy. Where've you been?"

"Out."

"Out where?"

"With Brandon."

"You know how I feel about him."

"Come on, Mom, it's not like I have a million friends up here." He glanced at his father, took a couple of steps away from him. "It's so freaking easy to make new friends in high school." He rolled his eyes.

His mother frowned. "So you couldn't have called?"

"It was a last minute thing. And you won't buy me a cell phone."

"You don't need a cell phone. Brandon doesn't have a phone in his house?"

"I didn't think of it. God. Why don't you back off?" Andy stormed out of the room.

Kevin watched the interaction between them without speaking, knowing better than to jump in where he wasn't wanted. Cindy slammed the saucepot hard on the stove, and then braced her hands on the counter, eyes squeezed shut.

"You all right?"

"You don't know how hard this is, raising two teenage boys by myself." Her eyes were still shut; she was talking to the counter.

"You want my help?"

"Yes." She straightened up and turned to look at him. "I guess."

He nodded. "I could stay, if you want." He said it without thinking about the consequences, without thinking about what it meant to stay here.

They all ate together, the kids doing their silent act again. It wasn't easy to sit with them. He found it hard to eat, but he smiled and nibbled whenever Cindy looked his way.

"Did you hear about that shooting in the Bronx?"

Kevin looked at Michael, not sure if the question was directed at him. "Yeah."

"Why'd they do that? Shoot the guy forty-one times like that?"

"It's what they do."

"Kevin." Cindy's voice was sharp.

Andy snickered.

Kevin put down his fork. "They thought he had a gun, so they shot him."

"He ran," she responded.

"He ran because he didn't understand what they were shouting at him."

"That wasn't a smart move," Cindy said. "He should have stood there, given up."

"Why would he stand there and give up? He didn't do anything. He didn't know they were cops. This sort of thing happens all the time. The pigs usually plant a weapon on the guy to make it look legit. I guess they didn't get a chance with this one."

Cindy glared. "For Pete's sake, why would you say something like that?"

He lifted his eyes. "You think it's not true?"

"I don't care whether you think it's true or not, you don't need to be talking like that in front of the kids. You think they need to learn your attitude? Seriously, Kevin—pigs?"

He looked at the boys. Andy had a sneer planted on his face and met his gaze. Michael was looking at his plate, pushing a meatball around with a piece of bread.

Kevin wasn't willing to let it go. "They carry extra guns—throw guns—so they can get away with it. Cops are all the same, all bullies. You remember that cop that tried to kill me? It was only because there was a witness that I'm alive to talk about it."

Cindy's mouth was working as if she didn't know where to start. Finally she just shook her head. "Most police officers are perfectly nice people who want to keep the streets safe. I hope you kids know that. Your father is just paranoid."

Kevin couldn't resist one last dig. "It's not paranoid if they really *are* out to get you."

They ate in silence for a few minutes. Then Cindy tried to change the subject. "So Andy, why are you finding it hard to make friends up here?"

Andy just shook his head.

"How about you, Michael? Are you having a hard time up here?"

Michael nodded. "The horses help."

"Yeah, with the girls," snorted Andy.

Michael glared at him. "At least I'm not hanging out with druggies."

"What the hell are you talking about?" growled Andy.

"Andy," said Cindy.

"Sorry, Mom," he muttered. He fished into the pocket of his baggy jeans and dropped a quarter into the jar in the middle of the table.

Kevin raised an eyebrow.

Cindy glared at him. "Don't you start," she growled.

"What?"

CHAPTER 5

He watched her leave for work, and tried to deal with the kids again. They still avoided him, disappearing into their rooms. He sat on the couch in the living room and thought about where he could be instead of here, what he could be doing, about money he was losing just by being here. Regardless of what he had told her, he wasn't sure he could stay. He wasn't sure he wanted to stay. Was all of this worth it?

He considered calling his boss, but didn't want to do it from this house. He glanced at his watch. Only seven-thirty, which meant a long wait. Too early to go to bed. No point in that anyway. He couldn't sleep. It was just too quiet here. He wandered back into the kitchen and sat at the table. Mrs. O'Brien paused in loading the dishwasher.

He nodded at her, tried another smile. "How long have you been working here?"

She turned to look at him, then back to the sink. "Since last September."

"You like it?"

"It helps pay the bills. My husband is retired."

"He doesn't mind you spending the night out here three days a week?"

She shook her head.

"Did Cindy tell you anything about me?"

"No, sir."

"You never wondered why she didn't mention a husband?"

"No, sir. I know how to mind my own business."

"Would it bother you if I stepped out for a bit?"

"No, sir."

"Do you want to give me a key?"

"The missus didn't give you one?"

"No."

She wiped her hands and walked over to a wooden key rack by the door and studied the keys. He got up.

"These are the keys? Hanging right here by the door?" He studied the glass panes. It would be a piece of cake to smash the glass, reach through, grab the keys, and unlock the double cylinder deadbolt. It made him nervous. He turned and headed back into the hallway to check the front door. This door was solid with just a small pane of glass high up. It had a regular deadbolt, which seemed sturdy enough. Maybe security wasn't as bad as he thought.

By the time he walked back into the kitchen, she had selected the keys for him. He went and found his jacket. The weight in the pocket reminded him that he still hadn't resolved the gun issue with Cindy. She was right, of course. He couldn't leave the weapon unattended around the kids. They were old enough to know better, but that didn't mean they wouldn't pick it up, handle it, and have it go off accidentally. It had happened before. She had nearly killed him after that episode. It had been the determining factor in her throwing him out for good. Until now.

Mrs. O'Brien glanced over at him just as he removed the big Colt .45 semiautomatic from the coat pocket and tucked it into the small of his back. He saw the look flicker through her gray eyes—saw her jaw go slack. He gave her a half-grin, and she turned away.

He sighed, shaking his head as he zipped up the leather bomber jacket and let himself out the kitchen door, locking it behind him. He walked well out into the driveway, dug out his cell phone, and made the call, dialing the number from memory.

"Manny, get somebody to call me back from an outside line." He hung up and waited, stomping his feet, jumping up and down, and smoking two Camels. It was twenty minutes before it rang.

"Hey, Boss."

"Hey, Justin. How's it going down there?"

"Tony's cooling off."

"Think I could come back?"

"Maybe."

"You got anything for me?"

"I don't know. I know he wants to talk to you. Can you be here Monday at noon?"

"Yeah."

"Oh, hey, Kevin?"

He hesitated. Justin never called him Kevin. "What?"

"Your mother died. I'm sorry."

It wasn't unexpected, but it still hit him like a punch to the stomach. "Thanks for letting me know."

"The funeral's Monday."

"I don't think I can do that." That would be way too complicated. The funeral could be watched by any one of the number of law enforcement agencies that were looking for him.

"Sure, I understand. Take care of yourself."

He hung up and stared at the phone for a minute, trying to avoid thinking of his mother. A sharp crack broke the silence, and he jumped, almost reaching for his gun. When he figured out it was just a tree branch, it struck him that it was cold. His fingers felt like they were going to fall off, despite the gloves. He glanced down at his feet to make sure they were still there.

When he let himself back into the kitchen, Michael was sitting at the table with a piece of pie on a plate. He looked up, then around, scanning for a way to escape. He finally settled back on the pie, stabbing the next piece.

Kevin took off his jacket, set it on the back of a chair, and sat down close to the wood stove. He fished out his package of cigarettes and lit one, then bent over to take off his shoes with the Camel clenched between his teeth.

Michael leaned over to watch as he peeled off his socks. The toes were white. Kevin saw the boy's eyebrows go up.

"You've nearly got frostbite there," the boy observed.

"They're a bit cold," Kevin agreed.

"You been outside for a while?"

"Yeah."

"You know how cold it is out there?"

"I know it's pretty fu... uh, cold."

"It was ten degrees the last time I checked."

"No kidding." Kevin was holding one foot, then the other, trying to warm them with his hands.

"Don't get them too close to the stove. You don't want to warm them up too fast." The boy had finished his pie.

Kevin was surprised he was still hanging around. He thought it might be worth trying to talk to the kid. "You ever get that horse you wanted?"

"Yeah. We bought him last week. We're keeping him over at my trainer's place until spring. She has an indoor riding arena." The boy looked down at the floor, then up to meet his father's eyes. "Thanks for buying him."

"No big deal." His feet were starting to feel as if knives were stabbing into them. "Damn."

"Told you not to warm them too quick." The boy stood up and put his plate in the sink, then headed up the back stairs. Kevin watched him go, wondering how a boy who had been raised in the city knew so much about cold. He got his feet to the point where he could feel them again and stood up with a quick glance at his watch. Nine o'clock. Close enough. He put out the cigarette in a pool of water in the sink, dropped it in the trash, then wandered down the hall until he found the guest bedroom, and stripped to his shorts and A-shirt. No point in even trying the tai chi, he was too cold.

His thoughts ran to his mother and his family. His father had been dead for years, his older brother before that, now his mother. It made him think of Cindy and the boys, the reason he was here in this cold house in the middle of nowhere. There were no tears, he was beyond that, but he lay awake under a pile of blankets for most of the night.

In the morning he sat with Cindy at the table in the kitchen again, allowing her to make him a bagel of his own this time. He shifted in his chair, trying to become comfortable with the 1911 stuck in the waistband at the small of his back. His solution so far to the gun problem was to carry it.

Cindy slathered butter on his bagel and set it in front of him. He picked it up and took a small bite, then put it down again.

"So what's up with you?" she asked.

"My mother died."

Her jaw dropped. "When?"

"Yesterday."

"Oh, Kevin, I'm so sorry."

He shrugged and concentrated on his coffee.

"Did I ever tell you I met her?"

He lifted his eyes. "No."

"I can't even remember when it was, maybe after the whole thing with Carlos. After you were..." her voice trailed off. "She came to the hospital." Cindy closed her eyes. "She seemed so much older than I thought she would be, I remember that."

"She had a rough life."

"She brought me a picture of you—the one on the wall in the living room—in the dress blues." Cindy sighed. "She sat with me for a while, just watching you breathe. I remember she said it looked like you weren't going to breathe. They still had you on a respirator, and nobody knew if you were ever going to come out of it."

Kevin looked at her. She was staring down at the table now, playing with a piece of fruit from the wooden bowl. "I never saw her again. I don't know whether she just lost track of me, with all the moving we did, or if it was too much for her, seeing you like that. It would have to be hard, seeing somebody you love so close to dying." She brushed a tear from her cheek.

"I'm sorry."

She looked up. "I know you are." She stood up, her breakfast untouched. "I just wish you'd really try to change."

"It's been a while since I've done anything quite that stupid."

"Oh, and last summer was what... brilliant?"

"It wasn't meant to work out that way."

"That's the problem, isn't it? That it never works out the way you expect it to." Her voice was rising.

He took out his cigarettes and tapped one out of the pack.

"Don't you light that in here."

He nodded. "I won't."

"You were smoking in here last night, weren't you?"

"Kids rat me out?"

"I can smell it, Kevin. You think I'm stupid?"

He shrugged.

"I need to get some sleep."

He watched her go, forced down another bite of bagel, and then stood up just as Mrs. O'Brien walked into the kitchen.

"Oh. Is, uh, your, uh, is Mrs. Winterling here?"

He looked towards the hall where Cindy had disappeared. "She just went upstairs. I can go get her, if you want."

"It's okay, I'll, uh, call her or something."

"No, hang on. I'm sure she wants to talk to you." He walked to the stairs and hollered up. "Cindy?"

She came down, hands on her hips. "What do you want now?"

He inclined his head at the housekeeper standing in the kitchen, staring at the floor.

Her voice softened. "Oh, Mrs. O'Brien. I'm so sorry. It's been a rough morning, that's all. Here, let me pay you." She hurried to the closet, grabbed her bag, and came back to the kitchen as Kevin walked out onto the porch.

He smoked the cigarette, listening to the murmured conversation, which he couldn't make out but seemed to be heated, at least on Cindy's end. Mrs. O'Brien came out as he was grinding the butt of the cigarette under his heel. He nodded at her, but she scurried past him without saying a word.

When he stepped back into the house, Cindy turned on him. "What did you do to that woman?"

"What?"

"She tried to quit. I can't afford to lose her. What did you do?"

"I didn't do anything."

"She thinks you're some kind of monster. She said you had a gun out last night and that you were asking her all sorts of questions. I don't know what she's thinking, but Kevin, I need that woman. How could you screw this up for me?"

"I guess I wasn't thinking, I just wanted to put the piece in a safer place."

"Damn right you weren't thinking. You can't do this to me, Kevin. I've made a good life here; I had this all worked out." She was shouting now.

He backed up a step, raised his hands. "Look, I'm sorry, okay? If she quits, I'll help you find someone else."

"You're going to find someone else? One of your goon friends, for instance?" She shook her head. "That's rich." She turned and stomped out of the room again. He followed her to the bottom of the stairs, watched her stomp all the way up, and heard her bedroom door slam.

CHAPTER 6

Kevin felt a bit lost, headed back to the kitchen, and found the boys fixing themselves bowls of cereal. "Hi, boys."

Michael nodded and set to eating. Andy fell on his cereal like he hadn't had food in days and didn't respond to his father's greeting at all. Kevin pulled out a heavy maple chair and sat at the table, close to the wood stove, rubbing his hands together.

"That your Jaguar in the driveway?" Michael asked.

"Yeah."

"It's cool."

"I've had it a while."

Michael nodded. Andy got to his feet and dropped his bowl in the sink with a crash. He yanked open the refrigerator door and took out a carton of orange juice. He opened it and drank straight from the carton, then put it back. He wiped his mouth on the back of his forearm and burped.

Kevin narrowed his eyes. Andy was wearing a long-sleeved thermal shirt and a pair of blue jeans that seemed two sizes too big. They were hanging low on his narrow hips, exposing polka dot boxer shorts. His stringy blond hair was too long, obscuring his eyes.

"How long are you going to be here?" Andy asked.

"I don't know."

"Between jobs?" Andy looked straight at his father.

"I'm cutting back."

Andy snorted. "How'd the last one go?"

Kevin lowered his eyebrows in a deeper frown.

"I heard it was a real mess."

"Where'd you hear that?"

Andy shrugged, hiked up his jeans, and left the room, thumping up the stairs.

"You know what he's talking about, Michael?"

Michael shook his head, placed his bowl in the sink, and walked out as well.

Cindy came back down at lunchtime, and they all sat together in the kitchen, eating tomato soup out of a can.

"I can start driving in ten days," said Andy.

Kevin lifted his head. "Really?"

Cindy nodded. "Really, fifteen and a half."

"That's cool. Have you practiced at all yet?"

"I've driven Mom's car down the driveway."

"That's an automatic, right?"

"Yeah."

"Mine's a stick." Kevin glanced out the window. "Hey. You ever think of putting in a garage?"

Cindy turned her head. "I never thought about it, no."

"Someplace to keep the cars out of the weather, you know?"

She shrugged. Michael and Andy both got up and put their bowls in the sink, headed out to the living room, and in a matter of minutes were absorbed in something that was making a lot of noise.

"I could pay for it. The garage."

"I guess."

———

He broke the news in the morning. "I've got to go back to the city today."

She nodded. "You working again?"

"Not really."

She stared at him. "What does that mean?"

"I'm not working on a job, not like I used to. I have to go down there to do something for my boss."

"Like what, Kevin? We all know what you're good at."

He shrugged his shoulders.

"So are you going to explain? I mean, to me, you're either working for him or you're not. You can't be sort of working, or not really working. It's like being a little pregnant. You either are or you aren't. What are you going to do, filing?"

"Filing?"

"A joke, Kevin."

"Ah, a joke." He sighed. "I'm not doing what I used to do. I told you that. No more. But I do have an obligation to this man. He's kept me going, given me jobs my whole life; I can't just walk away. If he needs me to do something for him, I have to do it."

"Regardless of what it does to your family?"

"I can come back next weekend."

"You're going to commute?"

"Why not?"

"Okay, whatever. I guess we'll see you when you get back." She stood and walked out. He could see the anger in the way she moved. It surprised him that he knew her so well after being gone for so long. He stood in the kitchen for a minute, baffled, then headed into the guestroom, gathered his stuff, and prepared to leave.

It was a five-hour drive to the Whitestone neighborhood where his boss was doing business. That gave him time to think about the whole family thing. He had to figure out a way to keep her happy and keep his boss happy at the same time. Work, make enough money to keep the family afloat, and make sure the boss was okay with him splitting his time. Commuting. That was going to be a long drive to make every weekend, but it was worth it. He was sure of that. Almost.

———

"Hey, Boss."

"How you doing, Justin?" Kevin lit a cigarette.

"Good."

"You have any idea what he wants?"

"Nope."

"He ask for me?"

"Well, you are late."

"I drove down from New Hampshire this morning. Seriously underestimated the traffic issues."

"You probably ought to head on up."

Kevin nodded, picked up his coffee, and followed Justin up the narrow stairs to the second floor. When he walked into the office, he turned to the heavy leather couch. There were three big guys sitting there, practically clones of each other. Kevin didn't recognize any of them, but he was willing to bet they were all made guys, and as such they were all higher in the pecking order than he was. He found an empty wooden chair in the far corner of the room. Sitting in the leather chair closer to Charles's desk was Tony Masiello. He turned and stared at Kevin, then returned his attention to Charles.

"We were just discussing Tony's problem with you." Charles raised a manicured hand and waved it towards Kevin. Kevin nodded. "Tony says you interfered with his business. You embarrassed him."

Kevin sipped at his coffee and said nothing.

Tony shifted in his chair. "I'm a made guy." He cleared his throat as though he was going to spit. "You're nothing but the hired help. Not even Italian."

One of the guys on the couch spoke up. "I think he's Irish or something, aren't you, Duke?"

Kevin let his gaze drift in that direction, ignoring the old nickname. "I was born in Brooklyn, not Ireland." One of the other guys on the couch said something crude in Italian about Kevin's mother and the other two laughed. Tony cracked a smile.

"The Dodgers were still there when you were born, right?" This came from the guy on the far end of the couch. He had black hair combed over a balding scalp and plastered in place with gel.

Kevin eyed him. "They left when I was five."

The three men all laughed again, but Tony shifted his attention back to Charles without a smile. "You need to do something about this."

"Duke is the best at what he does." The smile on Charles's face looked stuck, as if he had nothing keeping it there except muscle memory.

"There are plenty of other guys out there who can do what he does," Tony waved his hand at the three guys on the couch, "without attracting the attention he attracts."

Kevin shifted in his chair. His coffee cup was empty, and he didn't have any place to put it down. Charles looked at him. "What kind of attention?" Kevin knew Charles was worried about the Feds. Charles didn't like any kind of extra attention.

Tony leaned forward in his chair as though he had a secret to share with Charles. "You know he's wanted, right?"

Charles smiled. "He's been running from one thing or another for most of the thirty years I've known him. It's never been an issue."

"You don't think the cops will come here if they know he's here?"

"How are they going to know he's here?"

"Somebody sees him. Somebody calls the cops."

Kevin heard something in Tony's voice that worried him. He needed to cut this idea off at the knees. "Somebody disappears."

Charles cleared his throat. "That's enough of that." He leaned back in his chair, squeezing a rubber ball.

———

Sally Barnard was sitting in her cubicle, staring at the computer screen in front of her, trying to figure out how to check her email. Twenty years she'd been doing this job, and she was considering quitting to avoid having to learn this.

Thomas Neelon leaned in. "Hey, Sally."

She looked up at him. "Hey, Tom. Can you help me with this?"

"What's the trouble?" He sat down and sorted out the issue in what seemed to her a matter of seconds. "Other than the email, how are things going?"

She shrugged. "I'm doing court security next week. I hate that."

"I'm sure Dan will rotate you back into the fugitive work as soon as he can."

"He said he would." Sally clicked a button and the fugitive page on the Marshals Service website came up. "Look, he's on the main page again."

Thomas raised his eyebrows. "Your dead dog case?"

"He's out there somewhere; you know that."

"I know. Keep spreading the word. He's hard to miss, all six foot four of him."

She nodded. "He'll make a mistake. They all do. Have you talked to anyone in the Eastern District? That's where his boss is, right? Out in Queens?"

"Alleged boss. Yeah. Eastern District knows to keep an eye out. But come on, their plates are just as full as ours. Nobody cares about some ancient mobsters running bookies and loan sharking. It's all about drugs now."

"And Marconi has always been careful to avoid the drug business."

"Right."

Sally closed the website. "I'm not sure there's even anybody watching him at this point. Markinson could be there right now, and we'd never know."

"If I see him, I'll let you know."

She laughed. "Thanks."

———

Tony got to his feet and took the three guys on the couch with him as he left the room. Charles turned to Kevin.

"You're late."

"Yeah. Traffic."

"Let's go for a walk."

Kevin followed his boss out the back door. Charles wouldn't have a conversation that involved any sort of actual business inside his office. Instead, every time he needed to talk in any serious way, he insisted on going outside. They walked in circles in the parking lot with Manny leaning against the side of the building, watching.

"This thing with Tony is going to be a problem," Charles began. "Can you explain to me what you think is going on?"

"I haven't got a clue," Kevin said.

"He's talking about calling the cops. You know I have a certain amount of protection from that, but not when it gets to the Federal level."

"How the hell is Tony going to talk to the cops? He's a known associate. He goes to the cops, why would they trust him? Why would *he* trust *them*? How can he talk to them? He was calling me a fucking rat. You think he can just walk into the Federal building and start talking?"

"Do you?"

Kevin sighed and put his hands in his pockets. He was getting cold out here. "That'd be like *me* walking into the Federal building."

"Tony isn't wanted for anything."

There wasn't any point in arguing with Charles. Kevin glanced over at Manny, the big bodyguard working hard at holding up the building. "Tony starts talking to the cops, he's dead."

"You can't do that."

"You'd take his side?"

"He's family," Charles said with a shrug.

"And I'm not."

"Maybe you need to stay away for a while."

Kevin nodded. "I get it."

CHAPTER 7

Michael overheard his mother on the phone. "I guess we'll see you when you get here. Right. Bye." She turned. "Oh, Michael. I didn't see you there."

"Who was on the phone?"

"Your father. He'll be home tonight."

"Oh great. What, are we going to be one big happy family again?"

"Michael."

"Does he think he can just pop in and out whenever he feels like it?" Michael had a sudden flash of memories, of seeing his father at fast food places, or in hotels, a tall man bearing gifts. The man had never lived with them, not that he could remember. Although he did have some dim pictures that involved yelling that he was pretty sure had happened in some sort of home. "Why is he coming here again?"

"He wants to see us."

"Maybe I don't want to see him."

"This is his house, Michael. He has a right to be here, a right to see his family."

"Yeah, I forgot about that. He paid for all this, didn't he?" He paused to take a breath. "He can't do this; it's not fair."

Michael spent the night awake, watching for the headlights he knew would be coming up the driveway. He wasn't sure it would really happen, wasn't sure his father would show up. There'd been enough times when he was a kid, when his mother would tell them they were going to see their father, and he wouldn't come. He closed his eyes and tried to sleep. His eyes popped open again and he wondered if his dad would look different this time. It seemed like forever since he had seen him, even though it was only a few weeks. He almost found himself missing his father. He shook his head and rolled over, burying his face in the pillow, trying to avoid the expectations, trying to stay low. Trying not to care.

When Michael came downstairs the next morning, he spotted the little red car in the driveway. He looked around the doorway into the kitchen, checking to see if his father was there. No sign of him. He walked into the kitchen, grabbed a glass out of the cupboard, and filled it with milk. As he sat down he heard footsteps and almost got up to head out the back door, but it was only Andy.

"How's it going?"

"Okay." Andy pushed his long blond hair out of his eyes. He was wearing an A-shirt and baggy pants, nothing else, except polka dot boxer shorts that stuck out at the waist of his pants.

Michael spoke first. "Have you seen him yet?"

"No. Have you?"

"No. Do you know when he got here?"

"I think it was about two. I thought I heard voices then. Do you want to see him?"

"No."

Andy shrugged his shoulders.

They both turned as footsteps approached. Their father walked into the kitchen, ducking his head as he came through the doorway. He was wearing blue jeans and a sleeveless undershirt, no shoes. Michael realized that his older brother was almost the spitting image of his dad and that they dressed alike. That disturbed him. He had to blink and resisted rubbing his eyes.

"Morning."

Michael studied his father for a minute. His hair was blond again. It used to be long, in a ponytail, but his dad had cut it short last summer and kept it that way. He had cut it so short that it was nearly shaved. Michael remembered that it had been brown last summer and gray this January. He'd never really allowed himself to think about those sorts of things. Like why his father was always looking different, why he would disappear and reappear whenever he felt like it. He remembered the people at the house last summer, the Feds looking for him, and figured it was all connected.

The man glanced over his shoulder as Cindy came in behind him.

Neither boy spoke. Their mother set her jaw. Michael looked down at the table.

"Hi," he muttered, and then kicked Andy under the table.

His brother glared at him and said "Hi," without looking at his father.

His father opened the refrigerator, poured himself a glass of juice, and sat down. He took a pack of unfiltered Camels out of his back pocket, put them on the table, and started to take one out. Michael looked at his mom, and almost laughed when he realized that she was giving his father the same angry stare she had just used on him.

"What?"

"You are not smoking in this house," she said.

Andy snickered. Michael stared at him, panic rising in his throat. Some of his earliest memories involved his father exploding at his mother. He didn't want that now.

His father got to his feet, picked up the cigarettes, and walked outside, ducking his head as he went through the door. Michael looked at his mom, then got up and left the room.

Kevin was growing accustomed to living in the guestroom every weekend, even though he wasn't happy about it. He was trying to understand what was going on in Cindy's head. She was angry when he came back. Now she didn't want to let him back into her heart, and he didn't really blame her. But he still thought it was worth trying to save the marriage. Otherwise, where would he go? Picturing life without her was impossible; she'd just been there too long. He didn't want to give up on her, didn't want to give up on the kids. He wanted to try to make this work, refused to have the same regrets he had with his mother.

"You know how I feel about your work, Kevin."

"What does that have to do with how you feel about me?"

"I need to stand up for what I believe in. I think what you're doing with your life is wrong."

"Why'd you marry me in the first place, then?"

"I didn't know then. You know that. Besides, I've changed, grown up a lot since then."

"You know I told you I'm not doing what I used to do." He wouldn't come out and say it, he never had. He didn't really know if she knew what he did for a living. He could lie to anyone about anything, but it was hard to lie to her.

"But you're still with the same old people."

"You want me to cut off contact with my friends? Sever the only ties I have to any chance of making a living?"

"If you had any conscience at all, you would have done that a long time ago." She was polishing the dining room table. She wouldn't look at him; she never did when she was arguing with him. He thought it was because she was afraid of him. He knew he had been hard on her when they were first married. He had yelled way too much when he was drunk, thrown things, and threatened her. He'd never hit her;

he could be proud of that much. At least he hadn't followed in his father's footsteps there.

"Cindy," he tried.

"Why are you even here? Screwing up our lives?" She stopped polishing and glared at him, then started rubbing the table with new fury.

"You think that's all I'm doing? Screwing up your life?"

She shook her head, and he knew she didn't mean it, didn't mean any of it. But why was she so contrary? He pushed his chair back from the table as she reached the place where he was sitting.

"How's your leg?" She still wasn't looking at him.

"It's better."

"You look better than you did last January."

He shrugged.

"You're not drinking, are you?"

"No, I'm not."

"Jack Daniel's was your poison, wasn't it? I remember the trash can in our apartment overflowing with empty Jack Daniel's bottles." She stopped rubbing the table. "I was surprised. I had known you for so long, but I never knew until I lived with you how much you really drank."

"You should have seen how much I drank when I wasn't living with you. After you threw me out. After Andy..."

She sat down next to him. "Are your guns locked up?"

"Yes, ma'am."

"I do know how much you drank then. I talked to Justin and Charles almost every day. It was the three of us that conspired to get you into treatment." She looked down at the table. "You know how close you came to dying?"

He looked out the window, avoiding her. "I guess. When I was having blackouts and seizures."

"You had seizures?"

He shrugged.

"You never told anybody about that. Or the blackouts."

"Who would I tell? You threw me out." He fixed her with a steady gaze.

She stared right back at him. "You're not making this my fault, Kevin. You're responsible for your own behavior."

"Ancient history. Anyway. I'm back, and I'm clean." He paused, trying to sound softer. "I missed you."

She looked into his eyes; he could feel the green orbs penetrating his soul. She owned him. Always had. She smiled. "You're devious. You know that?"

He grinned at her and kissed her on the cheek. She blushed.

"I've got to get back to cleaning." She got to her feet.

He watched her go, wondering why, after all these years, she was still the only woman he lusted after. It had been too long, he thought as he got to his feet and pulled at the pants that were suddenly too tight in the crotch. Way too long.

CHAPTER 8

He found the place to keep his guns; it was under the back stairs. The windowless room was lined with shelves, complete with a locking china cupboard—a perfect place to hide the silverware and his guns. The key had long since disappeared, but that problem could be solved with a hasp and padlock. He removed most of the shelves to create a space tall enough for his long guns. He left a few shelves for ammo and handguns and installed a dehumidifier in the pantry.

"Whatcha doing in here?" Andy asked him, standing in the doorway, watching.

Kevin looked around. "Putting in a gun safe, sort of."

"Gun safe?"

"Yeah."

"How many guns do you have?"

"A few."

Andy nodded and walked off, shuffling in untied shoes.

Kevin was just putting the finishing touches on it when Cindy walked in.

"Andy told me you were building a gun safe in here."

"Yep."

"How many guns are you going to keep here?"

"All of them."

"So how many is that, Kevin?"

He didn't want to look at her. "Guess I'd have a shotgun, a long gun, a couple of handguns." He paused to think about it. "Don't know for sure."

"Do you have to have them?"

"Yeah, I do. I'm not going to feel safe here without them."

"Way out here in the middle of nowhere?"

He met her eyes now. "Yeah."

"Are they going to find you here?"

"I hope not."

"So do I. I wouldn't want what happened in the Bronx to happen here." She turned away.

He'd been coming home for months before he was able to sit with her, just the two of them. He considered it a good sign that she came looking for him after she cleaned up the dinner dishes. He'd given her a card at dinner just to let her know he hadn't forgotten that it was twenty-four years now, that this was the day he'd married her.

He was in the living room, staring out the big windows that overlooked the front field. She came and settled down next to him on the couch.

"Hey," she opened.

"Hey."

"Kids are out of the house for a while."

"Yeah."

"Good chance to talk."

Why did she always want to talk? "Yeah." He continued to stare out at the fresh snow glistening in the moonlight.

"It's pretty, isn't it?"

"Yeah."

"Poor man's fertilizer."

"What?"

"Snow this late in the year, it's called poor man's fertilizer. It won't last."

"Oh."

"Do you think about me when you're away?"

"Course I do." That wasn't entirely true; he often had to avoid thinking of her. It hurt too much when he knew he couldn't see her.

"I miss you sometimes."

He thought she said that as though she didn't want to miss him. He slid a little closer to her on the couch.

"You're a hard man to get along with, you know that?"

He didn't want to be sucked into an argument, so he nodded. He didn't care if she wanted to criticize him all the time, as long as she didn't throw him out.

"Do you still love me?"

"Yep."

"Say it."

"I love you." He didn't look at her.

She sighed and slid closer to him, leaned her head on his arm.

He flinched, and she sat up.

"What?"

"Nothing, it's okay." He shifted, reached for her, trying to put his left arm around her so she wouldn't lean on it.

She intercepted his arm and ran her fingers over it. "Does this hurt?"

He shook his head. "It just hurt when you leaned on it, you know, there." He gestured with his head, as she pushed the sleeve of his shirt up, looking at the divot in his arm, the scar that was still less than a year old, still sore.

"You ought to have seen a doctor."

"Cindy." He left the rest unsaid. He didn't want her to start bugging him.

She ran her fingers over the scar, and he flinched again, but not in pain. He lifted his arm and put it around her shoulders. She snuggled into his chest.

"So how did it get this way, this bad?"

He cleared his throat, suddenly hoarse. "I don't know. I guess it was infected. It was a real mess."

"What'd you do it for?"

"Do what?"

"Break out."

"When?"

She touched his arm again. "Start with last summer."

"Work."

"How about January?"

"Same thing."

"How long you think you'll be out this time?"

"Don't know."

"Is that why you came here, to work?"

He lied to her. "I told you. I'm not doing that anymore."

"Don't you want to turn yourself in, play it safe?"

"Good God, Cindy. What the hell are you thinking?"

"I'm thinking that if they come after you here, it won't be pretty." Her voice was quiet, and she was still stroking his arm. "I'm thinking of that poor man down in the Bronx, that Diallo guy, who didn't even have a gun on him."

He was confused again. She was turning him on, she was being sexual, but she was ragging him. "Ain't gonna happen. Nobody's going to find me here."

"How can you be so sure?" She took a deep breath. "Do you know what it would do to the kids to have that sort of thing go on here?"

"What sort of thing?"

"Police standoff..." She stopped.

"I know how to behave anyway, if they do find me."

"Do you?"

"Of course I do." He knew the routine, keep your hands where the pigs can see them, don't make any sudden moves, and always be polite. Whatever the hell you do, don't run.

He pulled her closer and let the silence settle on them again, breathing her scent, feeling her warm against his chest. Then he dug a jeweler's box out of the pocket of his jeans and handed it to her.

"What's this?"

"Open it."

She pried the box open. "Kevin."

"I know you don't wear a lot of jewelry, but maybe on special occasions."

She held the ring up. "It's beautiful."

"Those are the boys' birthstones."

She slipped it onto her finger and hugged him. "This is so sweet. I can't believe you remembered." She paused. "I didn't get you anything."

"That's okay." He settled back into the couch, staring out at the full moon reflecting off the April snow.

"Do you want to go upstairs?" Her voice was so quiet he almost didn't hear it.

"You inviting me to your bed?"

"Yes."

He allowed her to take his hand and lead him, his anger forgotten.

He hadn't even been in this room since that first night, the night he'd come home and she hadn't been here. He shut the door behind them, slid the bar home to lock it, then just stood and stared at her. She was standing by the bed, looking at him and then at the floor.

"It's been a while," he tried. His voice was raspy, and he cleared his throat.

"Come over here," she said, and sat on the bed, motioned for him to sit. "Kevin," she began.

He covered her mouth with his, not letting her finish.

———

He slipped into his jeans and searched for his cigarettes. She pulled on her clothes as well and followed him as he made his way down the stairs in the dark. He found his Camels in the guestroom, picked up the pack, and headed for the porch. She followed him out there too, surprising him. He stood in his bare feet in the cold and sucked the smoke into his lungs, with an arm around his best girl.

"You need to quit smoking." She at least waited until they were back inside before she said it.

He looked up from the couch, where he was studying the pack, trying to figure out how it got so light, he hadn't been smoking that much lately. "I know."

He perked up and got to his feet when a car came in the driveway, came to a stop in front of the house.

"It's okay, it's Michael," she said.

He stayed in the living room, in the dark, while she went to the kitchen. He could barely hear her asking the kid if he'd had a good time, and he couldn't hear Michael's response at all. Then heard the thumping on the back stairs that meant his youngest son was off to bed. He glanced at his watch. Ten o'clock. Michael was a good kid, knew enough to come in under curfew. Andy, on the other hand... that kid was going to be trouble. He looked up as Cindy came back in, silhouetted against the light.

"Where's Andy?"

"They weren't at the same party. Andy's not due till eleven."

Kevin considered telling her about the cigarette shortage, but decided to wait until he had a better idea of what was going on. She sat next to him on the couch and leaned into him. She fell asleep while he waited for the boy, luxuriating in her scent.

He moved her aside without waking her up when he saw the car coming up the driveway. Glanced at his watch as he got to his feet. Forty-five minutes late. He wasn't sure he had the right to bawl the kid out, though. He reached the door just as Andy was turning a key in the lock and stepped back as the youngster came in.

Andy almost fell over backwards. "What are you doing here?"

"I live here."

"Yeah, but isn't it late?" Andy looked at the clock.

"You're late. Right." Kevin leaned past him to lock the door, sniffing, checking for booze or cigarettes. "I need to talk to you."

"Look, I'm sorry I'm late."

"Not about that. About my cigarettes."

The expression on the kid's face changed. "You won't tell Mom, will you?"

"Tell Mom what? You're late, young man," Cindy said, entering the room, rubbing her eyes.

Andy slipped past his father and headed for the back stairs. "Sorry, I'm going to bed."

She watched him go, frowning, then turned to look at Kevin, who shrugged. Kevin headed for the front stairs, not wanting to bring up the cigarettes. He wondered how the boy could be so stupid as to expect him not to notice. But if he mentioned it to her, he knew where the blame would land. She never brought any cigarettes into this house. It was his fault.

He climbed the stairs with Cindy, fell into her bed and slept better than he had in years.

CHAPTER 9

Kevin was up early the next morning, coming down the stairs to find both boys sitting in the kitchen. They looked at him and then at each other. Kevin frowned.

"What's been happening to my smokes?"

Andy paled. "How would I know?"

"Cigarettes aren't cheap, you know. You owe me money."

"I didn't take them."

"The hell you didn't. You owe me money."

Kevin glanced at Michael, who made a point of looking out the window.

"All right. I owe you money." Andy nodded. "I just took a couple to try."

Kevin started to say something about the health risks of smoking when Cindy walked into the room. He bit his lip, gave the boy one last glare, and headed for the refrigerator to scout out some breakfast.

"I'll fix something. What do you boys want?" She smiled.

Andy and Michael stared at each other as though this was something their mother had never suggested before. Kevin backed away as she pulled the door open.

"How about eggs? You like eggs, right, Kevin?"

"Sure." He retreated to the table and sat beside Michael, who scooted his chair over as though he was afraid to sit too close.

Cindy began humming as she took a dozen eggs out of the refrigerator and grabbed a fry pan off the rack. The three guys looked at each other.

Kevin set up an informal range in the woods in an old sandpit off one of the trails that ran through the property. The walls made a good backstop, and it was far from any road. He'd retrieved his long gun from the storage shed in Concord where it had been for the last few months, spent some time getting it back into shape, and took it out to sight it in. He was wearing his usual gear, a Mets cap pulled low over mirrored shooting glasses, topped with a set of shooting muffs. After loading his rifle with five rounds of boat-tailed .308, he glanced downrange at his target, a sheet of plywood with a paper bull's-eye stapled to it. He'd thrown some sandbags on the ground here at the firing line, three hundred yards away. He had more space if he needed it, but this would do for now.

He lowered himself to the ground, feeling the creaking in every joint. He laid the stock of the Remington 700 on the sandbags, stretched out flat on his belly, and pulled the butt into his right shoulder. Wrapping the strap around his right arm and tugging the rifle in tighter, he sighted down the scope. He lined the crosshairs up on the center of the bull's-eye, and then raised the rifle a bit so the cross was above the center of the target. Then he waited for a few seconds, testing the crosswind. There was none to speak of on this late June day. The bugs were annoying, but he ignored them, driving everything else out of his mind.

Calculating the drop over three hundred yards and lowering the crosshairs just a tad, he slowed his breathing. He couldn't hear anything now; his brain was buzzing with the tension of the shot. There was nothing else in the world but that target and this rifle. He took a breath, let it out, squeezed the one and a half pounds out of the trigger, felt the recoil, and caught a glimpse of a sudden movement out of the corner of his eye. He was on his feet in a split second, letting the rifle point to the ground without dropping it. Yanking off the earmuffs, he looked around for whatever it was he had seen. He spotted a girl of about twelve in the middle of the trail, on a bicycle, of all things. Only she wasn't on the bicycle; she was on the ground next to it, looking up at him.

"What are you doing?" He reached down to help her up.

"I... I don't know."

"This is private property; it's posted." The last thing he needed was to shoot somebody by accident, never mind her telling people about the kooky old man in the woods with a gun.

"I'm sorry; I guess I didn't see the signs. I used to ride through here all the time." She had to crane her neck to look up at him.

That was logical. Cindy had only been here since last fall. The land hadn't even been posted for a year yet. "Don't let it happen again, okay?" He forced himself to sound less gruff as he slung the strap of the rifle over his shoulder. "Do you live near here?" He picked up her bicycle.

She nodded. "I'll go now." She got back on the bike and started to go back the way she had come.

"Go ahead through." He pointed in the opposite direction.

"Thank you." She pedaled along the path, and then glanced back as he stood cradling the rifle. He saw fear in those eyes and tried a half smile. She turned away and rode off.

He sighed and walked down to check the target. Not bad. He adjusted the scope to allow for the drop, let himself back down on the ground, lined the crosshairs up on the center of the target this time, and put four more shots into the middle. It was easy, all mechanical, all science. Anybody could do it; it just took a little practice. He grinned as he packed the rifle back into its case and walked back to the house.

Michael rode out of the woods onto the road and almost ran into a girl on a bicycle.

She stopped. "Is that your horse?"

"Yes." He sent Hammy into a walk along the side of the road.

"Are you going to Ridge Hill Farm?"

"Yes, I have a lesson today."

"I just started working there."

"Oh, yeah?" He looked down at her. "I work there, too. My name's Michael."

"I'm Jen. Haven't I seen you around at school? You're new, right?"

Michael nodded. "Yeah."

"Nice horse. What's his name?"

"Hammy."

"Do you live near here?"

"That trail I just came out of is on my parents' land."

"Really? I think I met your dad by accident, day before yesterday."

He gathered up the reins, angry. "I have to get going, or I'll be late for my lesson. I'll see you later." He pushed Hammy into a trot and glanced back to see Jen watching him.

CHAPTER 10

A couple of Sundays after the end of the school year, as Kevin was putting his duffel bag into his car, Andy approached. His father nodded at him. "Hey."

"Hey." The boy concentrated on the ground, running the toe of his black canvas high-tops back and forth. He looked up. "Can I come with you?"

"To the city?"

"Yeah. I miss it. I won't get in the way, I promise. Maybe I can hang out with Vinnie. Or Justin."

"Your mother say it was okay?"

"I haven't asked." Andy looked at the ground again.

"She won't like it. She'll think I can't keep an eye on you, or I won't feed you, or whatever." He glanced up at the house, scratched his nose, and said, "Okay, let's go ask."

"You mean it?"

"Yeah." The man started towards the house, long legs covering ground easily, despite the limp. Andy trotted to keep up.

She eyed them both. "How are you going to watch him while you're working?"

"Justin can help. Besides, he can hang out with Vinnie."

"Please, Mom. I haven't been down to the city since we moved. I'll call some of my old friends. It'll be cool."

She sighed. "All right. You'll keep an eye on him?"

"Absolutely."

"Okay."

Andy grinned like his face would split. "Thanks, Mom."

Kevin pointed upstairs. "Go and get your stuff packed; I'll wait for you."

When Andy came back out he walked up to the car. "Can I drive?"

Kevin stopped short. "Drive my car?"

"Yeah."

"You ever drive a stick?"

"Yeah. My friend Brandon, he's a year older than me, he's got a stick shift, he lets me drive it."

"On the road?" Andy just looked at the ground. "You have a learner's permit?"

"Don't need one. I just have to drive with an adult."

"Your friend Brandon isn't over eighteen, is he?"

"No."

"You at least stick to back roads with him?"

Andy raised his head and nodded with a grin.

"Okay, but just a little, all right?"

"Great. I've always loved this car." He tossed his backpack in and went around to the driver's side. "What year is it?"

"Nineteen seventy-four." Kevin settled into the passenger seat and fastened his seat belt. "Look, first is here; reverse is here. It's a four-speed; you see the others? Give it a try."

Andy turned the key and the little car lurched forward with the grinding of the starter.

Kevin closed his eyes and brought his left hand up to rub his forehead. "Clutch."

"Right. Sorry. Brandon's car doesn't do that."

"Clutch interlock was invented some time after this car was built."

The youngster managed to make it to the end of the driveway, and set out on the road, with a few jerks and mis-starts. Kevin let him take it on the highway and buried his face in his hands again as the boy punched the accelerator and the little car leapt forward.

"Andy, back off on the gas, okay?"

"Whoa, Brandon's car doesn't do that."

"This car has a twelve-cylinder engine. It's bigger than the engine in your mother's SUV. Try to keep it under sixty-five, okay?"

Andy eased up on the pedal, brought the vehicle down to a more reasonable speed. "This is so cool."

Kevin nodded and fiddled with the radio, settling on NPR. He stared out the side of the car, watching the trees flash by, thinking about how nice this was, driving with his kid.

"I love this car, Dad."

"Yeah, look, pull into that rest area, okay?"

"Why, we going to the liquor store?"

"No."

"Aww, come on Dad, let me drive it a little longer."

"No." Kevin got out of the car and motioned the boy over. He settled back in the driver's seat, buckled his seat belt and took it out on the highway again. "So what do you think of it?"

"It's a nice car, Dad. Thanks for letting me drive." He paused. "How fast does it go?"

"Pretty fast." Kevin glanced in the rear view mirror. "I've heard they'll do a hundred forty-five."

"You ever open it up?"

"That would be against the law." He pressed the accelerator, just a little, and the car responded the way he knew it would. He grinned.

Andy sat up straighter.

Kevin glanced at him and pressed it forward just a little further, watching the needle creep up. He moved into the left lane. He was having a good time with his kid, enjoying this, letting the car run like he hadn't done in years.

All the good feelings disappeared when he saw the blue lights in the rear view mirror. He brought the car back to the right lane, then the breakdown lane, letting it come to a stop. He leaned past Andy and pulled the registration out of the glove box, fishing his license out of his wallet. Andy slunk down in the seat.

Kevin put his hands on the steering wheel, at the prescribed positions of ten o'clock and two o'clock, registration and license in his left hand. He took deep breaths, forcing himself to stay calm, with one eye on the side mirror. He faced front, waiting, trying not to think about the weapon in the small of his back.

The trooper stepped up, but stayed back, wanting to throw Kevin off, and force him to turn. Kevin wasn't playing that game.

"You know why I stopped you, sir?"

"No, officer." Kevin was watching him in the mirror, refusing to twist around to see the cop.

"You were going pretty fast." The young man cleared his throat. "License and registration, please."

Kevin took his left hand off the steering wheel and handed over the paper and license.

"Is this your correct address, Mr. Williams?"

"Yes, sir." The address was an apartment in one of the buildings Charles Marconi owned but not the apartment Kevin actually lived in.

The cop disappeared back into his cruiser. Kevin let his eyes slide sideways. "You okay?"

"Yeah." Andy sat up and craned around in the seat. "You gonna get in trouble?"

"Probably."

"And you're just gonna sit there and take it?"

"That's what you do, Andy. You sit and take it. Think about it. What would happen if I took off right now? He's got my license and my registration. How hard do you think it would be for him to find me?"

"You can outrun him."

"Sure, until they set up a roadblock."

"They'd do that for a speeding ticket?"

"Not for a speeding ticket but for taking off. You see what I'm saying? If I take the speeding ticket, if I behave now, there won't be any consequences."

The boy turned around. "I get it."

The young cop came back up to the same spot, where the door pillar would have been in any other vehicle.

"Here you go, sir." He handed over the license and registration. "You were doing ninety in a sixty-five zone. That's more than twenty over the limit, so I'm not allowed to let you off with a warning." He almost sounded apologetic as he handed over a citation. "Instructions are on the back."

"Yes, sir."

"Take it easy, okay?"

"Yes, officer, I'll do that."

Kevin glanced at the boy now and then as they continued to drive south on Route 3, then 495. He wasn't sure when he had gotten so old, so big. Andy was staring to the side, listening to some awful music he had chosen on the radio.

"You want to get some money out for me, Andy?" Kevin handed the boy his wallet as they slowed for a tollbooth on the Mass Pike.

"Sure." The boy handed him some cash. "What's this picture?"

Kevin glanced over. "That's you and Mike and your mom. Like twelve years ago, maybe."

"You keep this in your wallet?"

"Yeah."

Andy stared at the picture for another minute. "Can I take some walking around money for the city?"

"Sure, help yourself."

Andy rifled through the bills. "How much can I take?"

"Why don't you take a couple hundred? That should do for the week, right?"

"Uh, sure."

"It's been a while since we've had a chance to be together like this, right?"

The boy snorted. "Try never."

Kevin lit a cigarette, inhaled the smoke, and blew it out. "You ever seen my apartment?"

"Nope."

"Nothing special, really, just a place to be."

"Can I have a cigarette?"

"No."

"So why are you going to the city this time?"

"I've got something to do."

"What is it you do anyway?"

Kevin reached over and switched off the radio. "What?"

"What do you do?"

"You tell me. What was it you came up with last winter, hammer?"

"Is that what you do?"

"Do you really want to know?" Kevin kept his eyes on the road, avoiding his son's gaze.

"That's what Vinnie Marconi says you do. He says you're a hit man."

Kevin snorted. "I think he's been watching too many movies." He looked at the boy. "Do you believe him?"

"I don't know. I mean, you've always got a gun on you, and you've got so much money, and you've got that look."

"What look?"

"I don't know. It's just a look." Andy cleared his throat. "Like you think you own the world; like you're not afraid of anything. Like nothing can touch you. I used to think you were so cool."

"And you don't any more?"

Andy sighed. "You're turning into just another square. You know what I mean? Coming down on me like Mom does."

"I talked her into letting you come down to the city with me."

"Yeah."

"So isn't that a good thing?"

Andy reached over and turned the radio on again.

When they reached the apartment Kevin hauled his duffel bag upstairs. Andy followed, dangling his backpack by one strap. "Where should I put my stuff?"

"You can sleep in here on the couch. I think I've got an extra blanket."

Andy sniffed, curling his lip. "You smoke in here a lot?"

"Yeah. What do you want for dinner?"

"What do you have?" Andy walked into the kitchen and opened the fridge. "Ew. How old is this milk?" He held the plastic container up to the light. "I think it's got lumps in it."

"Check the date." Kevin picked up the phone. "Chinese okay with you?"

"Sure. Just make sure you get something to drink." He paused. "I'll have a beer."

"Funny guy," his father responded. "Yeah, oh sorry, no, not you, I want some food delivered."

When he hung up the phone he looked at his son sprawled on the couch and wondered what he was going to do with the kid for a week.

The boy seemed to pick up on what his father was thinking. "So what the hell am I supposed to do anyway?"

"You're the one who wanted to come."

"You mind if I hang with my old friends from school?"

"Maybe. I figured tomorrow you could come with me and see what Vinnie's up to."

"I guess." Andy shrugged.

"All I ask is that I don't have to come down to a police station and bail you out, okay?"

The boy laughed.

Kevin took the boy out for breakfast the next morning at the bakery. Andy had three doughnuts and a large glass of milk. Kevin had his usual. Demetrios Mitro-poulos wouldn't let him pay for it, hadn't let him pay for anything since that time Kevin had bailed Tony out of trouble. He wasn't quite sure why, but he didn't force his money on the man.

"This your boy?"

"Yeah. Andy, meet Mr. Mitropoulos."

Andy stuck out his hand like a grown-up, surprising his father again.

"Nice kid."

Kevin nodded. "Thanks."

As they left the bakery Kevin lit a Camel.

"How long have you been smoking?" Andy asked as he climbed into the little car.

Kevin stepped into the driver's side as he pulled his old Mets cap down on his head. "Thirty-something years. I'd quit if I could. Been trying to quit for about a year now."

"Why'd you start in the first place?"

He started the car and glanced over at his son. "It just seemed like the thing to do. I was sixteen, invincible, trying to be cool."

"So why can't I do it?"

"Your mother would kill me."

"You're afraid of her?"

"I respect her opinion. Big difference. Besides, she's right on the money with this one. You don't want to start smoking. Bad for your teeth, bad for your lungs, all that."

"See, now that's what I was talking about. You sound like Mom."

Kevin snorted. "I never expected to sound like a parent at all."

"You say all this square stuff, like this is bad for you, but then you go and do it yourself."

"I told you I'm trying to quit. I told you I wish I had never started."

"It doesn't bother your health."

"Sure it does. I get sick." He paused. "You won't tell your mother this."

"Sure."

"I've had pneumonia twice in the last year and a half. It's the smoking that does it. I also haven't got the wind I had back when I didn't smoke."

"What do I care about wind?"

"Don't you play any sports?"

"Not in any serious way."

"You should, you know. Discipline would be good for you. Plus it'll help you get into college."

"I don't want to go to college."

"Why the hell not?"

"You didn't go to college, and look at you. You drive a fancy car, live in a big house, we have everything we need."

"Who says I didn't go to college?"

"Well, did you?"

"No, but that's beside the point. My life hasn't been all roses, you know. I worked hard, pouring concrete, doing grunt work. I wish I had gone to college. But you, you're young, you can make a decent life for yourself."

Andy just shook his head.

"Besides, didn't you tell me last winter that you didn't want to be like me?"

"Who says I'm going to be like you?"

"All this talk of not going to college, wanting to smoke, talking about my fancy car. Sounds to me like you're looking to be like me."

"Nah. I wouldn't want to go to jail like you."

"God, I hope not."

Andy cleared his throat. "What's it like?"

"What?"

"Jail."

Kevin swallowed. "You ever have nightmares?"

"Once in a while."

"Take your worst nightmare and multiply it by about fifty. There's people in there that ought to be in mental hospitals. You know, nut cases, that'd scare you so much you'd be crying inside of twenty minutes."

"How old were you, the first time you went to jail?"

"I was in a holding pen when I was sixteen. Scared to death, and that wasn't even prison. Went from there to a group home. Didn't do any real time until I was twenty-one, and that was minimum security." He turned to look at his son. "You want to hear all this?"

"Yeah, sure."

"I guess I was thirty-something before I went to medium. A year after that, maximum. That's where it got scary, but I was old enough to deal with it. Plus I had a rep."

"So what did you do when you were sixteen?"

"Stole a car. I was a little drunk." He laughed. "Okay, I was a lot drunk. It was a cop's car—his personal car, a little red Mustang. I was just joyriding, but with it belonging to a cop and all, they figured I needed to learn a lesson. Threw me in the tank with a group of bigger guys. I was scared out of my mind. Then my old man came and told them to keep me. He wouldn't let them release me into his custody."

"Why?"

Kevin sighed. "You have to understand, Andy, my old man was difficult. I don't think he liked what he saw in me. He thought he was a straight arrow. You know... like you said, a square. He was a disabled veteran, working as a security guard to keep his family fed." He rubbed his nose.

"So when he saw you in jail for stealing a car, he must have flipped."

"Yeah. He did."

"So you didn't get along with your dad? Big deal. Your dad was a square, and you're a square. I guess you'd expect him to get mad when you ended up in jail."

"Yeah, I guess you would. Except that he was a jerk who should have been in jail himself."

"Why?"

"He beat up my mother."

"So he was a hypocrite."

Kevin paused. "I guess."

"Know anybody else like that?"

Kevin glanced at his boy, then back at the street in front of the car.

Andy continued. "So your dad was this straight arrow, square guy, who beats up his wife and, let me guess, the kids, too."

"What makes you think that?"

"I know you. You think you're some sort of hero, you must have stood in the way."

His father nodded. "I did."

"You don't know anybody like that?"

"No."

"Maybe somebody who breaks rules but expects everybody else to follow them?"

Kevin got it then. "I told you, my life isn't exactly roses."

"So what? You're getting by okay. You can do whatever you want."

"No, I can't. I'm lucky to be walking around."

Andy didn't have a response for that.

CHAPTER 11

When Kevin pulled the car into the lot in Whitestone, Andy spoke up again. "What are we here for?"

"This is where I work."

"No way. Isn't the house down in Bayside?"

"We don't go there anymore. Too much heat." He got out of the car and walked over to the attendant. Andy followed. Kevin handed the pimply-faced kid sitting in the booth a twenty-dollar bill. "Watch my car." He started down the sidewalk with Andy trotting to keep up.

"That's not much money for the whole day. How can you be sure the kid will take care of your car?"

"He knows me."

"So?"

Kevin stopped and turned to look at the boy. "Okay," Andy said. "I get it."

"One thing you should be aware of," Kevin said, leaning in close to the boy. "This place is probably bugged, most likely under surveillance, and anybody could be wearing a wire. You keep your mouth shut, okay?"

"Yes, sir."

Kevin opened the heavy door, and Andy followed him into the darkness.

"Hey, Boss."

"Hey, Justin," Kevin responded.

"Andy?" The big guy looked surprised. "How you doin', man?" Justin lowered his voice and moved closer to Kevin. "You should be glad you weren't here last week. Feds came in and rounded up everybody with an outstanding warrant on them." They stepped through a narrow door reading "Employees Only" and headed up a dark, wooden staircase. "It wasn't a pretty picture."

"Who'd they nab?"

"Well, it was just the Feds, not the locals, so there weren't a whole lot of guys to go down, just Tony and Bunny."

"Who's Bunny?"

"You never met Bunny? He's part Native American, that's where he got the name. His people have this tradition of naming the kid after the first animal they see after the kid is born."

"He's lucky his mom didn't see a rat," Andy said with a laugh.

Kevin glared at him. "What did I tell you?"

"So anyway, Bunny had a warrant out on him for something or other, some kind of Federal charge. Tony was moving heroin, as it turns out. He was the one that brought down the heat." Justin shook his head.

A chair creaked as a huge man with a shaved head stood up, setting down a racing form. He didn't say anything, he just looked at the three of them.

"Anybody in there, Manny?" asked Justin.

"Just himself."

The three of them walked into the main office and shut the door. Charles glanced up at the visitors and raised his right hand. Kevin squirted some seltzer into a glass, carried it over to the couch, and sat down. Andy sat beside him. Justin stayed on his feet, leaning against the doorframe.

The man hung up the phone and smiled, revealing rows of perfect white teeth. "Who's this? Andy?"

Andy got to his feet. "Yes, sir."

The man shifted his gaze to Kevin. "So what's with the kid?"

"He wanted to come with me. We thought maybe he could hang with Vinnie."

Charles wrinkled his nose. "Maybe. Let me talk to Marie." He picked up the phone again and then announced to the room in general that Vinnie would be thrilled to see Andy. He followed up with the statement that they would all have dinner that evening.

"My wife will come and pick you up around noon. Vinnie has some kind of lesson this morning; I think it's tennis." Charles turned to Kevin. "Can the kid wait downstairs?"

"Andy, why don't you go hang out in the bar. Justin, you stay with him until Marie gets here."

When Kevin noticed the police car parked in front of Charles's house in Bayside, he almost drove on by. This Queens neighborhood was quiet, exclusive, all big old houses. Cops around here were unusual. He brought the Jaguar up to the wooden garage and climbed out. A quick glance back towards the street showed nothing out of the ordinary, despite the presence of the cruiser. When he walked in the back door, though, he knew something was wrong.

Manny looked up and called out, "Just Duke, no kids."

Kevin stopped and stared at the big, bald bodyguard. "What do you mean, no kids?"

Charles walked into the kitchen, looking ten years older than when Kevin had seen him that morning. "The boys are missing."

"Missing?"

"They went off by themselves."

"On foot or what?"

"In Marie's car." Kevin jumped when Marie walked into the kitchen followed by a cop in uniform.

"I'm afraid this is the best picture I have, officer." She stopped short. "Oh... ah... I assume Charles told you about the boys?" Her normally perfect hair was mussed, a few strands out of place.

"Yes, ma'am."

"Do you have a photograph of Andy?"

Kevin shook his head. "I'm sorry, I don't."

"Can you describe him for me?" asked the cop. He looked like he was about eighteen.

"He's fifteen, almost sixteen. Longish blond hair. Blue eyes. Maybe six one, about a hundred and sixty pounds."

"You're his father?"

"Yes, sir."

"What's your name?"

Kevin shot Charles a glance. Charles shrugged. Kevin refocused on the cop.

"Kevin Williams. We're visiting from New Hampshire."

"You don't have any pictures of your kid?" The cop looked at him as though this was a huge breach of parental responsibility.

"No, sir, I'm sorry."

He turned back to Marie. "Well, as I said, Mrs. Marconi, we haven't had any reports concerning two boys. I'll get this in right away and keep in touch."

Kevin watched the cop leave and looked at Charles. "Who do you have on this?"

"I only just found out, Kevin." Charles glared at Marie. "There was a police car in front of my house when I got home."

"Was anybody with them? Anybody keeping an eye on them?" Kevin asked.

"I want Vincent to have some freedom. He's sixteen years old; he doesn't need a babysitter." Marie didn't look at Kevin.

"Not a babysitter but a bodyguard, for chrissake. Have you even thought about what could happen to them? Never mind the fact that Vinnie is your son. They're kids."

Marie fell into a chair, and Charles settled down at the table across from Manny. He rubbed his chin, scratching at a day's growth of beard. Kevin sat next to Charles and tilted his head towards the big man. "When you were Vinnie's age, you had Manny following you around. Why doesn't your kid have someone watching him?"

"It's a different time, Kevin. Nobody knows me, not like they knew my father."

"Do you want to call your wife?" Marie asked Kevin.

"No. I've got a week before I have to tell her. I'm going on the assumption that they're just being kids, and they'll turn up hung over."

"I wish you had called me before you called the police, Marie." Charles spat out her name without looking at her.

"I didn't want to disturb you when you're with your mistress," she spat back at him.

"God damn it. You know I don't have a mistress. I keep telling you that." He turned to Manny, buried in the paper. "Manny, you're with me all the time, you tell her."

Manny replied from behind the pages. "He doesn't have a mistress, Mrs. M." Kevin hoped that Charles wouldn't ask him to make the same assertion, because he wasn't as good a liar as Manny was.

"What else is he going to say? If he tells me the truth, you'll have this man kill him." She gestured at Kevin.

"Hey," growled Manny, lowering the newspaper. "That's an insult."

"Regardless," insisted Charles. "You should have called me first. I don't want the police involved. Once you invite them onto the property, they can use any evidence they find."

Kevin interrupted. "Does Vinnie have a phone in his room?"

Charles turned his head. "Yes."

"Show me."

The two men went upstairs. Charles tried the knob. "It's locked."

"You don't have a key?"

"No."

"In your own house?" He hesitated. "You got any tools?"

"What kind of tools?"

"To open the lock. What do you think?"

"Why would I have lock-picking tools? I don't even know how to use them."

"Ask Manny."

Charles trotted down the stairs, returning with Manny. "Out of my way. Let the pro work." Manny took only a few seconds to open the door.

"What is that smell?" Charles asked, waving his hand in front of his face.

"You lead a pretty sheltered life for a gangster," Kevin responded. "You don't even know what pot smells like?"

"Pot? You let your kid smoke pot?"

"This is your kid's room. My kid's room doesn't smell like this."

"Well, how do you know that's what it is?"

"I've been around people smoking it."

"Oh, here we go," muttered Manny. "The soldier bit again, the I-went-off-to-some-god-forsaken-jungle-and-everybody-was-doing-drugs number."

"Shut the hell up, Manny."

"What're ya gonna do, soldier boy? Take me apart? Come on, man, try me."

Kevin shook his head as he walked into the room. "Is this the same line as the other phone?"

"No."

"Isn't there some number you can call to find out what the last number dialed was?" asked Manny.

Kevin looked down. "If I were you, I'd just push the redial button."

Charles stepped forward. "Who's this?" He waited. "What?" He glared at the phone.

Kevin held out his hand for the phone. "Hey, man, who's this?"

"None of your fucking business. What do you want?"

"I'm looking for some grass. I heard you can find me some."

"You sound like a cop. Why should I tell you?"

Kevin snorted. "You don't have to, but I got some cash to spend, and I'm looking for some good shit, you know?" Kevin looked at Charles, who was staring at him with his head cocked sideways. "My buddy Vinnie gave me your number." He waited, then wrote down the Woodside address the man gave him. "Thanks. Great." Kevin hung up the phone. As the three men walked out, Marie came towards them, her face white.

"The police found my car."

"But not the kids?"

"Not the kids. Just the car." Kevin thought she was going to cry.

He looked over at Charles. "Well?"

"Manny, you stay here with Marie. I'll go with Kevin, and we'll see what we can come up with, okay?"

Charles headed into the garage and opened a locked closet. He opened the safe inside and motioned to Kevin. "Take what you think you need."

Kevin grabbed a sawed-off 12-gauge pump shotgun and a box of 00 buck.

"That's it?"

"Yeah." Kevin nodded. "I've got a handgun."

"Okay, then."

"You know where we're going?"

"Yep."

Kevin shook his head. "I feel like I don't know the city anymore. Can't hardly find my way around."

"It has changed since you went away." He didn't have to say *to prison*. "You been over to your old neighborhood? Red Hook?"

"No."

"It's going yuppie along with everything else."

"You can't be serious. The crack capital of the world is going yuppie?"

"It starts with the artists, and they're moving in."

Kevin jumped as his cell phone rang. "Yeah?"

"It's me. What's happening?"

"Hey, Justin. We've got a situation. Can you meet us?" He gave him the address.

"On my way."

When they parked in front of a little bookstore, Kevin made no move to get out of the car.

"Well?" said Charles.

"I'm waiting for Justin."

"Oh."

Justin pulled up behind them on his motorcycle within a few minutes. "What're the kids doing here?"

"You know this place?"

"Sure. This is one of Tony's stores."

"We don't know that they're here."

Justin nodded. "They came here to get some pot, I'd bet."

"Vinnie?" Charles actually managed to look surprised. "Tony sells pot?"

"Tony sells more than that. You think it was just a coincidence that he got picked up?" Justin shrugged. "Let's go talk to the guy." He led the way into the dingy store. "Hey, Abe," he said to the man behind the counter, who jumped up. Justin was on him before he could move. "You know these guys?" He held him by his gray ponytail and waved his free hand in the direction of Kevin and Charles.

"Yeah, come on, man, you're killing me."

"They're both missing their kids. We have reason to believe you might have seen them today."

Abe twisted his head to look at Kevin and Charles. "I knew this was gonna happen. Look, I just sold them a little pot." He struggled. "Fuck, will you let me go?"

"Where'd they go?"

"How the hell do I know?"

"You talk to anybody else about them, like somebody that knew they were here, somebody who knew who they were?"

"Will you let me go?"

Justin released his grip and Abe sat back down, rubbing his head. "They could have run into someone on the street."

Kevin stepped behind the counter and brought his .45 out, had it up to the man's temple in one quick move. "You see anything, Abe?"

Abe turned white. "Take it easy, man. I didn't see nothin'."

"Leave him, Boss. He says he doesn't know anything, he doesn't know anything. Neighborhood like this, they probably just got rolled for the car."

"So where do we go now?" asked Charles.

"Let me make a couple calls." Justin took out his phone.

Kevin's phone rang at the same instant. "Yeah."

"Boys turned up in a hospital."

"No way."

"What?" asked Charles.

"Manny says they found the boys." He listened as Manny gave him directions. "It's not far from here. Let's go."

CHAPTER 12

Andy was sitting on a gurney, holding an ice pack to his head. Kevin felt a rush of anger as he eyed the boy, who looked as if he'd been run over by a rhinoceros. Andy's upper lip was swollen, both eyes were black, and he had stitches in a long cut along his right eyebrow.

"You look like shit," Kevin said.

Andy half smiled and winced.

"Hello," said a young Pakistani as he bustled into the room. "I'm Dr. Prouty."

"Kevin Williams."

"You're his father?"

"Yes, sir. Is he going to be okay?"

"Yes. Nothing too serious, just some bruises and a couple of cracked ribs. He has a concussion, so he ought to take it easy. I need you to sign some papers." He handed over a clipboard. "I'll be right back."

When the doctor left, Kevin turned to his son. The kid looked so awful it was hard for him to stay angry. He let out a sigh. "You got into a little trouble, eh?"

"I guess."

The doctor stepped back in. "All set. Here's a prescription for painkillers. No driving." He grinned.

"Thanks."

Kevin stiffened as a police officer stepped through the curtains.

"Can I speak to you, sir?"

"Uh, sure, officer. What can I do for you?"

"I just need to get a statement from your son. Maybe he can come down to the station, fill out some paperwork, look through some mug shots."

Kevin was hoping the cop didn't detect his sigh of relief. "Do we have to do that now?"

"Oh, no, sir, you can come by tomorrow. I know the boy's been through a lot." He handed over a card. "Here's the address and my name. Just ask for me, okay?"

"Yes, sir."

When they walked out of the cubicle, Charles, standing with the cop, caught Kevin's eye. He rarely had to deal with police; he had other people to do that for him. Kevin thought he looked a little lost. He said something to Justin, who began to talk to the cop while Charles walked over to Kevin.

"He okay?" Charles tightened the knot in his tie.

"Yeah. How's Vinnie?"

"He's lost a couple of teeth, and they broke his nose." He lowered his voice. "You find who did this, you take care of it, you understand?"

"Yes, sir."

On the way out, Justin turned to Kevin. "They found the car in Jackson Heights. You want me to find out more?"

"Yeah."

"Right, Boss." Justin took off on his Triumph while the boys climbed into the back of Charles's Caddy.

"You drive." Charles walked to the passenger side.

Kevin looked at the car. "Sure."

Kevin parked himself in a corner while Andy sat at the table and picked at cold ziti. He looked at his father, peering up from under long blond bangs. "You gonna tell Mom about this?"

"I think she's going to figure something out when she sees you this weekend."

"Can't we stay down here for another week?"

"We'll talk about it on Friday."

"I'm sorry I messed up."

"We'll talk later. Just eat."

The boy stared at his food. "I'm not hungry."

Kevin took out his cigarettes, got to his feet, and dragged himself through the door. He was halfway through the smoke when Andy came out.

"Can I tell you something, Dad?"

"Go ahead."

"It wasn't my fault."

"I don't want to talk about it right now."

"Dad..."

"I don't want to talk about it." He was growling through gritted teeth. He couldn't talk about it now; he needed time to digest everything. He needed to cool off so he wouldn't chew the boy out—or worse.

Andy poked at the pavement with the toe of his oversized sneaker.

Kevin woke up exhausted and dragged himself down to the kitchen. He'd just picked up a mug of coffee when his cell phone rang.

"It's a dead end, Boss." Justin sounded disappointed. "I talked to someone I know over there. The car was empty when they found it. No leads. I told him what happened, but he doesn't think there's anything we can do. I'm putting the word out on the street. I'll let you know."

Kevin thanked him and clicked off his cell phone. His boss wasn't going to accept that.

"Hey, asshole," said Manny from the other side of the room.

Kevin looked up.

"News?"

"Nothing."

"That'll make him happy." Manny grinned. "Maybe he'll let me break your legs." Kevin offered an obscene suggestion. Manny laughed out loud just as Andy walked in. "Look what's here. Fresh meat."

"Shut up, Manny. Go haunt a house," Kevin said.

Manny got up and walked out.

"Hey." The boy's voice was a whisper.

Kevin nodded. "How you feeling?"

"Like I got run over by a truck."

"You want to tell me what happened?"

Andy flopped down. "Vinnie wanted to go out. We took his mother's car. We got carjacked. They beat us up and threw us out of the car." He shrugged. "You know that money you gave me? All gone."

"You spend it on the pot or lose it to the punks?"

Andy lifted his head. "What?"

"We already talked to Abe."

"Oh." Andy looked down at the table. "You talk to Mom yet?"

"No. Don't change the subject."

"I lost it to the punks. Vinnie bought the pot."

"Where'd it happen?"

"Right outside of the little store where we bought the stuff."

"Really?"

"Yeah."

"They found the car a long way from there."

"They made us drive them around for a while. Then they pulled us out and beat us up and took the car."

Kevin sighed. "You ever have any karate lessons or anything like that?"

"No."

"You ought to at least know how to take care of yourself. I'll look into it."

"Mom won't like that."

"Your mom doesn't like anything." He paused. "I need you to talk to Justin, tell him everything you can think of. I want descriptions, what direction they came from, where they took you."

"What about the police?"

"They're no help. We can handle this."

"How about you teach me to shoot?"

Kevin lifted his head. "What for?"

"Then I can really defend myself."

"You're not old enough, haven't got the reflexes. You'd be more likely to get shot with your own gun. Besides, your mother would *really* not like that."

"How old were you when you started using a gun?"

Kevin glared at him. "That's different."

"No, really, Dad; I want to know. How old were you when you went into the Marines?"

Manny re-entered the room and laughed. "He was using a gun way before that."

Andy's gaze swung to Manny, then back to his father. "Well?"

"I've done a lot of stuff I'm not proud of."

Manny laughed again. "You're not going to tell him how old you were when you tried to stick up that store? Remember that? You must have been fourteen."

"I was sixteen."

"You stuck up a store when you were sixteen? I'm almost sixteen."

"I told you, I've done a lot of stuff I'm not proud of." He took his Camels out and got to his feet.

"Ha. He didn't get anywhere. He had a pellet gun. The storeowner laughed at him. Charles and I were in the back room, and I was going to break his legs."

"Yeah, but you didn't."

"I didn't because Charles wouldn't let me." He laced his giant fingers together and cracked the knuckles. "Any day, though. Soon as he gives me the okay."

Kevin turned to look Andy in the eye. "I joined the Marines when I was seventeen."

"Tell him why you joined." Manny was still grinning.

Kevin shifted his gaze to the huge bald man. "Manny, you can start minding your own fucking business any time now."

"Judge gave him a choice. Adult prison or the Marines."

Andy blinked.

"The next part's the best," cackled Manny. "They trained him as a sniper and sent him to Vietnam."

"Is that true?" asked Andy.

Kevin walked outside to smoke, listening to the laughter as Manny said, "'Course it's true."

CHAPTER 13

When Justin called back, Kevin was nursing his third cup of coffee. "Yeah?" he mumbled into the phone, turning away from Andy.

"I found the creeps."

"That was quick."

"I know a few people. They were working for Tony."

"They were what?"

"Tony's mad at you for some reason. You tried to get him fired or something?"

"Not really."

"Anyway, Tony got picked up last week, like I told you. Now he's pissed at the whole world and thought he'd take it out on your kid."

"You're serious?"

"Yeah. He found out your kid was with Vinnie. That was all he needed."

"Huh."

"I can take care of this for you."

"No. Charles asked me to handle it."

"So you delegate it."

"You know we can't touch Tony."

"I know that, but I've got the three kids. Them we can touch."

"Tell me where you are."

Justin let out a sigh and gave him an address. "I'll see you when you get here."

Kevin considered how he was going to handle this. He knew what Charles wanted done. He wanted revenge. But more than that, he'd want the thieves killed, an example made. Kevin got to his feet.

"Where you going, Dad?"

Kevin looked over as the boy entered the room. "I have something to take care of."

"Can I come?"

He hesitated. He could imagine what Cindy would think of that. Then again, he could keep an eye on the boy if he came along; he could sit in the car. Keep him out of trouble. "Sure. Why not?"

He directed the boy towards his car, while he went into the garage and got the shotgun. He tucked it into the trunk, then walked around to the driver's side and got in.

Andy was staring straight ahead. "Where're we going?"

"Told you." He backed the car out of the driveway. "I have something to take care of."

He drove into the parking lot of a worn-out warehouse. The door slid open when he honked the horn. "Stay in the car." He grabbed the shotgun, double-checked the 1911 in the small of his back, and walked across the empty floor.

Justin came out to meet him. "You don't have to do this. I can handle it."

Kevin shook his head. "I want to talk to them. What've you got?"

"Three boys."

"They admit anything yet?"

"We were waiting for you."

"Good." Kevin entered a partitioned-off area that might have been a workshop. He eyed three dark-haired kids, not much older than Andy, all tied to old wooden chairs. Although they seemed to be trying to hide it, they still looked scared. "Hey, guys. Did I miss the party?" He held up the shotgun, racked the pump, and sent a threatening grin their way.

One of the kids, a Hispanic with long dreadlocks, spat at him, hitting the floor well short of his target. "What you want, old man?"

"You guys steal a car yesterday?"

"'The fuck you care? You a cop?"

"By the time I'm done with you, you'll wish I *was* a cop."

He walked over to the spitter, a squat kid of about eighteen, wearing baggy shorts and a sleeveless flannel shirt. Kevin recognized something in the face and realized that he was the same youngster who had tried to hold Tony up back in the spring. That was an odd connection. He pushed it out of his mind and hit the kid in the face with the butt of the shotgun, hard, not holding back. Let the kid feel what he had done to Andy.

"You steal a car yesterday?"

The kid spat at him again, blood mixed in, connecting this time with Kevin's chest. Kevin pulled out his Colt, held it to the kid's temple, leaned in close as he thumbed off the safety.

"Maybe you didn't hear me. I asked if you stole a car yesterday. Two kids in it. Tan Mercedes station wagon. Sound familiar?"

"Yeah, man, we stole it. All three of us." This came from another kid, maybe a little older. "What do you want, the pot?"

Kevin snorted and lowered the handgun. "You guys don't get it, do you?" He took aim at the spitter's right knee and squeezed the trigger. Kevin barely heard the kid scream over the ringing in his ears. One of the other kids starting crying.

Justin stepped forward. "Boss, you don't have to..."

Kevin turned. "Shut up," he growled at the younger man. "This is *my* show. You want to help, go find me a sledgehammer."

The crying kid, the third one, began wailing even louder. "What'd we do, man?"

Kevin turned to him. "Which one of you beat up the younger kid—the one with the long blond hair?"

"He did... Julio did." With tears streaming down his face he tilted his head towards the first kid, the spitter.

Kevin studied the boy's face, twisted with pain, and then looked around for Justin. "Where's that sledgehammer?" He didn't see Justin. What he did see, ducking behind the doorframe, was Andy. He swallowed hard and walked over, lowering the Colt as he looked around the corner. Andy was there, with Justin beside him holding a nine-pound sledge.

"Here you go, Boss." Justin held up the hammer.

"Thanks." He looked at Andy. "You get back in the fucking car. Don't get out again."

"Why'd you bring him?" asked Justin as they watched Andy cross the warehouse floor.

"I don't know. Let's just get this done." He handed Justin the shotgun and took the hammer.

"Cindy'll kill you."

"She doesn't have to know." He re-entered the room. Julio had passed out. Kevin faced the other two. "Who beat up the other kid?"

"All of us." This came from the kid in the sweats. "We started on the older kid, he was driving. Then Julio grabbed the young one." The boy looked up at Kevin. "What's it to you anyway?"

"The blond one was my kid. The other one is my boss's kid. You get it?" He hefted the hammer and brought it down on the boy's foot. He had to swallow and turn away; had to try to tune out the screams.

"We won't do it again," the last kid cried.

"You're right; you won't." He hit this kid with the hammer as well, in the right shin. The youngster passed out.

Kevin hefted the hammer again, looking for another target.

"Boss."

He turned his head.

"Enough."

Kevin licked his lips. "You know he won't be satisfied with this."

"He doesn't have to know."

"How'd you get them here?"

"I've got a stolen van."

"Drive them to the nearest hospital and leave them, okay? Actually, have somebody else drive them. I don't want to risk you."

"Yes, sir."

"They'll be fine." He leaned over to look at the bullet wound. The bleeding had stopped. "Call me when you're all set, okay?"

"Right, Boss."

"Get somebody to clean this up." Kevin picked up the spent shell casing, dropped it into his pocket, and walked back to his car. Andy was staring straight ahead, legs drawn up to his chest, arms wrapped around his knees, shaking.

Kevin cleared his throat, standing beside the little car, looking down at his son. "Were those the ones?"

"I don't know."

He growled through gritted teeth, giving him an angry glare. "You'd *better* fucking know."

The boy still didn't meet his eyes. "Yeah, they looked like them."

"Get your fucking sneakers off my leather seat." Kevin motioned to the guy on the door, who nodded at him and pushed it open.

As they drove back Andy spoke up in a shaky voice. "Did you kill them?"

"No."

"What did you do?"

"I don't want to talk about it."

When they got back, Andy disappeared into the house while Kevin put the shotgun away. Kevin went into the house, and saw Manny in his usual spot. "Man, what'd you do to your kid? He looks like he's gonna be sick."

"Nothing. I didn't do anything to him. Charles upstairs?"

"Yep."

"Okay." He climbed the stairs and let himself into the office without bothering to knock. Charles was on the phone.

"See what you can do. She doesn't want that car back." He glanced up at Kevin and nodded. Kevin dropped onto the couch.

"I don't care if I take a loss. She wants a new one. Right. Let me know." He hung up the phone. "Marie won't go near that car. There's blood on the seats, a couple of dents, it smells like piss." He shrugged. "What can I do for you?"

"I took care of that little problem we discussed."

"Already?"

"Yes, sir."

"Good. You do it the way I wanted?"

"I think I covered the bases." He paused and cleared his throat. "We do have an issue though."

"What?"

"The kids were working for Tony. Tony's pissed at me."

"That little mother fucker."

"Yeah."

Charles took a deep breath. "You think he knew he was hurting my kid, too?"

"I don't know."

"You haven't done anything about this, right? About Tony?"

"No, sir. Just the kids, the ones that played it."

"All right, I'll take it from here then."

"You sure you don't want me to do anything about Tony?"

"You know the rules. He's untouchable. Hell, he's older than I am. He knew my father, for God's sake."

"But your father wouldn't have let him sell drugs."

Charles narrowed his eyes. "What?"

"You knew, didn't you? Knew that he was selling. You let it go on."

"Tony came to me this spring after he got held up. He said he needed more income."

"Your father wouldn't let this go on."

"My father is dead." Charles spat this at him. "It's a different world."

"People don't like drugs in their neighborhoods. Gambling, hell, everybody gambles. Prostitutes, well, you know. But drugs? This is what brings the Feds."

Charles was pacing now, shaking his head. "Tony's been with this family for God knows how many years. He's loyal."

"And when Tony's looking at going down for life for this, he'll flip."

Charles stopped pacing. "Did you flip when you went down for murder?"

"No."

"So what makes you think he will?"

"He's an old man with a family. Hasn't he got a daughter going to college?"

"I'll keep an eye on him, okay? But I don't want you doing anything, you got that?"

"Yes, sir."

Charles switched gears. "You should go home, take it easy for the rest of the week."

Kevin shrugged. "No, I'll stay down here. Give the boy a chance to heal."

"Hide him from your wife, you mean." Charles nodded as he walked back to his desk. "This is a real mess."

"Yeah."

"Never had a problem with this sort of thing before."

His boss was accusing him of causing this problem. "Nope, never have," he agreed.

"Your boy do this sort of thing on a regular basis?"

Kevin met the man's gaze. "No, sir." He wanted to get to his feet, stand at attention.

Charles looked down at the desk. "My kid's never been in trouble. Hell, he got honors at his prep school last semester."

His boss considered Andy the problem... which led back to him. He was going to lose the one source of income he had. His boss was going to fire him, and he was going to be out on the street on his butt. No apartment, no Justin, no more connections. He could feel his heart start to pound in his chest. Maybe this was the time to retire.

"Marie doesn't want your kid around here anymore, you understand?" This was directed at the pile of papers on the desk. Charles wouldn't even look at him.

Well, that wasn't so bad. "Yes, sir." It was bad, sure, but it wasn't as if he'd said that he didn't want Kevin around anymore. He relaxed, letting his eyes drift to the booze on the sideboard. He remembered all the times he'd stood there, downing one Jack Daniel's after another, wondering if the boss was mad at him for something.

"You can go, Kevin."

Dismissed. "Yes, sir." Kevin got to his feet and left the room. He found the guest room down the hall and knocked.

Chapter 14

Andy looked up as Kevin entered the room. "Oh, it's you." He was sitting on the bed, feet up, pillows piled behind his back.

"How you feeling?"

"I'm all right, I guess."

"When do we have to get those stitches out?"

"They said a week. Maybe we can do it Friday before we go home?"

"I'll make you an appointment with Doctor Williams."

"Sure."

"Tell me why you were in that neighborhood to begin with, why you had to do something that stupid." *Why you had to put my life in danger,* he wanted to add, but he didn't.

Andy shrugged. "It was Vinnie's idea."

"You always do whatever somebody else wants to do?"

"I thought it would be fun. Cool."

"You still think so?" The boy looked away. "You gonna do that again, or something like that?" He left the real question unspoken, the question about smoking pot.

"No." But his voice was defiant, rude.

Kevin didn't like that. He didn't believe the kid. "Did you ever get hold of any of your old friends?"

Andy looked up at him. "Never had a chance."

"Call around. See what you can do."

"Sure. That'd be great." His voice was flat.

"Pack your stuff." He turned and walked out of the room.

He stopped when Andy spoke. "Dad?"

"What?" Kevin leaned back around the doorframe.

"You won't tell Mom about the pot, will you?"

Kevin hesitated. "You stay clean, and I'll stay quiet. Deal?"

Andy nodded. "Okay."

He limped down the stairs and went out to the driveway to smoke. The cell phone chirped just as he finished the cigarette.

"Yeah?"

"All set, Boss. Friend of ours took them to the hospital. Made sure they got inside."

"Thanks, Justin."

"No problem. Anything else I can do for you?"

"I need an appointment for Andy with Doc. Can you do that? He's got to get those stitches out."

"I'll get right on it."

"Thanks, Justin."

Kevin closed the phone and stared at it for a minute. Andy came out the door, carrying his backpack. "I talked to my friend John. His mom says I can spend the day with them tomorrow."

"Fine."

"We goin' now?"

"I just need to talk to Charles. Say bye to Vinnie."

Justin called Thursday evening while Kevin poked at a carton of Chinese take-out with a pair of chopsticks. "Fun day today," he said.

"Yeah?"

"Yeah, I met that lady marshal you had trouble with, Sally Barnard. She's got a hard-on for you, I'll tell you that."

Kevin laughed. "She's a real pain in the ass."

"They brought me in for questioning. No charges, though; they couldn't keep me. They're pretty sure you're in town."

"What makes you say that? Did you pick up any information from them?"

"They think you're somewhere in the city. Sounds like they're working hard. I have no idea why. I even asked the lady why she was bothering with you."

"What'd she say?"

"She didn't give me an answer. I mean, come on, you're not federal. It's a state escape warrant. They don't think you're out of the jurisdiction."

"Remember that mess last winter? That whole witness thing?"

"Yeah."

"Barnard was watching her, and I grabbed her. That's what she's got against me."

"I think somebody told her you're in town."

"You think so?"

"Yeah. Like Tony."

"No way."

"I told you he got picked up last week; he was doing something with heroin. Let's think about it. How come they kicked him loose so fast?"

"No shit."

"You maybe ought to just head north and stay there."

"You think Tony knows about New Hampshire?"

"I don't think so. I know I don't talk about it."

"Thanks, Justin. I'm sorry you got dragged in."

"S'okay. I wasn't doing anything else today." He laughed. "But listen, because of all this, I'm running late. Can you get out to pick up Andy?"

"No problem. I've got it."

"You know where he is?"

"Yeah. I can find it."

He set the phone down and studied his half-eaten food. Sticking it in the fridge, he left the apartment.

When they got back Kevin flopped onto the couch, not hungry enough to finish his dinner. He pulled out his cigarettes and heavy silver lighter.

"Can I have one?" Andy asked.

"We've been through this."

"So I can have the secondhand smoke but not a real smoke. Is that it?"

"Yeah."

Andy sat on the far end of the couch. "How come we never met your family?"

"What?"

"Isn't your family down here? How come I never met them?"

"My parents are dead."

"I remember Mom saying something about your mother dying this winter."

"Right."

"You have any brothers or sisters?"

"Why the hell are you asking so many questions?"

"I don't know," Andy shrugged. "You don't have cable. There's nothing else to do."

"I have a younger brother and two younger sisters."

"So you were the oldest, too?"

"No. I had an older brother. He died on my sixteenth birthday."

"Oh, yeah?" Andy shifted on the couch. "My friend Randy, the kid whose house I was just at, his little brother has leukemia. They think he might die."

"That's too bad." Kevin took a long drag on the cigarette.

"So what happened to your brother? And your father?"

"My brother had something wrong with his brain, an aneurysm or something. He died during an anti-war protest, some cops threw him on the ground, and whatever was wrong with his head ruptured and he died."

Andy just stared for a minute.

"My father died in a veteran's home of liver failure. About twelve years ago. I guess he must have been in his sixties. I didn't see much of him."

"So is your family... like... cursed or something?"

Kevin frowned at him and leaned forward to crush out the cigarette in the ashtray.

"Sorry."

Kevin looked at his watch. "Is it too early to go to bed?"

"No. I can't wait to get these stitches out. They're wicked itchy."

"Yeah." He got to his feet. "I'll see you in the morning."

The next morning, Kevin sat in the examining room with his son, waiting for the doctor. He had lain awake most of the night, staring at the ceiling.

Doctor Williams came in. "Kevin. Good to see you. Been a while, hasn't it?" His eyes shifted to Andy. "What happened to you?"

"Uh, I..."

"Car accident," put in Kevin.

"The old standby. Why didn't you just say he walked into a door?"

"'Cause he didn't."

"Okay. You didn't hit him, did you?"

"No."

The doctor shifted his gaze. "I was sorry to hear about your mother."

"Thanks."

Looking back at the boy, the doctor continued, "If you want to talk to me without your dad here, Andy, we can arrange that."

"Will you quit it?" sputtered Kevin.

"Have you talked to Cindy yet?" the doctor asked as he set to work on the stitches.

"No. I'm looking forward to that later on today."

The doctor turned his head and raised an eyebrow. "I know you didn't hit your kid, Kevin." He turned back to the boy but continued to talk to his father. "Have you been taking care of yourself?"

"Yeah."

"So how's Cindy doing up there?"

"She's okay."

Andy jumped. "Ouch!"

"If you hold still, this will go easier. You like living up in New Hampshire, Andy?"

"I guess."

"This is a family tradition, you know. I can't tell you how many stitches I've taken out of your father's face and other body parts." He chuckled. "Can't say I'm happy to see you in the same shape, though."

"Wasn't really his fault," said Kevin. He caught the look of surprise that crossed Andy's face.

The doctor stepped away and began to wash his hands. "You're all set, Andy." He turned to Kevin as he threw a paper towel in the trash. "How's your arm?"

"Fine."

"Let me see you move it." Kevin obliged by swinging his left arm over his head, wincing as the scars pulled. "Lost some range of motion, haven't you?"

"I guess."

"The medical care in our state penal system is a joke."

"Uh, right."

"How's your leg?"

"It's okay."

The doctor leaned forward and studied the scar on Kevin's forehead. "Philistines." He shook his head. "They couldn't get a plastic surgeon to stitch this up?"

"I don't know; I was out at the time."

"Car crash, wasn't it?"

Kevin nodded.

"Must run in the family. Listen, you take care of yourself. I'm pretty backed up today, got a ton of patients waiting out there. Tell Cindy I haven't been able to find anyone as good as her to take her place."

"Okay."

He shook Andy's hand. "Stay away from car accidents, okay?"

"Sure."

"Kevin." He shook his hand. "Take care of your family." He paused, looking into the younger man's eyes. "Nothing is as important as that."

CHAPTER 15

Michael came in from the barn to find his parents having a loud argument. "I can't believe you didn't call me when it happened."

"I told you, I didn't want to worry you." His father cast a glance his way with a look in his eyes Michael had never seen. It was almost as if he was afraid.

Michael left the room, heading into the living room to sit for a minute, and found Andy on the couch.

"Whoa, what happened to you?"

Andy shrugged. "Got beat up."

"By who?"

Andy turned away from the TV. "It was a carjacking... a random thing."

"When?"

"Monday."

"Is that what Mom is yelling at Dad about?"

"Probably."

Michael was watching the TV later that week, late at night, flipping through the channels. A picture on the screen looked familiar. That was weird. He stopped channel surfing. The announcer was giving statistics:

"... height six foot four, weight one hundred sixty pounds, blue eyes, blond hair, forty-six years old, walks with a limp, several tattoos..."

Michael realized that the man was describing his father.

"Violent. Killed a police officer, escaped four times, decorated Vietnam veteran, ties to organized crime..."

Michael began to put the pieces together. Why his father was never home. Why he always carried a gun. Why Vinnie Marconi had said that Duke, as he called him, was a hammer. *When was that, last Christmas? A hundred years ago?* He hadn't believed Vinnie at the time; the kid was way too quick to talk like that. Andy had said he believed it, that he thought their father could easily be a hammer, a mob killer. But Michael hadn't accepted it. Until now.

"Kevin Markinson," said the announcer. Michael knew that name. He remembered how angry he had been when his mother told him they were moving and they were changing their last name. It was hard to get used to. There were times when he felt like an idiot because someone at school would say his name, and he wouldn't respond because he had forgotten his new last name.

He had known about prison, known that his father had escaped last summer. He hadn't realized that the man was only out now because he had escaped again. Michael had somehow imagined that his dad was out on parole or something, had served his time.

He sat and stared at the TV, watching as actors ran through a re-enactment of the original crime. An actor who looked like his father took a bullet in his chest from another actor playing a cop and then fired a gun into the man's face. Michael thought that seemed just a bit farfetched. *How could somebody do that?* The host of the show was talking again now, and the picture changed again to the mug shot. Michael looked into the eyes, trying to put the ice blue color of his father's eyes to the ones in the black and white picture, and continued to stare even when the program had moved on to a commercial. Then he punched the remote, watched the giant screen fade to black, and thought about what he was going to do with this knowledge.

He was half-tempted to pick up the phone, dial the 800 number they'd mentioned in the program, and turn his own father in. But that thought set him back, made him stop and think for moment. *What would happen if he did that?* They'd have to move again; there might be money problems. He'd almost certainly have to sell his horse. *Was that reason enough not to do it? How could he not have known? How could you know someone your whole life and not know something like this?* That was why those federal marshals came to the house last summer. That was why his old man associated with people like Charles Marconi, a reputed... *was that the right word?...* reputed mobster.

He went upstairs in a haze and spent the night awake in his bed, watching the shadows move across the ceiling, listening to the night noises, and struggling with his thoughts. He wondered how many more people in town had seen that same show. How could they not recognize him?

He was sitting at the kitchen table, trying to force down some cereal, when she walked in, just getting home from work.

"Mom. Can I talk to you for a minute?"

"Always, Michael." She stopped and turned to face him, setting her bag on the counter. She looked tired; her scrubs were rumpled and Michael was sure there were spots of blood on her shirt.

"Have you ever heard of this TV show where they put these criminals on to try to catch them?"

"No." She sat down across the table from him now and ran a hand through her hair. *There's more gray in it lately,* he thought, *since Dad has been around.*

He picked a piece of fruit out of the bowl and played with it, his cereal forgotten. He spoke without looking at her, focusing on the orange. "I saw Dad on TV. What did he do, Mom?"

"What did it say, Michael?"

He looked at her, wanting to see her reaction. "It said he killed a cop. Killed a cop and escaped from jail." She looked away. Michael felt even sicker than he had the night before. His mother's reaction was scaring him almost as much as the original information. "Is it true, Mom?"

"Your dad didn't kill that cop. He swore to me that he didn't do it. He did escape from prison." She met his eyes for a moment and then looked down at the table. "Four times."

"Four times? How is that even possible? I knew he escaped last summer, but I had no idea." Michael felt his stomach doing flips. He stared at the table. "What do I do now?"

"What do you mean?"

"How can you live with this? How long have you known?"

"I don't know, Michael. I..." She shook her head. "I've been living with this for a long time. I just try not to ask questions." She got up and walked out of the room.

He got to his feet and followed her, trotting to catch up. "Why did you marry him?"

She stopped and turned to face him. He was taller than she was, and she had to look up to meet his eyes. He glared at her, begging for some kind of answer. Some kind of explanation. He wanted his mother to make it right. He wanted a good reason, a simple solution to his questions.

"Why would you marry someone like him?"

She stared right at him. "I didn't know then. I was in love. I was young, and he was, well, different from anybody I knew."

"So what's your excuse now? Why do you stay with him?"

"Because I love him. We need each other." She shrugged.

"Then why do the two of you fight all the time?"

She shook her head. "I don't know."

"So you think this is a good way to live?"

"What else should I do?"

"Leave him. Throw him out. Turn him in. Do anything except what you're doing."

"Could *you* do that? Turn him in? Could you live with yourself knowing that you're responsible for something like that?" Her voice was louder, sharper. She shook her head again and turned to the stairs. "I couldn't do that. He's not a bad guy, Michael."

Michael frowned. "How can you say that?" He struggled with the thoughts running through his brain. *How could someone who does stuff that's wrong be a good guy?*

"Give him a chance."

He turned and headed for the kitchen as his mom climbed the stairs.

———

CHAPTER 16

Michael was just coming in from feeding the horses their lunch when his father spoke to him. "Your mother says you need something or other from someplace. A tack shop?"

Michael stopped. "Yeah."

"She got called in to work, and she wants me to drive you."

"Seriously? 'Cause I can wait. I don't need it right away. It's something we wanted to try for the next event—a different bit."

"Your mother insisted. She said you have that event coming up this weekend, and I have to take you to Plaistow."

"Okay." He shrugged and followed his father to his Jaguar. "Oh, you know what? I need a new muck bucket and other stuff that won't fit in your car. Mom will just have to take me tomorrow."

"We can stop at the hospital and switch cars."

Michael gave up. "Okay."

The ride down to Concord was silent. Michael stared out the window, avoiding looking at his father. Visions of that mug shot were burned into his retinas. After they moved into the Yukon, with the windows rolled up and the air conditioner on, his father cleared his throat.

"Your mom thinks I need to talk to you. She says you don't think much of me, and believes I can fix that by talking to you."

"Do you think you can change the way I think?"

"Nope."

"Then why bother?"

"It's a family thing. We're supposed to talk."

Michael snorted. "Yeah, right."

"I have some stuff I need to tell you, but I thought you might have some questions for me first. You had questions about me the other day."

"Did Mom tell you that? Tell you about the TV show?"

"She mentioned it."

"Is it true?"

His father cleared his throat. "I don't know; it depends on what they said."

Michael stared out the window.

"What do you want to know about it?" Kevin asked.

"Did you do it?"

"Do what?"

"What do *you* think?"

"Michael, you have to be more specific."

"God!" Michael shook his head. "Did you kill that cop?"

"No."

Michael wasn't sure if he believed him. The answer came so quickly, it was like he had practiced it so many times that even if it was a lie, he'd convinced himself it was true.

"I'm not very good at this father thing. I haven't had a lot of practice."

"No kidding." Michael paused and changed tactics. "Why don't you do what *your* father did? You had a father, right?" Michael turned to meet Kevin's gaze and wasn't sure what was there in those icy eyes. "Well?"

His father turned back to the road. "My father broke my nose when I was twelve."

Michael stared.

"He hit me because I was trying to keep him from hitting my mother."

Michael looked out the window again. "I'm sorry, Dad."

"I don't have a good example to follow. I never wanted to be a father. I didn't want to continue the cycle."

"So why did you have kids?"

"Your mother wanted kids. I went along with it. But I liked both of you, once I finally got to meet you. Not that she didn't like you. It was me she didn't like." He paused. "Did your mom ever tell you what I did when Andy was born?"

Michael shook his head.

"I was in prison. I was on a work release program, and I walked away because I wanted to see him."

"Why were you in prison?"

"Do you really want to know? You want the whole story from the beginning?"

"The truth, Dad."

"You really want the truth?"

Michael hesitated, thinking. "How much does Mom know?"

"She knows most of it. There's some stuff she doesn't want to know. The less she knows, the less she can be prosecuted for. You understand that?"

"Yeah. Sally Barnard, that marshal, came out to the house last summer with some other young guy. They told Mom they were going to arrest her for aiding and abetting."

He sighed. "They were bluffing. They didn't have anything on her. Justin has done time for it, just a couple of months. But they can't take her down, not without more proof."

"So what about the story?"

"I left home when I was sixteen. Got arrested for stealing a car. I took off, got thrown in juvie, and ran away from that. Ended up facing an armed robbery rap. The judge gave me a choice—prison or the Marine Corps. I was seventeen years old, with a tenth grade education. I figured I was invincible." He hesitated. "I went to Vietnam as a sniper. I had no idea what I was in for."

"I've seen the movies," Michael interrupted.

"The movies don't even come close, not that I've seen them." He sighed. "I got hurt a couple of times, got promoted, got demoted, got hurt bad, and got sent home."

"So did that clear your record?"

"Yeah."

"So how did you end up in prison?"

"I came back to the world with two really painful injuries. My neck still hurts nearly thirty years later. I got my GED, but I had no real skills. Took me a couple of months to find a job, then I lost it." His voice got quiet. "What was I supposed to do? I didn't want to go to my old boss, the one I had before I went to Vietnam, but I had to eat. And he really wanted me.

"I went to work for him—Charles—the guy I still work for now. Doing whatever he wanted me to do, you understand?"

Michael nodded, not wanting to say anything.

"God, I need a drink." He took a deep breath. "I got tagged leaving a nightclub with a gun. There was a dead guy inside. I was acquitted but got a year because of the gun. I served six months, got out on parole, played that game for a while, and then had to run for a different reason. That was the first time I came to New Hampshire, which is where I met your mom. You sure you want to hear all of this?"

"It's you, right? There's no reason why I wouldn't want to hear it." He tried to catch his father's eye, but the man wasn't looking at him.

"I fell in love with her the first time I saw her twenty-five years ago. I went back to the city, got her to marry me, and brought her down there. She didn't know what I did then. She thought we would live in a little house somewhere with a white picket fence, I'd go to work every day, and she'd stay home with the kids. I never told her about my father... never told her I didn't want kids.

"We moved ten times in the first four years." He paused, took a deep breath. "I couldn't stay in one place."

"You were wanted, right? You escaped from jail."

"Right." His father turned his head. "Did I say that? You can't tell anyone that." He looked back out the windshield. "I guess there's not much of this you can tell anybody anyway. She finally talked me into having kids, and then I got arrested.

"When Andy was born I walked away, like I said. Some idiot kid on drugs came to give me a ride. He ran a red light, we got stopped by a cop, and the kid tried to shoot him. I reached for the gun, and I got shot by the cop. The idiot kid shot the cop in the face and took off. I told your mom I didn't do it. I don't know if she believed me."

Michael saw the re-enactment from the TV show in his mind then, rearranged it to fit what his father had said, saw that it made more sense the way he told it. "She believed you, Dad. She told me you didn't do it."

"I went down for that, hard time. I broke out after a few months. Went back to work. Your mom got pregnant again."

Michael nodded.

"I got shot in the leg right before you were born. I had a real hard time after that. I started drinking heavy. I couldn't deal with life anymore, so I tried to drop out. Drank like that for two years. Your mother threw me out after a year of it."

"Andy fired your gun."

The man's head swiveled around. "She tell you that?"

"I think I remember that."

"You were only about a year old. Is that even possible?"

"It's my first real memory. Maybe I just remember Andy talking about it."

"I'm sorry." He picked up the pack of Camels from the dashboard. "Would you mind if I smoked?"

"Yeah, I would."

His father nodded and put his cigarettes back. "I collapsed a few months after she threw me out. I wasn't eating, and I was drunk most of the time, maintaining. I had some kind of weird reaction, some kind of vitamin deficiency, and I ended up in the hospital. Went through detox, and I haven't had a drink since.

"Then your mom told me she didn't want any more kids. I figured that was it, she was done with me. I didn't go home after that."

"It was a long time between visits."

"You remember the visits?"

"I remember Mom would say we were going to see you, and then we wouldn't. You used to send things. Toys. Presents."

"She finally got to the point where she asked me to come home. I got nailed a few months later by a dirty cop. He beat me up, we sued, that money paid for your house down in Queens, then this house. I stayed put in prison for a while after that business until last summer. You know what happened then, right?"

"Not really."

"I broke out, got shot, missed my ride because I fell off the fu... uh, train, and I was in some stupid pipe under the tracks for two days. Then this kid about your age helped me. Some idiots broke out of minimum security, walked into his house, and took us hostage. They beat me up, but I got out alive. Turned myself in a few days later because the screws led me to believe they were going to send the kid to jail for helping me. Somebody broke me out to do a job in January, and here I am."

"And that's the whole story?"

"That's it."

"What kind of job?"

"I can't really talk about it."

"So what do I tell people when they ask what my father does for a living?"

"Tell them I'm retired."

"You're retired?"

"Yeah, pretty much." He slowed the car as they neared a huge red barn perched on the edge of the road. "Is this the place?"

"Yeah." Michael paused before getting out of the car. "Thanks Dad."

CHAPTER 17

Michael was eating a quick breakfast at six on Saturday morning, in preparation for a competition, when his father walked into the kitchen. Michael almost choked on his Pop-Tart.

"Hey," the man said, sitting down on the opposite side of the table. He looked worse than usual, like he'd gotten about two hours of sleep.

Michael nodded at him. "Just coming in?"

"What time do you have to leave?" His voice sounded like gravel.

"My dressage ride is at eight-fifteen. Takes about ten minutes to ride over, half hour to warm up. I guess I should ride out by seven-fifteen."

"Your mom has to work. She called and said I take you, to help you out."

Michael stared. His father knew even less about horses than his mother. Even with the horses here, Michael was pretty sure that the closest his dad had ever been to a horse was the carriage horses near Central Park. "That's okay, Dad; I can handle it by myself."

"No, really, Michael, your mother insisted. She said I have to drive the truck over. I switched cars with her on the way home; she's got my car at work. She said I have to haul water buckets, walk the horse for you—the works."

"There'll be a lot of people there, Dad."

"So?"

Michael looked down. "So do you really want to go?"

"I've never been to one of your events. I've always wanted to see you ride."

Michael looked at him, staring into those icy eyes rimmed with red. He couldn't tell whether Kevin was telling the truth.

"Okay." Now Michael had to figure out how he was going to work with someone who had never handled a horse. He finished eating, watching his dad prowl around the kitchen, scrounging for food. "Pop-Tarts are in the cupboard to the right of the refrigerator."

His father opened the cupboard to the right of the refrigerator, but the wrong one, the high one instead of the low one. "No, Da—" he started to say, but it was too late. A cascade of plastic containers fell out, hitting the counter and his father.

"Holy sh... uh, shoot," Kevin stammered as he jumped back. "Does that always happen?"

Michael smiled in spite of himself. "Mom likes to save plastic containers. She has enough to keep leftovers for an entire army." He shook his head. "Bottom cupboard."

Michael rode down the trail at exactly seven-fifteen. He found himself waving at his old man. He wasn't sure how he felt about it. He had to force himself to forget the TV show, to think about the horse show instead.

His father parked the SUV, filled up two water buckets, and parked himself in a director's chair set up by the truck, back against the vehicle. Michael glanced at him now and then as he warmed up Hammy. He was nervous today, more than he had expected to be. This was familiar territory, his home farm. He shouldn't feel so unsettled. Michael set his gaze on his father once again, realizing that he was the cause of the nerves. His dad looked like he always did—wearing blue jeans, combat boots, an untucked polo shirt, the stupid Mets hat that he had worn for a hundred years, and the usual mirrored sunglasses.

His dressage test went better than he expected. When he arrived back at the truck Michael handed the reins to his father. "You hold him while I take off my coat, okay?" He had to struggle to keep from laughing out loud as his dad held onto the end of the reins while Hammy kept trying to check the man's pockets for carrots.

"Is this thing gonna bite me?"

"Probably not."

"Probably not?" His father shot the horse a "Don't even think about it" glare.

Michael grabbed Hammy and took off the bridle, slipped on his halter, and then took off the saddle. His father held Hammy, and Michael was surprised at the way he held the lead folded in his hand instead of wrapped around it, as though someone had taught him horse safety.

"I walked my cross-country course yesterday, so I don't think I need to walk it again today. I do have to be ready to ride at ten, though." Michael glanced at his watch. "You can let him graze."

"Right."

After he changed, Michael walked over to where Hammy had dragged his dad. He took the lead from him, noticing that he was on the correct side of the horse—the left. That surprised him.

"Thanks."

"No problem." Kevin limped back over to the chair and sat down, stretching his left leg out in front of him. "Fuck." Then he looked over at Michael and said, "Sorry."

Michael realized he'd never known a time when his dad didn't limp, yet he had no idea what had caused it. He took a deep breath. "What happened to your leg?"

"Huh?"

"Your limp, Dad. Was that something that happened in Vietnam?" Michael had never asked his father about his war experience, but then, he had never really asked his father about anything before this week.

"No."

Michael started to walk away. "I know, you don't want to talk about it." His dad never wanted to talk about anything.

Kevin looked around. "You want to know what happened?"

"Sure." Michael shrugged then turned around.

"I took a .357 magnum slug just above the knee." He took off his sunglasses, closed his eyes, and pinched the bridge of his nose.

Michael stared at him.

"If that had happened in 'Nam, I would have lost my leg. I was able to get to a hospital, which happened to have a pretty good orthopedic surgeon. The end of the femur was shattered; there's still some pins in my leg. It hurts like... uh, heck, it hurts like heck." He put the sunglasses back on, drew in a deep breath, and sighed. "I got into a car accident last winter. Tore some ligaments. Lately, it's been hurting more..."

Michael looked at the ground for a second. "I want to walk over and see if they've posted the scores yet." He looked at his father. "Want to come?"

"Sure." He got to his feet. "Just don't ask me to follow you around the cross-country course."

Michael laughed, surprising himself.

Michael stared at the scores and couldn't believe his eyes. He was in first place. Of course, there was still cross-country and stadium to go through. He walked back to the truck almost in a daze. He had never been in first place after dressage before.

He tacked up for cross-country, then he slipped on his protective vest and strapped on his helmet. He was a little nervous about the course. He had schooled over most of these fences before, but this was his first time doing a novice-level course. He put on the bridle and swung up onto the big gelding's back.

"Do you need me for anything?" his father asked, looking up at Michael for once.

"No, Dad, you can stay here."

"Good luck." Kevin smiled.

"Thanks, Dad." Michael headed off to the warm-up area. After warming up over a few fences, and having a gallop to get the blood flowing, Michael headed to the start box. When it was his turn, he guided Hammy into the box, leaving him facing the back.

"Ten, nine, eight, seven, six, five..."

Michael turned Hammy around.

"Four, three, two, one, go! Good luck," the starter called as Michael and Hammy left the start box and headed for the first fence.

Hammy felt really good, smooth as silk, galloping like a metronome. They went clean over the first six fences, not even a hesitation. He'd been worried about the ditch in the woods, but Hammy took it in stride. Michael checked his stopwatch as they passed the halfway marker. *Just a tad fast, but that was okay.* He wanted to be as close to the optimum time as possible, but if he was over time he'd get penalty points. A little under would be okay, again not too much because there were penalties for going too fast as well. He maintained the same pace and continued clean over the last five of the eleven jump course. Michael clapped Hammy on the neck as they cantered through the finish flags.

His coach, Jane, was walking in his direction. "How'd you do?"

"Great, just great."

"Good for you."

———

After cross-country, Michael jumped off and led his horse back to the truck. His dad had a bucket of fresh wash water ready, and he held Hammy while Michael untacked and washed him.

"So how did it go?'

"He is such a great horse, Dad. Totally clean."

"So you're still in first?"

"Yeah." Michael removed his helmet and vest, then took the lead from his father. "I'll walk him." He started off, then something struck him. His dad had paid for this horse—had made all this possible. He walked by and said, "Hey."

His father looked up.

"Thanks, Dad."

"No sweat."

After Hammy was cool Michael walked back over to his father. "Did Mom make us a lunch?"

"No. Don't they sell food here?"

"Yeah. You want to hold Hammy? I'll go get us something to eat."

"Okay."

"What do you want?"

"Nothing."

"Nothing?"

"No, I'm not hungry. Let me give you some money though; you get what you want." Kevin pulled a wad of bills out of his pocket.

Michael stared. "Dad, how much money do you carry around?"

Kevin looked up with his eyebrows drawn together. "I don't know, it's just walking around money." He peeled off two twenties. "Is forty enough?"

"Uh, sure Dad." The bills on the outside were hundreds; there had to be close to a thousand dollars in his dad's pocket. Michael didn't want to think about why his father was carrying that much cash.

"Aren't you worried about getting mugged or something?" he asked.

"Around here?"

"Well, no, I guess not, but what about in New York?"

His father laughed. "Nobody messes with me, Michael. Listen, get me a cup of coffee."

"Okay. I need to check the scores, too. Are you going to be okay with Hammy?"

"Sure, I think we can come to an agreement." Kevin shook his fist at the horse, with a smile.

"Okay, I'll be back." When he looked back, his father was stroking Hammy's neck, running his fingers along the horse's coat. Michael almost walked into someone, staring at his old man, convinced now that his father did know something about horses. At the same time, though, something he had said bothered him. *Why didn't anybody mess with him? Did everybody in the world know who his father was? Did he really have that much of a reputation?*

He thought again about the TV show, the mug shot burned into his brain. He wanted so much to have a normal life, to have a dad he could trust, a dad he could talk to. But every time he started to get comfortable with the man, he'd remember what he knew, and everything would sour for him. He found himself shaking his head as he went over to the scoreboard, trying to drive his worries out of his mind and focus on the task at hand.

He bought three burgers, added some fries, a Coke for himself, and the coffee for his dad. Then he grabbed two chocolate brownies. When he got back to the truck, his dad was sitting in the chair with the end of the lead in his hand, Hammy grazing next to him.

"Hey, Dad. I brought you some food just in case." Michael grabbed a burger, and Hammy started pestering him. He fed the horse a piece of the bun.

"Dad?"

"Huh?"

"You know how to handle a horse, don't you?"

"Yeah."

"How do you know that?"

The man sighed. "When I was in medium, upstate, they had this program. They brought in retired racehorses, and the guys who behaved got to work with them, and rehabilitate them. I worked with a big old gelding named Spud."

"I never would have guessed that you would do something like that."

His father shrugged. "I was so fucking bored sitting in that cell, I would have taken up bullfighting if they offered it." Kevin's head came up, and he got to his feet, causing Michael to turn around and see what he was looking at.

He saw Jen coming towards them. She had a man with her, somebody that Michael didn't recognize. Michael noticed out of the corner of his eye that his father was fading back, moving around to the other side of the car. What was his dad doing?

"I just wanted to introduce my dad to you." Jen motioned towards the big man by her side. He looked like her—the same brown hair, the same easy smile. He was wearing a baseball cap, blue jeans, and a dark blue tee shirt with a DARE emblem on it. There was a small radio attached to the left side of his belt.

Michael shook the man's hand as Jen made the introductions. "Nice to meet you." He looked around for his father. "My dad is around here somewhere." He appeared from the front of the truck, moving slowly, as though he was feeling out the situation. "There he is. Dad, this is Jen; she works with me at the barn. This is her dad, Ned McKenzie."

Kevin stepped forward. "Kevin Winterling. Nice to meet you."

Michael was nervous, though he didn't know why. There was something about Jen's dad that he couldn't quite place. Something about the way the man moved, the way he carried himself. It reminded Michael of his father.

"Nice to meet you, too." Michael saw the man's eyes go to the *Semper Fi* tattoo on his dad's forearm as he shook his hand. "Which division?"

"Huh?" Kevin looked down. "Oh, yeah. Uh, First."

"Yeah? Me too." Ned pushed up his sleeve to show off a diamond shaped tattoo, blue background with a red number one in the middle.

Michael's father didn't volunteer any further information. "DARE?"

"Yeah, I'm the chief of police here in town. I do the DARE program at the school. Drug abuse resistance education."

"Chief of police. That sounds interesting."

Michael thought he was going to faint. That was the worst possible thing, right? Why didn't his dad look scared? Wouldn't this guy know him?

"Well, it's not all that interesting. We don't have a lot going on in this town."

"I've got a brother who's a cop, down in western Mass."

"Is he busy?"

Michael decided he didn't want to listen to any more of this. He walked away with Hammy. Jen followed. "I never knew your dad was a cop."

She shrugged. "It's no big deal."

Michael glanced over to where his father was talking to the police chief. He felt his stomach churn. He walked back, with Jen following him. As he grabbed his drink he could hear his father talking about basketball.

"Yeah, I used to be pretty good."

"I could really use another coach for the little kids' teams. We play every Tuesday night at the elementary school, during the school year. It's a way for the kids to get to know some of the police officers, learn that cops aren't the enemy. I have some other parents helping out, but we can always use someone who's good at basketball."

Michael's dad had a half-smile on his face, standing with his arms folded.

"He must have gotten my dad going on that basketball program," said Jen.

Michael wished his father would take off the sunglasses so he could tell what he was looking at. "Yeah."

"I used to be a pretty good ball player myself. Oh, I know I don't look like it now, but I played all through high school," said Jen's dad. "Your boys are pretty good at basketball, I've seen them play."

Michael saw his father's eyebrows go up. He really wished he could tell what the man was thinking. At any moment, Michael expected the cop to draw a gun and throw his father against the truck. Why didn't his dad recognize the danger? Michael grabbed his second burger, and held out the fries to Jen.

"No, thanks, I get too nervous to eat when I'm riding."

"You have to eat something, Jennifer," said her father. "You'll faint from lack of food."

Jen took a few fries. Her father shook his head. "I'll tell your mother, young lady. Of course, she'll figure out some way to make it my fault." He looked at Kevin. "You have a good marriage?"

Michael watched his father nod, wondering if that was the truth.

"I think we're on the verge, you know what I mean?" The heavier man gave a sideways glance at his daughter. "Holding it together for the kids. At least so far." He shrugged.

Michael saw his father nod again.

"You folks just moved in, what, last fall?" Ned directed this question at Kevin. Michael felt himself draw in a sharp breath. He didn't want his dad answering questions, didn't want his dad talking to cops, didn't want anybody to find out who his dad was, to have this whole thing end badly. To have to move again.

"My family moved up here last fall, I'm generally only here on weekends. My job keeps me away during the week." The smile was gone, replaced by a blank slate.

Michael knew what the next question would be.

"Oh, yeah? What do you do?"

Kevin took a deep breath through his nose. "Well, I'm pretty much retired, but I do some troubleshooting, consulting."

"Cool." McKenzie nodded his head. "Like computers?"

"No. More diversified than that, I cover everything."

Michael felt the need to interrupt. "Dad, can you take Hammy for me? I want to go pee." He didn't mention his urge to throw up, just handed his dad the lead rope and walked off, shaking his head. Troubleshooting. That was rich. Shooting and trouble were both accurate.

CHAPTER 18

When Michael returned, his father was alone, sitting in the chair, and holding the end of the lead while Hammy grazed. His dad looked exhausted.

"You okay, Dad?"

"Yeah. Just tired. You were pretty close when you asked me if I was just getting in at six. I got home about two. Got off work late, and traffic was insane. Seems like everybody in the world was going north on ninety-five, and there was an accident in Hartford."

Michael took the lead and leaned against the car. "What do you do for work, Dad?"

"I can't talk about it, Michael."

Michael looked at the ground, and then turned away to prepare Hammy for the next phase.

Michael was in first place; all he had to do was get around the course. He pushed the whole thing with his father out of his mind and rode.

He rode clean, received his blue ribbon and trophy, and walked back to the car.

They packed up, and Michael rode Hammy home. His father met him in the barn and gave the horse a peppermint.

"Congratulations, Michael."

"Thanks, Dad."

He watched his father limp back towards the house with mixed feelings, wondering why he felt an affinity for a man he hardly knew.

When he came into the house his mother and father were sitting at the kitchen table. He opened the oven to check on dinner. It was his mother's lasagna.

"Hey, Mom, how come you're so good at cooking Italian food? You're not Italian, right?" Michael glanced at his father. "You're not Italian either, are you?"

"I learned from some of your father's friends." There were bags under her eyes, and she sounded like she was exhausted.

"Like Vinnie's mom?"

"Yeah." His mother's voice was almost a whisper now, her eyes on her husband.

Michael looked harder at his dad just then and realized the man's eyes were closed. As the boy watched, the man grimaced.

She had seen it, too. "What hurts?"

Michael hadn't thought about it, but now that she mentioned it, that was what it looked like. His father was in pain.

The man focused on his wife. "I'm okay. Just walked a lot today."

She frowned. "I should have told them I couldn't do a double. I should have gone with Michael instead of asking you to do it." She got up. "What do you want for it?"

"I already took some ibuprofen. I'm all right. Really." He closed his eyes again.

Michael blinked. He thought about what his dad had told him, about his leg being shattered, about the screws in it. He realized that his dad must be in constant pain to begin with, never mind walking around on it all day. He cleared his throat.

"When did it happen, Dad?"

The man opened his eyes again and looked straight at his son. "Thirteen and a half years ago."

"And it still hurts?"

"It will always hurt," his mom said. "I've seen the X-rays." She walked over to him. "You really ought to think about using a cane when you've got to do any real walking."

Michael caught the venom in the stare his father gave her. "No, thanks."

That would be a sign of weakness, Michael knew that. No way could his old man use a cane. He felt as if he was beginning to understand the man, starting to know what made him tick. He watched him during dinner, remembering what he had eaten for lunch—a couple of fries and half a chocolate brownie—expecting his dad to be hungry by now. But again the man ate next to nothing, just a few bites of lasagna and a piece of bread with butter. He drank a bottle of root beer and sat back, staring into space. Michael picked up the tension in his mother's voice when she asked about it.

"Is that all you're eating?"

"I had a big lunch."

Michael frowned at the casual lie, told without hesitation, without even a blink. His dad was good at lying, wasn't he? Michael cleared his throat and reached for his own root beer. He caught the quick glance from his father, the anger in the eyes, the dare. His father thought he was going to rat him out over something this little. Michael just shook his head.

"What'd you eat for lunch?" His mother was directing that question at her husband, but she gave Michael a sideways glance as she did.

"I don't know, dear, french fries, burger, chocolate brownie, cup of coffee. I think. I wasn't paying attention."

"You could use another twenty pounds, you know."

The man just shrugged at that.

"What's it called, Mom... Anorexia?" Andy had a smile on his face as he asked the question.

Cindy gave him a sharp stare. The grin vanished. Michael wondered if she was going to keep pestering his dad about food until he gave up eating altogether. That was the way he could see it going. His father was not the kind of person who gave in on anything, and he could hold out longer than she could, Michael thought. His dad seemed to live on air, and it showed in the lack of meat on his tall frame. He could see that was why his mom bugged him about it.

Tuesday morning his mom sat down as he was eating breakfast. "Michael, your dad wants to invite Jen McKenzie and her family over for dinner this weekend. Would you ask her when you see her at the barn?"

Michael stared. "Mom, do you know who her father is?"

"No. Should I?"

"He's the chief of police."

Cindy raised her eyebrows. "What is your father up to now?"

"I don't know, Mom; he met Jen's dad at the event last weekend. The two of them seemed to hit it off." Michael looked down at his plate. "Is he insane, Mom? He can't want the police chief here in this house."

"No, Michael, he's not insane. He probably has some sort of plan. He's always thinking five steps ahead." She paused for a minute. "He calls it down-range thinking."

His father had come in late again, or early, depending on the perspective. He wandered around the house with an unlit Camel in his fingers.

"What are you doing?" Cindy asked him.

He was sitting on the couch, holding the unlit cigarette in one hand and a bottle of liquid antacid in the other, staring into space. He turned his eyes to her. "What?"

"What is all this for? Why are you doing it?"

Michael leaned in the doorway, listening.

"Recon." Kevin sucked on the bottle.

Cindy frowned. "So you're trying to find out how much this cop knows?"

"Sort of. Threat evaluation. Trying to determine if I'm safe here."

"And what about the rest of us?"

"Window dressing."

She advanced on him, looking like she was going to slap him. Michael looked at his father, noting the look of what appeared to be grim amusement on his face.

She stopped and stared at him as though she was just realizing what he had said. "Is this some kind of game with you?"

"It's not a game."

"It's also not a war."

He narrowed his eyes.

"No guns, Kevin." Her voice was hard now.

He moved his eyes to look at Michael, and then looked back at her.

"Not here, not in this house, not around the kids. You can do your stupid threat evaluation, play your stupid war games, but you are not going to endanger the lives of my children. Do you understand me?"

"Yes, ma'am."

"Don't patronize me."

"I would never do that."

But Michael thought from the way a smile played around the corners of his lips that that was exactly what he was doing.

CHAPTER 19

They all sat around the huge table in the dining room. Michael couldn't remember the last time they had eaten in here. He was sure his father had never been here for something like this. His parents were both well dressed; his father was wearing a shirt and tie for once, but still blue jeans and sneakers. He had cleaned up a little—actually looked like a human being. His attitude was better and there was a bit of a smile on his face, despite the dark circles still present under the eyes.

His mother's face was set in an almost permanent frown. She was scurrying around, trying to get everything ready, and barking at anyone who got in her way. Michael realized she was nervous, too.

Michael was wearing a shirt and tie with his chinos and loafers. Andy was wearing baggy pants and a huge shirt with another one of those rock and roll stars on the front. That was something he had in common with his father; he liked to wear those concert shirts, although not the same bands his father favored. Michael knew his dad brought the shirts back from New York on a regular basis. He didn't know where he got them, but he thought it had something to do with Justin Stewart.

As it turned out, it was just Jen, her little brother Will, and their father who joined them for dinner.

"My wife and I are in the process of getting a divorce," Ned explained. "Going downhill fast. She didn't want to come tonight. I'm sorry." He handed Kevin a bottle of wine as he came through the door.

Michael saw his father recoil, like a vampire confronted with a cross, and hand the bottle off to Cindy. "I don't drink."

"Oh, Jesus, I'm sorry." Something attached to his belt made a squawking noise. Michael saw his father stare at it. "Police radio. I'm not on duty tonight, but I need to keep my ears on. I can turn it down a little."

The seven of them sat around the huge table, eating lasagna, green salad, and fresh bread.

Ned McKenzie was quite a talker. Michael could tell that his dad was just as happy to listen, and then he realized that his father was pumping the police chief for information.

"Well, you know, this being a small town, we don't have that much of a drug problem, but I still think it's important to try to prevent it. The sooner you get the kids thinking that drugs are bad, the less likely they'll be to experiment when they get older."

"So for prevention, you have this DARE thing?"

"Yes. It's meant to teach the kids to avoid the stuff."

"What kind of stuff?"

"Oh, you know—stuff like marijuana, cocaine, crack, inhalants, and methamphetamines."

"Heroin?"

"Well, I don't think we have much of that up here. I think the kids are more likely to get involved with stuff that doesn't involve needles."

"You know they snort it now... or smoke it."

"Yeah, I heard about that, but I haven't seen it here."

"What about stopping the traffic? Getting the dealers?"

"Well, I'm not sure we have a whole lot of dealers here in town—at least none that operate on any large scale." He paused. "We do have the State Police and the DEA to help us if we go after the bigger fish. We don't really have the manpower to go after them."

"So what do you spend most of your time doing?"

"Traffic stuff. We occasionally have summer house break-ins and trouble with kids and vandalism. You know, simple stuff. We don't have a lot going on in this little town."

After dinner the two men went into the living room, still talking. Michael and Jen followed.

"Did you go to college?" Kevin asked as he sipped coffee out of a heavy stoneware mug, sinking back into one of the overstuffed chairs.

"Yes, dropped out after two years and went into the Marines. Then I decided to go into this line of work."

"Where were you?"

"Vietnam, believe it or not. I was an MP, spent my thirteen months watching some colonel's back. Didn't see much action. After that, I decided I liked police work, came home, and got a job on the police force here." He looked over at Michael's father. "When were you in?"

"Tail end of the Vietnam War."

"Where were you?"

"I Corps. Hue City..."

"'Nuff said." McKenzie shook his head. "I was glad I wasn't on the front lines. Although nowadays, it's like some kind of big deal to be a 'Nam vet. Everybody likes to think they're hot stuff, you know? Everybody wants you to think they were out on the front. I was happy to be in the rear."

"I guess." He paused. "I would have preferred to have not been out front."

"What'd you do?"

Kevin wrinkled his nose. "I was a sniper."

"That's got to be rough, doing that kind of shit. You get hurt?"

"Yeah."

Ned shook his head again. "The whole war was just so... I don't know." He shrugged his shoulders. "And then coming home, that was even worse. Nobody ever wanted to talk to you. It was like having the plague. I noticed a change, though, after the Gulf War. It was okay then; people started recognizing us again. Started inviting us to the Memorial Day parade and all. And now, like I said, it's a big deal. You have any trouble when you came back?"

"Little bit."

"You were out in front, too. You got hurt. You ever have flashbacks?"

Kevin cleared his throat. "I don't care much for helicopters."

"Hell, I have problems with choppers, too. Brings back memories."

Kevin changed the subject. "So what about this basketball program?"

"Oh yeah, let me tell you more about that."

Michael got up and walked into the kitchen, where his mom was doing dishes. Jen followed. "They could be talking all night," said Jen.

"They're certainly getting along well." Michael shrugged. "That's the most I've ever heard my father talk about the war."

His mother turned her head. She dried her hands on a towel, walked over to the living room, and leaned against the doorjamb, listening. Michael followed. The two men were alone in the darkening room, both of them staring at something else while they talked. The subject had come back to Vietnam.

Ned was speaking, conjuring up images of green jungles, of young kids fighting for something they didn't understand. Michael had to strain to hear him. "I'd see a lot of kids come through—fresh kids, with bright eyes, ready to go out and kill. They'd come back—if they came back—with dead eyes, like they had killed themselves somehow and forgot to lie down. I never knew what it was like; I never had to go out there and face Charlie. My boss was important, and I had to stay on his six. I didn't mind." He paused. "I don't know how anybody could go out there and come back whole. How anybody could keep their sanity." He stopped again and turned towards Kevin. "What about you? How'd you do it?"

Michael looked at his father, anxious to hear the answer. Kevin cleared his throat. "I drank a lot."

"Oh." Ned looked like he had been slapped across the face, as he reached a sudden understanding. "Hey, man, I'm sorry. You doing the twelve-step thing now?"

"Yeah." He shook his head. "What is it I'm supposed to say? My name is Kevin, and I'm an alcoholic."

"You think it helps?"

Kevin raised his head and looked hard at the other man. "No."

"But you kicked it."

"No. I don't drink. If I was to drink, I wouldn't be any different than I was. I just don't drink."

Ned paused and stuck out his lower lip. "So you didn't have any trouble getting booze in the jungle?"

"It was easy. But I didn't drink when I was on duty." He stopped and cleared his throat again, then took a drink from his coffee cup. "When I was working."

When he was working. Michael felt his jaw drop. *Working.* Wasn't that what he was doing last winter when they saw him in Concord? Working?

"Sniping?" Ned asked.

"Yeah." Kevin cleared his throat again and shifted in his chair.

"So you think the booze kept you from going nuts?"

"I kept myself pretty anesthetized. I didn't think about any of it. I still don't." His right hand was clenched around the coffee cup, the fingers of his left hand drumming on the arm of the overstuffed chair.

Michael turned to look at his mother. She was hanging onto the door frame, biting her lip. She looked like she wanted to run to her husband, but she stayed put.

The police chief spoke again. "It's hard to talk about it, isn't it? I don't talk about it much. It's like nobody understands, you know? Nobody but somebody who was there." He let out a short barking sound that Michael assumed was a laugh. "Hell, my wife is leaving me because she says I won't talk to her. I spend hours staring at things that aren't there. I probably drink too much myself."

Kevin nodded. "How can you talk about something like that? It's only the other guys—the others who were there that can even begin to understand." He turned his head and stared right at Michael and his mother standing in the doorway. Michael saw the surprised look in his eyes harden, and he knew there wouldn't be any more revelations tonight.

Kevin excused himself and walked out of the living room, and McKenzie gathered his kids to go home, thanking Cindy and saying goodnight. Michael found it odd that his father didn't appear to send off the guests, but he shrugged it off. It wasn't until later that he understood, when he went up to go to bed and heard his parents arguing.

He paused outside their door on the way to his room, startled by the sound of his mother shouting. "Why won't you talk to me? You'll talk to a complete stranger before you'll talk to me. How do you think that makes me feel?"

Michael couldn't hear his father's quiet reply. He was astonished by his mother's behavior, so much like the way his father had acted for so many years. His father had always been the one with the temper, the one doing the yelling, the one storming out. His dad seemed to have lost the will to fight tonight, though, responding to her shouts with quiet replies.

"You don't ever think about anybody else, do you? Why don't you just go ahead and get drunk?"

Michael wanted to tell her to stop, tell her to leave him alone. *Let him be, Mom, just let him be.* He turned at that thought and walked to his own room, surprised by his sympathetic feelings towards his father. He flopped down on his bed and stared at the ceiling, thinking hard about this man he barely knew.

Michael had always just sort of known, without anybody telling him, that his father had been in the Marines, that it was in the early seventies, and that he must have been in Vietnam. But nobody ever talked about it. He'd never asked his dad about it until recently. He'd never heard his father talk about it. And the drinking thing? He knew his father didn't drink, but nobody ever talked about that either. He'd never heard his father admit that he had been a heavy drinker. He remembered his mother talking about it last winter—trying to talk his father into going to a meeting—but he hadn't understood at that time, hadn't made the connection.

Nobody ever talked about anything in this family. That was just the way it was.

CHAPTER 20

At the sound of Cindy's voice, Kevin snapped out of his daze. "Kevin, would you mind taking the trash to the dump?"

He looked up from his coffee. "The dump?"

"Yeah. Dump... transfer station, same thing. It's down to the other side of the river, off 103. The trash and recycling are in the barn."

"All right."

"Use the Yukon."

Well, duh, he wanted to say... but didn't. He folded the backseat down and loaded the stuff into the truck. The transfer station was crowded. It took a bit of doing to find a place to park. As he was unloading the bins of glass, cans, and paper, he heard someone call his name.

"Hey, Kevin."

He turned, thinking about the weapon in the small of his back, but waiting, wanting to see who it was. It was the police chief, Ned. He was out of uniform in a polo shirt and jeans, but he had his BPD ball cap on.

"First time I've seen you here." Ned stuck out a hand; Kevin pulled off his gloves and shook it, sizing up the guy.

"Yeah, Cindy asked me to do this." Kevin waved at the bins and trash bags. "Kind of busy here."

"Saturday morning at the dump. It's the place to be." Ned grinned. "Let me give you a hand." He reached into the truck and grabbed a plastic bin full of cans. "Of course," he continued as he walked towards the Dumpsters, "nobody calls it the dump anymore. It's the transfer station. It's not politically correct to call it a dump." He laughed as he upended the bin.

Kevin tipped his bin of glass bottles into the next Dumpster, not quite sure how to respond.

"The old dump is right over there." Ned pointed to a sagging plastic snow fence. "Filled in an old sand pit over the course of some fifty years. Now the state wants us to properly cap it, but they won't give us the money to do that. So here it sits." As they walked back to the Yukon for another load, Ned stopped. "There comes trouble." He pointed at a rickety stake truck coming through the gate. "This is why I'm hanging around here today. The dump manager said old Will Brown was giving him shit last week about some used motor oil he wants to get rid of."

As Ned crossed the parking lot, Kevin wondered if he had backup here, if he was expecting trouble. He didn't even know if Ned was the only cop in the whole town, much less if he was the only cop on duty.

Ned was leaning against the driver's door now, talking to the big guy in the truck, who had a white beard that looked like it belonged on a mall Santa. There were a couple of long guns in a rack in the back window of the truck, something that wasn't unusual around here. It still made Kevin nervous, even after seeing the rusty pickups with the gun racks parked every day outside the hardware store. He turned away and carried his bags of trash over to the compactor.

"Morning." The manager leaned out of his booth. "Go ahead and toss those in, then step back, I need to cycle this through."

Kevin nodded and threw the bags, then looked back over at Ned as the machine roared to life. The police chief looked like he was having a heated conversation with Mr. Brown. He had stepped away from the truck and was gesturing with his left hand. His right hand was quiet, hovering near his right hip, where his untucked polo shirt was most likely covering his duty weapon. That touched off Kevin's nerves, and he had to swallow the bile that rose in his throat. He headed back to the truck, watching Ned, hoping there was backup here he hadn't seen.

When Mr. Brown jumped out of the truck with a shotgun in his hands, Kevin almost jumped into his own truck. He didn't want to get involved with this. But Ned was backing up, his hands empty, and the white-bearded guy was waving the shotgun around. The crowd parted, getting out of the way, but there wasn't a lot of screaming that Kevin could hear. Mostly he could hear the compactor grinding away on the trash. That seemed to be where Mr. Brown was heading with Ned, gesturing with the shotgun. This was just stupid. He had to know he wouldn't get away with any of this. Where was Ned's backup?

Kevin felt his shoulders sag as he made up his mind. He covered the short distance between his truck and the compactor in a few strides. When he was between the compactor and the old man, he turned and waited. The machine was still roaring away. Kevin wasn't sure if it couldn't be shut off in the middle of a cycle or the manager just hadn't noticed the guy with the gun. Just as Kevin was thinking about it, the machine shut off with a hiss. At the same time, Mr. Brown focused his attention on Kevin, who gave him a steady stare.

The old man's eyes were watery and glazed. Kevin thought he might be drunk, although it was early in the morning for even a serious drunk. Brown swung the shotgun towards him. "Who the hell are you?"

"Don't do it, Will," Ned warned. "You don't need to get into any more trouble. We can work this out."

Kevin let his eyes shift towards Ned, just enough to see Ned clear his Glock and aim it at Brown. He refocused on the old man, staring straight down the double barrels of an ancient twenty-gauge shotgun.

"Get the hell out of my way." The old man moved his finger to the triggers. Kevin contemplated the effect of twenty-gauge ammo on the human body at a distance of less than ten yards, wondering if the man had bird shot or buckshot loaded. At least the holes would be smaller than a twelve gauge. Kevin took a step back with his left foot, making his stance more stable, turning his body to make less of a target. His vision was narrowing. He couldn't see Ned anymore. He wanted to pull his weapon, but he didn't have a permit, and there'd be questions.

"Will. Come on." Ned's voice was pleading now.

"You youngsters come into my town and start trying to run my life. Keep raising taxes on my property. Now you're telling me what I can do with my trash. I'm tired of it, I tell you."

Ned kept trying. "Will, I've been here all my life. You know me; you knew my father."

Kevin shifted his focus enough to see Ned moving forward as he spoke.

"Come on, Will. Look at me. Do I look like I want to ruin your life?"

The old man turned his head that way, lowering the shotgun just a bit. That was all Kevin needed. He threw himself at Will, aiming for the knees. The old man spun back and fired the shotgun, but it went high, over Kevin's back as he slammed into the guy's lower legs. He went down hard and Kevin rolled away, his ears ringing. But now Will was unarmed, as the shotgun went clattering into the trash compactor.

"Don't you move."

Kevin was sure Ned was talking to him, and he had to fight to remind himself that he wasn't. He looked over at Ned, who was covering Will. The old man was lying on the ground in a heap, sobbing.

"You okay, Kevin?"

He could barely hear Ned. "Yes, sir." Kevin struggled to his feet. "Goddamn motherfucking pussbucket ."

"Did you get hit?" Ned was helping Will to his feet, tucking his own weapon away.

"No, just getting old." Kevin rubbed at his left leg, already aching from hitting the ground hard.

"Thanks. You really saved my ass."

Kevin met his eyes now. "Sure thing. Can I go home?" He realized all of a sudden that the crowd around them was applauding.

Ned nodded as he guided the handcuffed old man towards his car. "Go ahead. I'll give you a call if I need a statement. Take it easy. Thanks again, man."

Kevin watched as Ned pushed Will into the backseat of the patrol car. His hands were shaking so hard he had trouble getting the key into the ignition. When he got home, he sat in the vehicle with his forehead on the steering wheel, wanting a drink. He was damn sure that he wasn't ever going to take the trash to the dump again.

CHAPTER 21

Andy came in late—something that was becoming regular with him. Michael was sitting on the couch, watching television. He glanced up at his brother. "Where's Dad?"

Michael shrugged. "I don't know."

"Want to see something?"

"What?" Michael asked.

Andy pulled a gun out of his pocket. A tiny little thing, easily held in the palm of his hand.

"What's that for?" Michael said, wide-eyed.

Andy just shrugged his shoulders. "I just wanted it, that's all."

"It's not one of Dad's, is it?"

"No."

"What do you want it for?"

"Dad's got a million of them; why shouldn't I have one?"

"You gonna do what Dad does?"

"Shoot people?"

Michael didn't answer, just turned his head, and nodded.

"No. Probably not. I just want to have one."

"What are you doing?"

"What do you mean?"

"You're messing around with pot, aren't you? And tonight you smell like booze."

"What difference does it make to you?"

"I thought you didn't want to be like Dad."

"I'm not going to be like him. I'm going to be successful." Andy dropped the weapon into his coat pocket.

"You think he's not?"

"He got caught, didn't he?"

Michael frowned. "You know what he's going to think of this, don't you?"

Andy shrugged. "I don't give a fuck what he thinks."

————

"Mom."

Cindy turned her head to look at Michael. "What?"

"Andy's getting into trouble."

"What do you mean?"

"You won't tell Dad, will you?"

"I have to tell your dad if it's bad enough. Why don't you tell me what's going on, and I'll decide what to do about it."

Michael sighed and looked around the kitchen. "Where is Dad?"

"I don't know. I don't ask."

"I think Andy's doing drugs."

She turned away from the sink, dried her hands and sat down at the table. "Tell me about it."

"He's going to parties. He hangs out with the wrong people. He's drinking. I know that, and I think he's doing pot, too."

"Your father will kill him."

"That's why I don't want you to tell him."

"What do you want me to do about it, Michael?"

"Talk to him; tell him to straighten up. I told him I'd tell you if he didn't quit, and he hasn't. Maybe you can use Dad as the next level."

"Your father will kill him." She was shaking her head. "How does he hide it?"

"He comes in late a lot; he goes out to parties when you're at work. Dad isn't as sharp as he thinks he is, I guess."

"Actually, Michael, your father probably already knows." She met Michael's eyes. "I'll have to talk to both of them."

Kevin walked in, looked at her, and instantly knew there was something wrong. He set his green duffel down.

"Sit." She pointed to a chair. He only stayed sitting for half of the story. He was on his feet, pacing, by the time she finished.

"It's my fault. I should have seen it coming." He remembered the problems with Vinnie. "Goddamn that kid." He shook his head, fished a quarter out of his pocket, and dropped it into the jar on the kitchen table.

"What are you going to do?"

"I need to talk to him."

"I want to be there when you do."

He hesitated. "Fine." He took his Colt out of the small of his back and walked to the pantry. "Is he here?"

"Yes, I grounded him. He's not going anywhere for a while."

"Let's talk to him then." He closed his eyes and sighed. He was exhausted from driving, and his leg was throbbing. He wasn't looking forward to this.

She knocked.

"Go away."

"Andy, we need to talk."

Kevin tried the door. It was locked. "Open the door, Andrew."

He heard the footsteps coming across the floor, the sound of the lock turning.

Kevin walked in and glared at his son. Andy flopped down on the bed, wearing baggy black cargo pants and a black tee shirt sporting a large red cannabis leaf picture. Kevin rubbed his chin, scratching at the stubble. "On your feet." Andy glared at his father, but stood up. He shrank back as Kevin approached him. "I've never hit you, have I?"

"No."

"No, sir."

Andy made a face. "No, sir."

Kevin stepped up to the boy, towering over him. Andy was tall at nearly sixteen, but not as tall as his father was. "You have a problem, and you know that. I'm going to help you with that problem, because you're a minor, which makes it my problem." He turned away from the boy and began to pace. "Suppose you got arrested?"

"It's a misdemeanor. I'm not selling the stuff."

"I don't care!" Kevin shouted, stepping into the boy's face. "You get arrested for anything, and I go down. Do you see that? No, you *don't* see that, because you're so fucking stupid you can't see past the end of your own nose!"

Andy backed up a step.

"Kevin," Cindy warned.

He ignored her. "Where did you get this stuff? Who gave it to you? I want to know who else in this town is doing this." He began to pace again.

"You drinking, too?"

Andy looked at the floor and nodded.

"Oh, shit," his father said. "Look at me, Andy." The boy looked up at his father. "I'm an alcoholic. You know that, don't you?" Andy shrugged. "I don't drink because I *can't* drink." Kevin paused, frowning. "I never told you this before?" He looked at Cindy. "Don't the kids know this?" He closed his eyes for a minute. "I told Michael; I *know* I did. I didn't tell you?"

He stared at Andy again. "You shouldn't drink. It's genetic. My father was an alcoholic; he died from it. You can't drink." The boy just shrugged. "You're a teenager. I know what it's like to be sixteen years old—invincible."

He looked around the room, walked over to Andy's desk, and sat in the chair. He ran a hand through his practically nonexistent hair. "Hell, I started drinking when I was sixteen." He sighed. "I want you to stop. No more booze. No more pot. No more parties."

"I'm *fifteen*. And you don't know *anything* about me. You've never been here."

"Fifteen, sixteen—what's the difference? You are *not* going to do this anymore, you got me?" He stood up.

"Whatever," Andy mumbled, but Kevin didn't hear him. He walked over to the boy, swallowed hard, and reached out to him, putting a thin hand on the boy's arm.

"One more thing. You sit down and write down everything you know. You tell me where you got the pot, who sold it to you, who sold it to him, if you know that. Do you understand me?"

Andy muttered something.

"You have to look at me when you talk to me."

The boy looked into his father's eyes. "Yes, sir."

"You told me you weren't going to do this again."

Andy shrugged.

"So what good is your word? Do we need to keep you locked up like an animal?"

"No."

Kevin leaned back into the boy's face and shouted at him again. "No, sir!"

"No, sir," Andy muttered.

She leaned against him in bed, resting her head on his chest, touching the scars. "He *does* know, Kevin. He knows about your drinking; he knows how much you hate drugs."

"Then why is he doing this?"

"He's trying to get your attention."

"He's got it."

"What did you mean when you were talking about him doing this before?"

"When I took him with me to the city, back in June, he bought some pot with Vinnie."

"And you didn't tell me?" She rolled away from him and sat up.

"I told him I wouldn't."

"But you're telling me now."

"He didn't keep his end of the bargain."

"You should have told me, Kevin. You have no right to keep something like that from me. This is really incredible. Anything else you want to tell me?"

"Nope." He rolled over, facing away from her, and stared into space.

CHAPTER 22

Sally Barnard climbed the stairs, not in any hurry to get where she was going. One more mobster caught dealing drugs who claimed to know something that somebody thought was relevant for her. She walked into the tiny interrogation room, shook hands all around, and sat down. The mob guy was old, wheezing up a storm, and patting his forehead with a soiled handkerchief.

"So why am I here?" she asked the room in general.

"Go ahead, Tony, give her that info you said you had for her."

"You're Sally Barnard?"

"Yep." The voice sounded familiar. Maybe she had talked to this guy before.

"I called you a couple of months ago about a fugitive, a guy named Duke. Duke Markinson."

She sat up. "Right. I remember. We brought in one of his known associates, but got nothing. Markinson was gone."

"I know where he went."

"You do?"

" Yeah. I want a deal, though."

"I can't promise anything. You tell me where he is, and if it pans out, I'll see what I can do."

"He's in New Hampshire." Tony sat back and smiled as though this was a great piece of news.

"Where in New Hampshire?"

"I don't know."

"It's a pretty big state."

Tony looked puzzled. "I thought it was just some podunk little place."

"I think you're thinking of Rhode Island." Sally got to her feet. "Thanks."

"Hey, what about me?"

"I'll put this in your file."

"So where does that leave me?"

She shrugged as she walked out the door. When she arrived back at the office, she called the New Hampshire office in Concord and let them know that she had reason to believe that a fugitive was in their area. She faxed wanted posters to every major police department in the state and some smaller ones near Concord, remembering that he had been in that area earlier this year. Then she waited.

Cindy put down the phone, tears starting in her eyes as she felt his hand on her leg. "What?" he said, always conserving words, as if there was a limit on the amount of language he was allowed to use.

"That was my mother. My dad died just about an hour ago."

"I'm sorry." He rolled away from her, turned on his bedside light, and grabbed his watch.

She blinked and sat up. He reached for her, touched the tears on her cheeks, and slipped an arm around her shoulders. "You want to go to the funeral?"

"I don't know. I guess so. I should." She tried to remember how long it had been since she had seen her parents.

"You want me to go with you?"

"How?" she sniffled.

"Hey, nobody knows me up here."

"Don't you think there might be somebody there? Some Fed looking for you?"

"I doubt it. I'm a small fish." He rolled out of bed.

"We could all go." He nodded, got to his feet, and limped to the bathroom. "Do you really think it would be okay?" she called after him.

He didn't answer; she could hear him using the toilet, and washing his hands. He washed for a long time, trying to wash off years of accumulated guilt. She had no idea what was going on in his head lately. He'd been living here full time for a few weeks now. She knew he wasn't working anymore, even when he would disappear.

"Do you really think it would be okay?"

He climbed into bed again. "Yeah, sure. Why not?"

She touched his shoulder. "What about that guy—you know, who went to ground—and his brother is a politician in Massachusetts? They harass his brother all the time."

"I don't think you can compare me to him. That was a federal thing. I don't think there are any FBI agents looking for me."

"The funeral will be in two days." She looked at her wrist where her watch should be. She tried to figure out what day it was. "Saturday."

He put an arm around her, pulling her in close. She rested her head on his chest. "How did you feel when your dad died, Kevin?"

"Relieved."

She'd forgotten for the moment that he hadn't gotten along with his father. That even now, after his mother's recent death, he still had very little contact with his family. "I'm feeling a little different, I guess." She felt a tear run down her nose. She didn't have any siblings; it was just her mom and dad and her, and she hadn't seen as much of them as she would have liked.

"Hey, it's okay." He touched her nose. "Let's try to get a little more sleep."

She settled down into his arms and let the memories wash over her.

She was almost proud of him. Them. Kevin and the boys. They were all well dressed, even Andy, who never wore anything other than black tee shirts. All three of her men were wearing dark suits and ties, white button-down shirts, and polished black shoes. Kevin had taken the boys shopping, getting them all outfitted for the funeral. As far as she knew, he'd only ever owned one suit in his entire life—the one he'd married her in.

He didn't tell her how much trouble he'd had with the boys, but she could imagine. Andy had never worn a tie before. She looked over at Kevin as she walked up to the church. He was standing off to one side, hands clasped behind his back. He was wearing dark glasses, and she thought that all he needed was an earpiece stuck in one ear to look like a Secret Service agent. As she approached, he leaned on his cane and followed her. Her boys flanked him. They were wearing the same glasses, looking like clones of their old man. She only hoped they weren't.

She sat with her mother in the front of the church, Kevin beside her, the boys next to him. Her mother kept looking over at him, giving him funny looks. Cindy tolerated it.

She rode to the burial with her mother in the limo behind the hearse. Kevin drove her car, and the boys went with him.

"Why is he here?"

"Who, Mother?"

"Your husband." She was twisting her wedding ring on her finger as she whispered.

"You can't even say his name?" Cindy paused, gathering herself. "He came because I wanted him to." Cindy watched her mother fiddling with the ring, wondering if she would still wear her own ring when her husband was dead. She realized that she had never really thought about it despite years of it being a possibility. He could have died... what, three or four times in the time she had been married to him? Or was it even more than that? She'd sat beside him on at least two of those occasions, holding his hand, willing him to live.

"Wasn't he worried about somebody seeing him here? Isn't he still a fugitive?"

"I'm not worried about it, Mother, although it's certainly nice of you to be so concerned. I would appreciate it if you wouldn't use the word fugitive in public, okay?"

"Okay." Her mother turned to look out the window.

Cindy swallowed hard. "So why didn't you tell me Dad was sick?"

It took a moment for her to answer. "He didn't want to worry you. He really didn't think he was going to go so soon."

"I would have liked to see him again instead of having to come to his funeral."

"I know, Cindy. I'm sorry." She paused. "We didn't think you could."

"That's presumptuous of you."

Her mother changed the subject. "Your boys look great."

"Their father took care of everything."

"Really?" She sounded surprised.

"Really." Cindy sighed. "Look, I know you never liked him. Neither did Dad. I guess Dad would be surprised to see him here. But I love him, Mom, and he's given me a decent life."

"I understand." She sighed as well, sounding almost the same as her daughter. She stared out the window for a few moments. "You know your father cheated on me."

Cindy almost fell off the seat. She hadn't known, had never even suspected. She was surprised her mother would bring it up now at the man's funeral.

"Our whole marriage was a sham. It started right after you were born, when I was still sick. This pillar of the community slept with every woman he could convince to sample his manhood." She paused, looking down at her lap again. "So I guess I do know how you feel. I put up with it because I knew I needed him. And in some way, he needed me, as well."

"I would have left him in a minute," Cindy growled, surprised at her own sudden anger.

"Really? You would have left the man you loved over a few simple indiscretions?"

"But you said he cheated on you for your whole marriage. That's not a few simple indiscretions, Mother."

"Off and on. But I still loved him. And he was still providing for me and you. Think about the time period, Cindy. What could I have done... a divorcée with a small child and no education?"

Cindy looked out the window. "I wish you hadn't told me."

"I needed to tell someone."

"I didn't want to know."

"Now you know why I feel I can understand your situation."

"This isn't anything like my situation. My husband has never been unfaithful."

"Your husband is a murderer."

"Who says?" Cindy found herself wondering why she was defending him. She had seen him standing in courtroom after courtroom, wearing orange jumpsuits and shackles. She had heard the sentences, she knew the charges. Of course he was a murderer. He had admitted as much to a judge. But at least he was faithful. She never doubted that. Her husband was honest. She knew that. Or at least she knew she could tell when he was lying. "So is there anything else I should know? Like a half-sister or something?"

"Not that I know about." Her mother brushed a tear from her cheek. "I suppose it might be possible, but I never heard anything like that."

"He probably would have taken care of any little problem that came up. He was a doctor, after all." Cindy muttered this under her breath, not really wanting her mother to hear it.

"We did want to see more of you, you and your boys."

"But not my husband. That was the problem, Mom."

Her mother seemed to ignore her. "Such nice boys. We enjoyed the times you came up for Thanksgiving."

"Mother, I'm married. You can't just ignore him—pretend he doesn't exist."

Her mother shook her head. "Your father wouldn't even discuss it. He never understood what you saw in that man. Of course, your father was right."

Cindy almost said, "Mother, it's this sort of behavior that keeps me from visiting you, do you understand?" But she bit the words off, refusing to rise to the bait.

"Here we are," her mother said as the limo pulled into the cemetery.

Cindy stood beside the grave, next to her mother, listening to the pastor. Kevin put a hand on her shoulder when she backed up after placing a rose on the coffin. She backed into him when the bugler played Taps, wanting to be close. She watched her mother take the triangle of flag from the two young servicemen, wiping tears as she did.

She wrapped an arm around her husband as they walked towards the car and felt the familiar lump of steel at the small of his back. He wiggled away from her hand and she grabbed his arm, pulling him down to her level.

"At my father's funeral, Kevin?" she hissed in his ear.

"Please don't attract attention, dear."

"I can't believe this." She was angry now, angry for all the times over the years he had spoiled things, had created problems. Suddenly angry at him for the rift in her relationship with her parents. "Why do you think you need that at a funeral, for God's sake?"

"You never know." He straightened up and scanned the horizon.

She moved a step away from him as he continued to walk to the truck. "You're paranoid, you know that?" She wanted to scream at him, beat him with her fists. She remembered the first time he had gone with her to meet her parents, he'd had a gun with him then, too. Nothing had changed.

He looked around, kept walking. People were giving them curious looks. The boys were staring at the ground.

Michael spoke. "Come on, Mom, can we just go?"

She bit her lip and followed her three men to the vehicle, shaking her head.

"Can I take this tie off now?" Andy asked after they had settled in the car.

"We still have to go and eat." She glanced over at Kevin, who was loosening his tie. "I guess it will be okay for you to take it off. You can leave off your suit coat as well, if you want."

"Thanks."

She glanced at the backseat where both boys were squirming out of their coats and taking off ties.

She focused again on Kevin. "Why do you have to carry that at my father's funeral?"

"I have to protect myself. You were the one who suggested there might be somebody here looking for me."

"And what were you going to do, shoot it out over the headstones?"

"No."

"Go quietly?"

"I don't know. I just feel better with some kind of backup, okay?" He paused. "How long do you expect this to last?"

"I don't know. Dad's Legion buddies put this together. I've never been to anything like this before." She hesitated. "I haven't been to a whole lot of funerals." Something to do with being out of touch with the family, with not having many friends.

They parked outside of the old Quonset hut that served as the Legion hall.

"Can't you leave that thing in the car?" she asked.

"No."

She got out of the SUV, and Kevin limped along behind her as she went in with a son on each arm.

"How are you, Cindy?" A large, pale man in a tight sport coat approached, holding out a hand. "Long time no see. I was so sorry to hear about your dad."

"Uh, thanks." She freed her right hand and offered it to him. "Bill Hannaford, right?"

"Right." His eyes widened. "Is this your husband?"

"Yes, Bill. You remember Kevin, I'm sure."

Bill backed up a step, looking up at him. "Uh, yeah."

Cindy saw Kevin smile. He was still wearing the glasses. As Bill scurried off she turned to him. "Are you going to keep those on in here?"

"Yep."

"How can you see?"

"I'll manage."

They found a place to sit, Cindy avoiding her mother. She had no desire to hear any more true confessions.

The boys loaded up paper plates with mounds of food. Cindy looked at Kevin. "You going to eat?"

"Nope."

She started to speak, then thought better of it as he raised his eyebrows.

"We have a deal."

"Okay." She nodded. The deal was that she didn't get to bug him about anything. She wasn't allowed to complain about his eating or his smoking, and he would stay around. Besides, she'd had her quota for the day, bugging him about the gun. She turned in her seat as a heavy-set woman approached the table and Kevin got to his feet.

"Cindy?"

"Louise?"

"Yes. I'm so sorry." She leaned over, wrapped her pulpy arms around Cindy's neck. "Is this your family?" She ran her eyes up and down Kevin as though sizing him up.

Cindy nodded. "My husband, Kevin, and my sons, Michael and Andrew. This is my cousin Louise."

Louise sat down. "I was just talking to your mother, and I had to come see you. I'm so sorry about your father."

Kevin took his seat. The boys sitting across from them looked up from their food and then resumed eating without speaking.

"Did you want to get something to eat, Cindy?" Louise asked.

"Uh..."

"I'll get you a plate, hon, you stay and chat." Kevin got to his feet again.

CHAPTER 23

As Kevin approached the people in line for food, he caught a glimpse of Bill talking into a cell phone. As he watched, the man turned towards him, and Kevin could just see what he thought might be a weapon on the man's hip. Too dark to see for sure. Not worth taking off the glasses. He remembered Bill from a time before he and Cindy were married, before he and Cindy were even dating. He did remember that the guy had been proud of his service in the National Guard. The man in front of him turned to him and looked up. Kevin smiled, trying hard to be polite, trying to be nice. The man stuck a pudgy hand out.

"I'm Dick Wilson."

Kevin shook the man's hand. "Kevin." He didn't offer a last name, avoiding the awkwardness of having to explain why nobody had ever heard his last name before.

"How are you related?"

"He was my father-in-law."

"Really?" The man looked up, focusing on Kevin's face. "You're Cindy's husband?"

"That's right."

"I'm her cousin. I'm surprised we've never met. How long have you been married?"

"Twenty-four years."

"Twenty-four years? I don't remember your wedding. Where have you been hiding?"

Kevin gave him a half-grin. "We lived in New York for about twenty-two of those years. Didn't come up this way a lot." He leaned on the cane as he moved forward in line.

"What'd you do to your leg?"

"Car accident. Long time ago."

Dick turned to the dishes, and Kevin sized them up. Lasagna, green salad, baked beans, potato salad, Swedish meatballs—all the usual potluck fare. Kevin dished out a small amount of the foods he thought she would prefer, realizing that he had very little idea what she liked.

"You have kids, don't you?"

"Two boys." Kevin looked at the table, and then picked up some plastic silverware and a napkin.

Dick followed his gaze. "There she is. How's she doing?"

"She's okay. She's tough." Kevin limped towards the table and realized that Dick was following him. He sat down next to Cindy just as Louise stood up, patting him on the shoulder like a child.

"No, dear, don't get up again." Dick and Louise nodded at each other, and Dick took her seat.

Kevin slid the plate of food over to Cindy, set the plastic ware on the napkin, and spoke to her. "Did you want a drink?"

"What do they have?"

"The usual. Beer. Soda. Kool-Aid." He smiled. "You want me to get you a Bud Light, sweetheart?"

"I'll have whatever you're having. But hey, don't you walk all the way over there again." She looked across the table. "Michael."

The boy was staring at the photographs of soldiers on the wall as he chewed his food. He turned to look at her.

"Go get sodas for your father and me. Please."

"Okay." He looked at them. "What do you want?"

"Get me something with caffeine in it," Kevin said.

Cindy made a face. "I'll have root beer, Michael."

The boy nodded and ambled off.

"So, Cindy, your husband tells me you've been hiding in New York for a long time."

"Hiding?" Cindy glanced at Kevin. He shrugged. She refocused on Dick. "Yes, Dick, we lived down there for a while. Now we're up this way again."

"What do you do for work, Kevin?"

"I'm retired."

Andy snickered.

"Retired?" Dick asked with a quick glance towards Andy.

"That's right."

"How old are you, if you don't mind my asking?"

"Forty-six."

Dick glanced at Cindy, then back at Kevin.

"What did you do that you could retire so early?"

"Business consulting. Troubleshooting."

Andy snickered again.

Michael returned with the drinks and handed his father a Mountain Dew.

Kevin turned to Cindy. "I'm going to go in the bar and have a smoke, okay?" She frowned, but nodded. He removed his sunglasses as he entered the dark room and sat on a stool at the end of the bar. He turned to the room, back against the wall, needing to feel safe. There were a few other guys gathered at the opposite end, but he wasn't interested in conversation. The group was spreading, though, and he soon found himself sitting next to a vociferous character with a Green Beret perched on his salt-and-pepper Brillo-like hair.

He listened, puffing on a Camel, sipping his soda, as the man talked about his time in the service. He finished the soda and ordered a seltzer. Then he narrowed his eyes to stare at the newcomer with the familiar face who was joining in.

Somebody at the far end of the bar asked, "Weren't you in the Army in the sixties, Bill?"

The large, pale man nodded, causing his multiple chins to jiggle. "I'll tell you, you don't know fear until you've looked down the barrel of a rifle at another man ready to kill you." He looked around.

The audience was mostly old men, many of them veterans, with a few civilians thrown in. Kevin figured the majority were of his father-in-law's vintage, WWII, with a few Korean vets and a couple of 'Nam vets thrown in. Nobody younger. As he leaned forward to listen to what Bill had to say, the vet next to him gave him a nod. He returned it.

"You know this guy?"

Kevin nodded again. "As a matter of fact I do."

"What did he do, really?" The man looked around and lowered his voice. "I'd bet my ass he was never in country."

Kevin shook his head. "He wasn't, he was in the Guard, defending the Portsmouth Naval Shipyard from the godless communists."

"What about you?"

"What about me?"

"You've got that look. You've been there."

Kevin shrugged and looked away, searching for something to look at other than the man's intense green eyes. "I was there."

"So was I." He offered a big, callused hand. "John Fitzsimmons. What do you say we unmask the pretender over there?"

"He's not doing any harm." Kevin shook the man's hand and focused on Bill for a minute, listening. Someone was buying him a drink, and he was talking about Khe Sahn.

"So there I was, lying in a hole, and one of the new guys gets shot. I had to crawl the whole length of the trench with tracers going over my head, you know, and I was so sure I was going to die."

A couple of the older men were nodding.

Fitzsimmons gritted his teeth. "I don't want to listen to this shit. I lost friends at Khe Sahn."

"He is going a little overboard. Khe Sahn was a Marine battle. He couldn't have been there." Kevin raised his eyebrows and nodded. "Go ahead then. Tell him I told you to tell him to shut up. He knows who I am."

John got up and walked over to Bill. He tapped him on the shoulder and leaned close to his ear, then pointed at Kevin as he whispered.

Bill turned even whiter than his normal color and looked over at Kevin. Then he closed his mouth and turned away. He walked out of the bar, and the group focused its attention on the two men who had driven him out. Kevin wanted to melt into the woodwork. Fitzsimmons sat down again and lifted his beer once more, then glanced at the group.

"What the hell are you looking at?"

The crowd turned away as one, and Kevin heaved a sigh of relief.

"Fucking rubbernecks," muttered Fitzsimmons. "Let me buy you a drink." He leaned forward and spoke to the barkeep. "Another one of whatever he's having, okay?"

The bartender placed another glass of soda water next to Kevin's two-thirds full one.

"So what'd you do over there?"

Kevin cleared his throat and took a drink. "Sniper."

"No shit. Army or Marine?"

"Marines."

"Totally different programs. Were you any good?"

"I was young, but yeah, I was pretty good."

"I was in the Army."

"Yeah, I saw the cover."

The man chuckled. "I guess I don't bother to keep it a secret anymore."

"Uh-huh."

"So what'd you do after?"

Kevin shrugged. "Different stuff. Knocked around the world a little. Restless, you know?"

The other man nodded. "I know. I've gone through four marriages." He laughed. "Every one of them has a piece of me. Vicious women." Then he sighed. "I tell you, though, there's nothing worse than those fakers—those guys that want people to think they were there. It's bad enough to have gone through it—to come back and have everybody hate you—without having to lose what little dignity you have left to some idiot who was never there."

Kevin stabbed out his cigarette. "I better get back to my wife."

"You part of this funeral thing?"

"Yes, sir. My father-in-law died."

"Your wife taking it okay?"

"So far." He got to his feet. "It was nice talking to you."

"You, too. Semper Fi and all that." The older man raised his glass and Kevin nodded.

CHAPTER 24

When he got back to the table Cindy was listening to Dick as he explained how her mother needed to get out of that big house and settle into a retirement community. "Where do you folks live?" Dick asked as Kevin sat down. "I can let you know what there is nearby. I'm sure you'll want to keep an eye on your mom, Cindy."

"Um, well, we're near Concord."

"You know she's not well off financially, right?"

"No, as a matter of fact I didn't."

"The house is mortgaged to the hilt. She'll have to sell it. The bank has been giving her a break on the payments because of your father's illness." Dick leaned in closer to Cindy and lowered his voice. "I'm not sure your mother even understands how serious her situation is. You probably ought to have a talk with her."

Cindy cleared her throat. "Thanks for letting me know, Dick." She looked around the room. "I'll see if I can track her down."

Kevin got to his feet as Dick left. Cindy turned to him. "I need to find my mother. We should give her a ride back to the house and make sure she's okay."

"We're not staying over, right?" asked Michael.

"No. Will the horses be all right if we are a little late?"

"I can call Jen and ask her to bring them in."

"Great, I'd appreciate that, Michael. Did you bring your phone?" Michael shook his head. "Kevin, you have a cell phone, don't you?"

Kevin frowned at her and handed the phone to Michael, watching him as he dialed and talked to his friend. Cindy got up and craned her neck to locate her mother.

He was on his feet once more when Cindy returned with her mother in tow. "I think Mom is getting a little tired. Can we go now?"

At that moment, Bill walked up to them and said, "Can I talk to you outside for a minute, Mr. Markinson?"

Kevin frowned and stared down at the man. "You must have me confused with someone else."

"No, I don't think I do."

Kevin let his eyes wander for a moment, looking at Cindy and her mother standing there with her mouth hanging open. When he returned his gaze to the pale man in front of him, Bill had unbuttoned his coat, and he could see the Glock semi-auto resting in a holster on the man's hip.

"We can do this here in front of your family, if that's what you want, or we can take it outside." Bill had a smirk on his face now.

"Cindy, stay here. Keep the boys inside. I'll clear this up and be right back." He touched her shoulder, then leaned on the cane and headed for the front door. As they stepped outside, Kevin hesitated to allow his eyes to adjust to the bright sun. Bill stepped up beside him.

"So what are you, Bill, a cop?"

"Yes."

"What do you want with me?"

"There's a felony arrest warrant out on you from New York State."

Kevin continued walking, putting some distance between himself and the building with his family in it. "Where'd you get that idea? Small town New Hampshire cops always keep up with the latest from New York?" He wasn't watching Bill as he talked; he was scanning the horizon, checking the streets and the parking lots. There were no cop cars in sight. Was this man stupid enough to be trying to do this alone?

"Would you stop right there, please?"

Kevin stopped, but still didn't turn to face the man. He could hear the footsteps though, knew the guy was approaching. He half turned, keeping his right hand clear, waiting for an opportunity. He looked at the cop now, expecting to see the big gun in the man's hand, but it wasn't. "Look, Bill, you're mistaken. I'm not who you think I am." He saw the man reach now, and steeled himself, ready to draw if he thought he could, but Bill took a folded sheet of paper out of his pocket.

"Look familiar?" Bill unfolded a fugitive poster. Kevin made a show of squinting at it, even though he knew what it was. "The US Marshal's Service faxed this to me yesterday. I talked to some broad on the phone, Sally somebody, who said she was looking for you, and would I check out your father-in-law's funeral."

Sally Barnard. Kevin knew the name. The photo on the poster was grainy, taken a couple of years ago, but the description was pretty good. "So this is where you got the name Kevin Markinson?"

"That's right."

"It's not me, you know."

"Course it's you."

"What's that say, 'armed and dangerous?' Do I look dangerous to you? Dear God, I'm just an old man attending a funeral with my family. If I was this guy—this Markinson guy—would I take this kind of risk? Do something this stupid?" Kevin was counting on the man looking at the poster again as he spoke, and he took that opportunity to get his hand on his weapon. If Bill had backup that Kevin hadn't seen, this move would get him shot. But Kevin was counting on Bill's ego, and quite possibly a reputation in his department as a loose cannon or, at the very least, an idiot. He hoped that would mean he was doing this on his own.

Kevin slipped the weapon out of his belt, but kept it behind his back as Bill looked up at him again. Kevin could see the doubt in the man's eyes. This was why he wore sunglasses, so nobody could see anything in his eyes. He brought the weapon around, the big 1911 feeling heavy in his hand. His eyes were moving now. He had to know if anyone had seen him. There was not a lot of foot traffic on this street, but he didn't need anybody walking out of the legion hall right now.

Bill gulped.

"Where's your backup, Bill?"

The man tried to go for his gun, but Kevin waved him off.

"Don't do it. I'm armed and dangerous, remember?"

"What are you going to do now?"

"What do you think I should do? Oh, wait, I'm a cop killer." He switched the gun to his left hand and took Bill's gun with his right. He tucked Bill's weapon into his waistband. Then he motioned to the side of the building, towards the Dumpster. "Move."

Bill was shaking.

"Don't worry. I'll tell you a secret, Billy boy." He leaned closer to the man as he followed him. "I'm *not* a cop killer. You can't believe everything you read." Kevin was thinking as fast as he could now, but had no idea what to do with the idiot. A roll of duct tape would come in handy about now.

If he killed the man, he'd be looking at yet another murder sentence. A cop killing that he actually committed, no less. If he didn't kill the man, Bill would tell the world where Kevin was. That was not a good alternative either. Even if people thought he was an idiot—if Bill repeated the story often enough—somebody would investigate it. Cindy's mother had her cell phone number. How long would it be before somebody made the connection and traced it to him, stolen credit card or not?

It took him a minute to realize Bill was whimpering. "What the hell is wrong with you?"

The man quit whining. "You gonna kill me?"

"I already told you; I'm not a cop killer. Give me your handcuffs."

"What?"

"Cuffs, Bill. Where are your cuffs?"

"Left hip pocket."

"Get 'em out."

"Okay." The man was sweating now, huge patches spreading down the sides of his shirt. Kevin took the handcuffs.

"You got keys?"

"Yeah."

"Hand 'em over."

"Right." He handed over a ring of keys.

"Did you talk to anyone about this?" Kevin asked as he slapped the cuffs onto his right wrist.

"No. I called the number for that Deputy, Sally Barnard, but she wasn't in. They were going to have her call me."

"That reminds me. Cell phone."

Bill handed him the phone. Kevin patted him down to make sure he didn't have any other weapons.

"You were just going to be a hero, right? Do this on your own?"

Bill looked away, forehead glistening with sweat.

"So." Kevin sighed as he attached the other end of the handcuffs to the rail on the front of the Dumpster. "What are we going to do now?"

"I don't know."

"You think New York will pay for extradition?"

"What?"

"You know how these things work. The state with the warrant has to pay for transporting the prisoner back. They might not want to do that."

Bill looked confused.

"Your department will just get mad at you for the extra paperwork."

"Really?"

"And then they'll kick me loose." Kevin knew this wasn't true. Any state, even if it was as far away as California, would pay for extradition on a charge like this—the murder, the felony escape.

Bill frowned.

"Of course, that's only if I am who you think I am. You know you're mistaken about me, right?"

Bill raised his head. A glint of hope appeared in his eyes. "Right. Mistaken."

"So you're not going to follow up on this, are you?"

"Oh, no. No sir, I won't."

"You won't bother me or my family again."

"Of course not."

"Good choice, Bill." Kevin kicked the magazine out of the Glock, emptied the bullets, reinserted the mag, and handed the weapon back. "I don't want to see you around, Bill."

"Right. Yes, of course." Bill nodded as he tucked the gun back into his holster.

Kevin tossed the keys into the Dumpster. "Who should I call for you, to come let you loose? What town are you with?"

Bill kind of shrugged.

"You work here?"

He shook his head. "I work up in, well, near Pittsburg." He cleared his throat. "I'm not really a cop. I'm a dispatcher."

"You're not a cop? What the hell were you thinking?"

"I don't know. I thought maybe if I brought you in—if I could fool you—then maybe I could get a job on the force. I did the part-time academy, but all I could get was this dispatcher's job. Been doing that for so long now, I just wanted to be a real cop. I saw that poster, and I knew Cindy when she was in school. I remembered you from... well, anyway." He looked at the ground.

Kevin almost felt sorry for him. He shook his head, then leaned on his cane and turned away.

"Wait, what about my phone?"

Kevin turned back. "You gonna call someone?"

"I have to get out of this; you can't leave me here. I need the phone."

Kevin dropped the phone in the Dumpster next to the keys. "I'll call 911 when I'm away from here."

Bill looked over the edge of the Dumpster. "Okay."

Kevin turned once more, heading back to the building. Back to his family.

"Are you ready to go now?" Cindy asked the minute he walked in.

"Absolutely." Kevin led the way back to the door, holding it open for his wife and mother-in-law.

"What do you need that cane for? Makes you look like an old man."

Cindy groaned. "Mom, he hurt his leg last winter. It's hard for him to stand and walk for a long time, so I made him use the cane."

The old woman nodded. "Glad he listens to you."

Kevin drew himself up to his full height, and Cindy shot him a quick glance. "You want to ride with your mother, Cindy?"

She hesitated. "Okay."

Kevin resisted the urge to check around the corner and look at the Dumpster. Instead, he climbed into the car with the two boys. "You guys ever been up to your grandmother's house?"

"Once," said Andy. "Thanksgiving. I think I was maybe five years old."

Kevin followed Cindy in her mom's car, staying behind her to avoid losing her. He had no idea how to get to the house on his own and didn't want to get lost up here. Never mind the fact he could use his phone to call her mom. He didn't want to get lost in the first place. He was still rattled by the whole incident at the wake—the whole Bill thing. He wondered if Bill really had talked to Sally Barnard. If he had, that meant she was still watching him, looking for him. What made her think he was even in New Hampshire? How in the world could she still be active on his case? They had to have other things to do down there. That brought it back to what he was worried about, that it was personal with her, that she was using her own time and resources to chase him.

He pulled into the driveway, surprised by the resemblance to their house—same color, same big trees lining the long driveway. It was a little eerie.

"I remember this now," said Michael.

Cindy was just getting out of the car, looking over at Kevin and rolling her eyes. He could see that as he approached. He smiled, in spite of himself.

CHAPTER 25

Michael was sitting at the kitchen table, looking at a tack catalog while he ate a sandwich. He'd just finished feeding the horses their lunch. He'd noticed his father's car in the driveway, but hadn't seen him at all yet. He looked up as the screen door slammed and his father walked in. Kevin took off his sunglasses and looked at him. Michael felt a stab of pain in his stomach. His father looked like he was ready to kill someone. His face was set in a firm frown, eyebrows drawn low over ice-cold eyes, with the cords in his neck standing out.

He set down the long black plastic case he'd been carrying, dug into his pocket, and dropped a handful of bright brass on the table.

"What's this?"

Michael looked at the objects. "Shell casings?"

"Right. They yours?"

Michael shook his head. "I don't shoot." He looked up at his father again. "Where'd they come from?"

"I have an informal range set up in the woods by the sand pit. I found these out there."

"Maybe it's one of the neighbors? Somebody hunting maybe?"

"It's an unusual round. A handgun round. A twenty-five. Not the sort of thing a lot of people would have. Definitely not a hunting round." He sat down, took off his baseball cap, and scratched his head.

Michael noticed there was more and more gray there, even though it was cut so short you could hardly see the color. His dad was getting old. He looked back down at the table again.

"Know anybody with a small handgun?"

Michael remembered his brother showing him a tiny pistol. He kept his eyes focused on his plate. "No." He wasn't ready to give up his brother. Not yet.

Kevin sighed and scooped up the shell casings. "So what are you up to?"

Michael looked at him. The facial expression had changed; the rage was gone. His dad was like that—angry for seconds at a time, then cold again. Even without the anger there was no warmth in the eyes, no compassion, no real interest that Michael could see. He wasn't sure why his father bothered.

Michael shrugged. "Nothing much." He thought about asking his dad what he was up to. He figured it wasn't worth the trouble. He saw something change in the man's expression and turned his head to see what he was looking at.

Andy sauntered into the room, wearing his usual black nylon wind pants, a black tee shirt, and a black suit jacket that looked like it might have been popular in the twenties. His black combat boots were untied. He wore black wrap-around sunglasses, even in the house. The boy stopped short when he saw his father.

Kevin tipped the brass back out onto the table, watching his son for a reaction. Andy licked his lips. "Hey, Dad. Didn't know you were here. I was just on my way out." He headed towards the door.

"Hold it."

Andy stopped.

"Turn around."

The boy turned.

Michael could feel his heart pounding. His stomach felt as though someone was twisting a knife in it. He watched as his father picked up a shell between his thumb and forefinger. "You know what this is?"

Andy started to chew on his bottom lip. He shoved his hands into his pants pockets in a sudden move. Michael caught another quick movement out of the corner of his eye and realized his old man had a gun in his hand. Two of the shell casings rolled onto the tile floor, hitting with a soft plinking sound that was way too loud in the sudden silence of the kitchen.

"What the fuck?" muttered Andy.

"Take your hands out of your pockets."

"Dad..." Michael tried.

Andy took his hands out of the pockets and turned the palms out so his dad could see they were empty.

Michael looked from his father, tucking the huge blue-metal weapon back into his pants at the small of his back—his face filled with that rage again, the eyes looking like they could burn a hole through concrete—to his brother, whose face had gone white beneath his long blond hair. There was something else going on here, some kind of interaction between these two that Michael had never seen before.

"These yours?"

"No."

"Don't you lie to me, boy. I'm much better at it than you are." He turned his head to look at Michael. "You don't need to be here, Michael."

"I'll stay." Michael knew he was risking his father's wrath, but he felt the need to stay and protect his brother. Now would be a good time for their mother to wake up.

His father cleared his throat. "Look, Andy, I'm not going to beat you up over this, but if you have a gun, I want to know about it."

Andy turned his head from side to side, scanning, Michael thought, looking for a way out of this. Maybe looking for Mom, the same way he was. He finally returned his attention to their father. "Yeah, I have a gun."

"Where is it?"

Andy started to reach inside his coat, and his father reached for his own gun. Andy withdrew his hand and raised both hands above his head.

"Inside coat pocket." The boy swallowed.

His father got to his feet and took the weapon from the pocket. He sat down hard, as though it was difficult for him to stay upright. He studied the weapon, sizing it up, took out the clip, cleared the chamber, and then dropped the little gun onto the table. He looked up at Andy again. "What's it for?" Andy shrugged. "Somebody threaten you?" Andy shook his head. "Why then?"

"I don't know. Maybe I wanted to be more like you." Andy curled the right side of his mouth into a pretty good imitation of his father's half-grin.

Michael shifted his gaze to his dad, wanting to see his reaction to this. Kevin's face was blank, just staring at his son. He blinked and swallowed, and Michael felt that perhaps Andy had actually struck a nerve. That was obviously what the kid wanted to do. His father got to his feet again, moved closer to Andy, looking him straight in the eye.

They stood in silence, the two of them locked in some sort of staring contest. At last Andy dropped his gaze, looking at the floor.

His father spoke first. "Christ, Andy. Why the hell would you want to do that?" He glanced around the kitchen, looking for something. Then he grabbed the left leg of his jeans and pulled it up past the knee. His jeans were baggy; it was easy enough to expose the damage to his knee. Michael leaned forward to get a better look.

"You see this? You know how much it hurts?" He looked up again at Andy. "You want to take a bullet?" He rolled the pant leg back down and tugged off his sweat-shirt, yanking it over his head, then the undershirt as well. Michael almost fell back in surprise. There was a divot in his father's left shoulder, right below the joint, as if someone had taken a shovel and removed a huge chunk of flesh. There was also a neat round scar in the right side of his chest, with accompanying scars from surgery.

"Maybe I'll be careful."

"Careful in what way? You think I'm *not* careful? I'm forty-six years old. You think I got to be this old without being careful?"

Andy looked away now. Michael thought his father was losing his attention. Then their mother walked in.

She stopped just inside the doorway and cocked her head sideways. Her husband looked at her and put his shirts back on. He scooped up the gun and dropped it into his pocket. "What's going on?" she asked, looking from Andy to Kevin to Michael.

"Nothing," said Andy.

"Just showing off some scars." The man gave her a half-grin and sat back down in his chair.

"What's with the gun?"

"Nothing."

"Nothing?"

"We're just working something out." Kevin cleared his throat. "Just having a little discussion, that's all."

"Can I join you?"

Andy looked at Michael, who looked at his father. Kevin was staring at his wife, his face impassive. He motioned to a chair. "Have a seat."

She sat, then motioned for Andy to sit as well, which he did. "So what are we discussing?"

"The effect of high-powered ammunition on the human body. You should fit right in, with your medical knowledge." Michael noticed that his father was not looking at his wife as he spoke. His eyes were focused instead on Andy.

"Is there any particular reason you're discussing this?"

Kevin took the small gun out of his pocket and laid it on the table. His gaze never wavered. "You want it back?"

Andy shook his head.

"You son of a bitch," Cindy said. "You see what you've done? You bastard..." Her voice trailed off, her mouth working like a fish. Then she set her lips in a hard, thin line, the corners turning down. "It's like some sort of disease! Don't you see that? Don't you see how it's spreading?" Her voice cracked. "You're poisoning him."

"Don't see how you can blame it on me."

"What are you, stupid? You think he learned this stuff from me?" She paused. "So what are we going to do about it?"

Kevin shrugged. "I can keep it if you want."

"That's not really what I was worried about. You don't see the deeper problem here?" She looked at Andy. "Will you please take off those ridiculous sunglasses?" The boy removed the glasses, revealing red-rimmed eyes with nearly black half-circles beneath them. "There's other stuff going on here."

Kevin lifted his eyebrows. "Like what?"

"You are so clueless sometimes. He's still doing drugs."

He twisted his head and glared at the boy. "Are you?"

Andy cleared his throat. "Yes, sir."

"You're not even going to deny it?" Kevin asked.

Andy shrugged. "Just pot. Nothing hard."

"We send him away, right?" He turned to look at his wife. "That's what we decided. One more chance, then we send him to rehab."

She nodded, dropped into a chair. "Do we give him one more chance?"

His father kept his gaze on his older boy as he spoke to Michael. "Michael, we need you to go now." Michael nodded and left the room, wondering what was going to happen to Andy.

Andy spent two weeks visiting what his mother called an outpatient adolescent treatment facility. When he finished he was different; Kevin saw that immediately. But he wasn't different in the way his parents had hoped. He was tougher, hardened, stealthier. He had learned from his mistakes, all right—but not what they had expected him to learn.

He took up running, surprising both his parents. Kevin thought it might just be a way to get out of the house, since his mother refused to allow him to go anywhere, and the running kept him away for long periods of time. Kevin would sometimes watch him stretch in the driveway in the morning. He remembered when he used to do that, wishing he could still run, and felt old.

Andy had gotten into a driver's ed class with his father's help. The school-sponsored class was full, but Kevin agreed to pay for private lessons. By the time Andy turned sixteen, he was ready to get his license.

Andy's birthday fell on a Friday. Cindy was still at work when Kevin made his way down the stairs and poured himself a bowl of Raisin Bran. Andy was already at the table, freshly showered, and wearing just a pair of cutoffs. He was tanned and tall, his long blond hair pulled back into a ponytail now. Cindy hated that; Kevin found it amusing. It was only a year ago that he'd chopped off his own ponytail. Kevin had a feeling that was why Cindy hated it so much.

"How you doing?" Kevin asked.

Andy shrugged.

"You want to go get your license today?"

"Yeah. I guess Mom will take me this afternoon."

"You have an appointment?"

"No, it's walk-in."

"Where do you have to go?"

"Concord."

"I can take you."

Andy lifted his head to meet his father's eyes. "Okay."

"Let me just finish my breakfast. You go get dressed. Put something halfway decent on."

"Why?"

"Cause if you dress like a druggie they won't give you your license."

"If I pass, I pass."

"The driving test is subjective."

"How'd you do on yours?"

Kevin had to think for a minute. "Never took one."

"How'd you get away with that?"

Kevin shrugged.

"So your license that you have now, is that legitimate?" Andy asked.

"Yep." That lie was as easy as telling the truth.

"But you didn't have to take a test to get it."

"Right." He watched the boy head up the back stairs, then he finished his breakfast and went to get dressed.

He knew Cindy had taken care of the parent permission form getting Andy added onto her insurance, and set aside the paperwork she had planned on taking in. There was also a birth certificate, which Kevin knew to be a forgery, and a passport—not a forgery—obtained with the help of the fake birth certificate. He sat at the desk for a minute, studying the pile of papers, and wondering how life had gotten so complicated. Maybe he should just let her take the boy in to get his license.

"Dad?" Andy was standing in the doorway, wearing jeans with a shirt and tie.

"I'm ready." He scooped up the papers and got to his feet. They went down the front stairs. Cindy was sitting at the table.

"Hey." She sounded tired. "What are you guys doing?"

"I was going to take him to get his license."

"You?"

"Yeah. Is that okay?"

"You know where the office is?"

"No."

"It's at the Department of Safety in Concord."

"So?"

"So, the State Police have their headquarters in the same place."

"So?"

"Kevin." Her voice was lower now, close to a whisper. "Don't do this."

He looked over at the boy, then back at her. "I just wanted to take my son to get his first license."

She looked down at the table. "You just like to play with fire."

"What the hell does that mean?"

She looked up at him again. "You need the excitement, don't you? You need to be where the action is. You want to walk in there and smile and wave at those troopers. You want to get caught."

"I do not."

"Then why are you spending so much time hanging around with the Police Chief? Why do you keep going down to New York? Why do you drive ninety miles an hour on the highway?"

He shot Andy a quick glance. The boy looked away. "This isn't about me."

"If it wasn't about you, you wouldn't care if I took Andy to get his license. It's all about you; it always is." She paused to take a breath. "What is it, a death wish?"

Kevin glanced over at Andy again, standing there with his eyebrows drawn down, his hands shoved into his pockets. "Okay. I give up. You take him."

The next day he handed Andy the keys to his car and motioned for him to come out to the garage. "I need a ride."

"Where we going?"

"I've got something to do."

"Okay, but where do you want me to go?"

"Bow. I'll tell you where when we get there."

"Okay." Andy drove to the highway, merged carefully with the couple of other cars on the road. "Can I open it up?"

"You're funny."

"No, really." Andy glanced in the rear view mirror. "I don't see any cops."

"You get a ticket, you lose your brand new license for ninety days."

"Only if I get caught."

"Not worth the risk."

"I guess." Andy shrugged. "So where are we going?"

"Get off at the end of the highway and take a right." Andy obeyed. "Now take a right here."

"Into the car dealer?"

"Yeah."

"What for?"

"I thought you might like to pick out a car. I've got one in mind, but if you don't like it, we can discuss alternatives."

"You're kidding."

"Come on." Kevin unfolded his long legs and walked towards the building. "Bring my keys, okay?"

"Sure." Andy trotted after him.

Kevin leaned on the counter. "Ann Diprimo, please."

"That's me, what can I do for you?" A black-haired woman turned around.

"I'm Kevin Winterling. We spoke on the phone. I want to see that Miata."

"A Miata?" gasped Andy.

"Is this the lucky kid?" the saleswoman asked, coming around from behind the desk with a dealer plate and a set of keys.

"Yes, this is my son, Andy. He got his license yesterday."

She shook her head. "I wish I'd gotten this kind of birthday present when I was your age." She led the way to the lot.

Andy spotted it from the door, a red convertible, used but still in good shape. "It's perfect."

"You like it?"

"I love it."

"I figured since Michael has that expensive horse, I could get you something nice."

"Mr. Winterling, I just need to make a photocopy of your license. Why don't you guys check it out?" Kevin fished out his wallet and handed the woman his own brand new New Hampshire license.

"So will this do, Andy?"

Andy was opening the doors, crawling inside, checking the trunk. "This is so cool, Dad. It looks brand new. What year is it?"

"It's a ninety-seven. Last year they used the pop-up headlights."

"And it's really mine?"

"It's yours as long as you stay clean."

"What?" Andy climbed out of the car.

"You stay clean, you keep the car. You slip up once, I sell it. You got that?"

Andy just stood there, staring at his father.

"You boys ready to take it out for a test drive?"

"Thanks, Ms. Diprimo."

"Oh, call me Ann. I'll see you when you get back, okay?"

Andy drove the little car on the highway, took the tight exit ramps too fast, grinning like his face would break. When they got back to the dealer they sat for a minute before Kevin got out of the car.

"What do you think?"

"I love it, Dad."

"Can you live up to your end of the bargain?"

Andy scratched his chin. "Yeah, no problem."

"Okay. Let's go pay for it."

CHAPTER 26

He didn't know how he had let himself get talked into this. He was sitting on the beach—well, not technically on the beach. He was in one of those silly folding web chairs, and that was on the beach. Sitting right near the Atlantic Ocean, which was so cold that he didn't even want to put his feet in it. The boys were swimming.

"How can they stand that water?"

Cindy looked over at him. "This is the only time of year it's warm enough to go in. It'll be warmer in September, but of course by then the boys will be back in school, and we won't have time for this." She reached for his hand and squeezed it. "I'm so glad you decided to come."

He resisted the thoughts that came to mind, the unspoken words behind what she said, the hidden meaning. The "you never go anywhere with us" meaning. The "where have you been for the past however many years it's been?" Instead, he raised one corner of his mouth in a half grin. He didn't reply to her, just let his eyes wander up and down the beach.

This place was making him nervous, although he didn't know why. Just too many people, he figured. "Is it always this crowded during the week?"

"Yeah, especially when it's hot like this."

"Don't these people have jobs?"

"I don't know; maybe they're all on vacation."

He leaned back in the beach chair, pulling his hat lower over his eyes. He wasn't wearing his Mets cap today; he was wearing a hat Andy had bought for him. He got the impression it had been a joke. He wasn't really supposed to wear it; it was just supposed to rub him the wrong way. It was a boonie hat in a Vietnam Tiger stripe camouflage pattern. He'd plopped it on his short-cut hair this morning as they prepared to leave, cinched up the chin strap, and hadn't taken it off since. He hadn't really minded the way it looked in the mirror. Hid that gray that was starting to show.

He was also wearing swim trunks, though he had no intention of going near the water. Cindy had bought these for him just this summer for reasons he couldn't fathom. Bright red with broad orange and blue stripes, they came practically down to his knees. He refused to go so far as to remove his shirt, but he was wearing a big, floppy tee shirt—black, with a picture of Bruce Springsteen on it. He was uncomfortable here, not just because of the whole casual atmosphere—the carnival atmosphere even; it was more than that. There was something about big groups in small places that made him tense. There was a lot of beach here, but too many people were spread over it.

It only added to his discomfort that he didn't have any place to hide a weapon. He'd left his gun in the glove compartment of the SUV. Cindy had given him a hard time about bringing it at all. He sighed, fished out a cigarette, and lit it—which brought another dirty look from her. He glared back at her, but turned away as he exhaled the smoke.

He didn't want to be here with the screaming kids and the searing sun. "When do we get to go home?"

She frowned at him. "Can't you be normal for one day?"

He clenched his jaw and looked over her head for a moment, the dark sunglasses keeping that fact a secret.

She cleared her throat. "You want a drink?"

"I guess."

"What do you want?"

"Root Beer."

She had forced Michael to drag a wagon bearing a loaded cooler over the soft sand, and now she opened it and pulled out a brown bottle.

"Thanks."

"So how are things?"

"What kind of things?" He had absolutely no idea what she was talking about.

"Oh, I don't know, life, work, you know, whatever."

"Okay, I guess." He shifted in his chair. He wasn't about to talk to her about work. He wasn't sure he would even be comfortable talking to her about life. Maybe he could get her to talk about *her* life instead. "You busy at work lately?"

"Off and on. It follows the cycles of the moon."

"Really?"

"Sure. More babies around the full moon, more emergencies—more nuts, too."

He glanced up at the sky, wondering if the moon was full at the moment. Something was making him uneasy. Maybe it was just the situation. He honestly couldn't remember the last time he'd sat and had a real conversation with her.

"It's been nice having you around full time."

"Uh-huh."

"This going to be a long-term thing?"

"Should be."

"Everything going smoothly for you?"

"As well as can be expected."

"You worried about Andy?"

That was out of left field. "Are you?" Turn that back around to her; she brought it up.

"I don't know. Do you think he's staying clean?"

"It's hard to tell. He's got that attitude all the time, which is pretty normal for him, being a teenager and all. Won't talk about anything; keeps everything a secret." He stared out at the two boys standing in the water, wondering where the taller one had gotten that attitude. Maybe the same place he'd gotten the blond hair that was always in his eyes. The boy reminded Kevin of himself at that age. Maybe that was the problem.

"He needs a hobby."

"A hobby?"

"Yeah, like Michael has his horses; it keeps him out of trouble. Andy has never had any real interests. He just sort of floats along."

"Okay." He nodded. "I know what you mean."

She took a deep breath and let it out in a sigh. "I did the best I could with them, Kevin. I really did."

He tried to keep himself from thinking of the undercurrent again, the unspoken criticism of his absence. He looked out at the two boys once more, body surfing on the not-so-big waves. "They're good kids, honey; you did okay."

"I feel like I messed up with Andy. I don't know what I did wrong. Should we have forced him into rehab? Do you think we made the right choice?"

"He seems to be staying out of trouble now, right? I haven't seen any more signs that he's still using. Have you?" He squinted out at the water, watching his two boys, and wondering what he should be looking for. Andy hadn't wandered off to find a drug dealer in the time they'd been here today, as far as he could tell.

"I didn't see the signs in the first place."

"He'll be all right."

"Do you really think so?"

"Sure," he lied. There was way too much she didn't know; way too much he didn't want to tell her.

She was silent for a few minutes. Then she got to her feet and tugged off the big tee shirt she had been wearing over her suit. "I'm going in. You want to come?"

"It's too cold for me."

"That's probably true, with your lack of body fat. You'd get hypothermic." She walked off. "I'll be back." He shivered as he watched her wade into the ocean.

Lunch consisted of sandwiches washed down with homemade lemonade. Kevin watched his kids eat. "Aren't you going to eat?" Cindy asked him.

"Not very hungry."

"Got to watch your weight, eh, Dad?" Andy grinned.

His father frowned at him, ignoring the dig, staying cool. He'd always been thin; lately he actually *had* gained some weight. He just wasn't hungry here. Sand in the food and all that.

They stayed until late afternoon, and then dragged the stuff back over the dunes to the car. Kevin eyed the traffic on the narrow road outside the State Park. "Hon, why don't we wait till the traffic clears out a little?" He hoped she'd listen to reason. He hated getting trapped in traffic.

"It'll be okay; it seems to be moving anyway."

The older boy piped up now. "I'll drive if you want, Mom."

"You will not drive, Andrew. Now get in the car."

He watched the two boys clamber into the back, then climbed into the passenger seat. He had no intention of driving in this kind of traffic in a strange place. He wanted to be able to watch what was going on. Then again, he considered, would it be better to drive, to be in control? He thought of saying something as she started the engine, but he didn't.

They eased out onto the narrow beach boulevard, creeping along with what seemed like a million other people. They moved about two hundred yards, then came to a stop. She crept forward, impatient, until the bumper of the SUV was almost touching the trunk of the Civic in front of them.

"Honey, would you mind leaving a little more space between us and the car in front of us?" he asked.

"Advice from the anti-terrorism school of driving," snorted Andy.

Kevin turned and glared at the boy, then swiveled back around to watch what was going on outside. Nothing was moving. It was long line of traffic along the boardwalk, all the way up to Rye, most likely. He cocked his head sideways, staring at the cars in front of them, when a sudden movement caught his eye. From a side street to his right a burly man with a graying beard stepped out, gripping a baseball bat. He strode up to the car in front of theirs and smashed the passenger side window.

"Cool," said Andy. "Did you see that?"

"Yes, I did see it—and it's *not* cool." Cindy was looking around, scanning for an exit. She looked in the rear-view mirror; the Nissan behind her was almost as close as she was to the Honda in front. The man with the bat was stuffing something into his pockets and turning away from the car.

"Do you have your cell phone on you, Kevin?"

"No." Of all the days to forget the stupid phone. He checked the mirrors. No way out. Trapped like rats. Get out of the car and run? He unbuckled his seat belt and hesitated. How could he protect his family like that?

"Can't you do something?" Her voice was rising; he could hear the fear in it. That clinched the decision. He didn't want her to be afraid, and that overrode his desire to stay out of trouble. He opened the glove box, took out his Colt 1911, and held it in his lap. Then he waited—staying cool—as the man, who was singing something now, approached their SUV.

"Mom," said Michael, in an almost squeaky voice. "Move the car."

"I can't." She leaned on the horn.

Kevin hit the switch on the window, lowering it as the man approached.

"Show me the way to go home," he bellowed, off key, raising the baseball bat. "I'm tired and... Good day to you, kind sir." He bowed next to the car. "Would you mind handing over your cash?"

Kevin frowned, easing the safety off. The big gun was locked, cocked and loaded, always ready to go. Seven hollow-point rounds in the magazine—one in the chamber. .45 ACP. He didn't even have to raise the weapon; he could shoot the idiot right through the car door. Of course that would ruin his wife's car.

Cindy inched the Yukon forward, and the man swung the bat, taking off the side mirror. She screamed above the sound of breaking glass as the mirror hit the pavement.

"Get the hell away from my car." Kevin said it in a level voice. No anger. No yelling. Still cool.

"Hand over the money, bud, or I'll ventilate your rear window." Black eyes flashed within the tanned, wrinkled face.

Michael unbuckled his seat belt and scrambled to the middle of the car.

"Kevin, please." Her voice was pleading now, terror clear in it. Kevin shifted towards the center seat and raised the weapon in his right hand, lifting it until it was just high enough to be seen above the door. He brought his left hand up and added it to the handle, tightening just enough to depress the grip safety. He cleared his throat as the other man held the bat with both hands and took a practice swing. Horns were blaring on all sides now, and Kevin could just hear a siren above the din.

"Hey, asshole."

The man brought his eyes to focus on Kevin again. "What the...?"

Kevin growled, "Back off," and brought his trigger finger inside the trigger guard.

The thief dropped the bat, turned, and ran.

Kevin lowered the weapon, re-engaging the safety. He kept his eyes moving, looking for cops now. He dropped the semi-automatic back into the glove box. "Keep moving if you can. I don't want to answer any questions; you got that?"

She nodded, tears running down her face. He slid back over by the door and raised the window again, putting on his seat belt.

"Michael, get back in your seat. Put your seat belt on." He was barking orders still, even with the danger past. Although he wasn't sure it had passed. He closed his eyes for a second as the car continued to inch forward. When he reopened them, a cop on a bicycle approached them. A bicycle of all things. Where was this guy five minutes ago? The car in front of them pulled over into a parking lot, and the cop began to wave at them, trying to get Cindy to pull over.

"Keep driving."

"Kevin, he wants me to stop."

"Keep driving. Wave at him and keep moving."

She continued to inch along in traffic, past the bewildered cop, who approached the car even as they inched forward. Kevin rolled the window down again, about halfway.

"You folks need to pull over, I need to get a statement from you."

"That's okay, officer. We just want to get home; no harm done. He ran off; didn't steal anything from us." Kevin started to close the window again.

"You need to pull over now. You witnessed the robbery of the car in front of you."

Cindy had stopped, and Kevin waved his left hand at her, trying to get her to keep going.

"I need you to give me a description of the thief."

"I really didn't get a good look at him, officer."

"Kevin," Cindy muttered under her breath. "The nice officer wants us to stop."

"Keep driving, dear." He leaned a little closer to the cop and hardened his voice. "Look. We don't want to press charges against the guy, and I can't give you a description, so unless you plan to charge us with something, we're going to go home now."

The young police officer backed away from the car and threw up his hands. "Okay, folks. If that's the way you want it. Move along."

Kevin leaned forward against the seat belt and buried his face in his hands as Cindy pressed the accelerator to bring the vehicle back to a snail's pace.

As they reached the highway and cruising speed, Kevin lit a cigarette with shaking hands.

"Not in the car with the kids, Kevin." Her voice was as shaky as he felt.

He ignored her and took a deep drag on the Camel.

Andy started a fit of simulated coughing.

"Kevin," Cindy repeated.

"Leave him alone, Mom," Michael said.

Cindy was silent for a few minutes, and then looked over at her husband. "I appreciate what you did back there."

"I didn't do anything." He rolled the window down a bit and tapped the ashes outside the car. He cleared his throat as he put the window back up. "You understand what I'm saying? I didn't do anything. The guy just took off when I talked to him. Maybe the sound of the sirens scared him. I don't know. But I didn't do anything."

She turned back to the road. "We're okay now, right? The police can't come after us, can they?"

"Cindy, they're already running the plates. I wouldn't be surprised if there's a state trooper in our driveway when we get home. They'll want us to give them a description, tell them where the guy came from, where he went. If they catch him, they'll call us in to testify, under oath, about what happened. Do you see why I'm worried about all of this?"

"But you didn't even fire the gun," Michael protested.

Andy muttered, "It's a fucking federal crime just for him to have the gun."

"Watch your mouth, young man." Kevin wheeled around to glare at his older son, startling himself that he could sound so much like a parent.

"Oh. I didn't even think. Oh, no." She shook her head. "Do you want me to drop you somewhere? Do you want to run?"

He couldn't believe she was asking this so calmly, like she was asking what he wanted for dinner. She was asking despite knowing that it would blow the whole life he had made here, would take him away again. He turned to stare out the window. "Fuck."

She kept driving while he thought about it. He didn't want to run. He'd spent too many years on the run. That was why he'd missed out on so many of these lovely trips to the beach. He shuddered.

"Kevin, what do you want to do?"

"I don't know."

He didn't even have so much as a change of clothes. There was a little cash in the car, in the back, hidden with the tire changing equipment. Enough to get him to New York, to get him to his next stash of cash. He stuck the cigarette in the ashtray, unbuckled his seat belt, and climbed into the back seat.

"Watch it," growled Andy.

"What are you doing?" asked Cindy, watching him in the rear view mirror. "Do you want me to pull over?"

"Just drive." He climbed to the rear and scooted over next to the compartment that held the jack. Fiddled with the latch, popped it open, and reached deep into the well. Nothing. He withdrew his hand and thought for a moment. He was sure he had put some emergency money in here—at least a thousand bucks. He looked up and noticed Andy craning around to look at him. He poked his hand back into the compartment and felt around the tools.

"What's going on, Kevin?" Cindy called back.

"Nothing." He glared at the boy, who turned around to face front again. The kid had taken his cash; that was obvious. He climbed back over the seats and resumed his place in the front.

"Do you want to go to Manchester, to catch a plane or a bus?" Cindy asked. "Now's the time to say so, before we get past it."

"No." He picked up the cigarette again and sucked on it.

"Are you sure?"

"Yeah, let's just get home."

So he wasn't going anywhere today. Still, he could take his chances, let her testify maybe, avoid the subpoena. Maybe they wouldn't be persistent; maybe they'd never catch the jerk. Maybe nobody else had seen the gun. He watched the scenery change from strange to familiar, and they pulled into the driveway.

"If you see a cop car, I want you to take it into the garage. Don't stop outside; just go straight into the garage. I need to ditch the piece. You understand?" He hoped his voice wasn't as nervous as he felt. He hoped that local cop at the beach hadn't recognized his face. He hoped there wouldn't be a trooper waiting for them.

The state cop was there all right, sitting in his vehicle.

Cindy hit the garage door opener as they came close enough and drove right into the building.

"Stall him," Kevin hissed through gritted teeth as he opened the glove compartment and grabbed the gun, tucking it into his waistband and pulling the shirt down over it.

Cindy got out of the truck and headed out of the garage, meeting the young man in the Smokey Bear hat as he approached.

"Is there a problem, officer?"

"Cindy Winterling?"

"Yes, that's me."

"I'm Sergeant Stubbs." He reached out a hand.

She shook his hand, and walked to the house, leaving the officer no choice but to follow. "What's this about, Sergeant?"

"You were at the scene of a crime earlier today. You left without giving a statement. The officers on the scene were hoping you'd reconsider. Maybe go back and talk to them, or even talk to me." The man turned as the two boys came up behind him.

Kevin watched them walk away, then carried the weapon to his Jaguar and stuffed it under the driver's seat. He couldn't hear what the cop was saying now; they were almost at the porch. He moved to the door of the garage and stood there, waiting and watching, not sure he wanted to go any closer. Cindy was standing on the porch, looking down at the trooper with his hat in his left hand, running his right hand over his short-cut hair. He turned and Kevin knew he'd been spotted. The man was still talking to Cindy, but he was looking in Kevin's direction. Then he was walking back towards the garage, and Cindy was following him. Kevin could just about make out what she was saying, something about harassment.

He jammed the hat down further on his head and stepped out of the garage, remembering his etiquette for dealing with cops—keeping his hands in sight and well away from his body.

Cindy said loudly, "That does it. I'm calling my lawyer."

Kevin almost smiled at that. Instead he nodded at the trooper as the man approached. "What can I do for you, officer?"

"Are you Mr. Winterling?"

"Yes, sir."

"Mr. Winterling, all we're asking is that you answer a few simple questions, just give us a description of the man. We have witnesses who said he was threatening you; he damaged your car. You must have seen what he looked like."

"Frankly, Sergeant, uh..."

"Stubbs."

"Right, Sergeant Stubbs. We didn't get that great a look at the man. Something scared him, and he took off. I assume it was the approaching sirens."

"Yes, but..."

"Now if you'll excuse us, we're exhausted. We've had a rough day. I just want to get cleaned up, okay?"

The young man looked from Kevin to Cindy, who was standing with her arms folded, glaring at him, and back again. He sighed, put his hat on, and walked to his cruiser. Kevin watched him drive off, then grabbed his cigarettes out of the car and walked to the porch. He sat down hard in one of the wooden chairs and lit a Camel. Eyes closed, he leaned back, took a deep drag, and let it out in a long sigh.

"Do you think that's the end of it?"

He opened his eyes to look at Cindy, who was now standing on the porch again. He shrugged. "We can only hope."

"I'm sorry," she said. "I never expected anything like this to happen."

He nodded and stared out at the driveway, Watching, and waiting for more cops. Trying to stay cool.

CHAPTER 27

He finished the cigarette and headed into the house, looking for Andy. He wasn't that angry. He wasn't sure whether the kid had stolen the cash when he was still using or if he had stolen it recently. If it was recent, it meant the kid was probably using again. Using what, Kevin didn't know. The boy had tested positive to alcohol and marijuana when he started his counseling at the treatment center. He was probably back on them. Kevin knew how hard it was to give up alcohol. He could still taste it, could still feel it sliding down his throat. He shuddered.

Andy wasn't in the living room, or in the kitchen. Kevin limped up the stairs, leaning on the railing. He was washed out, ready to fall asleep. He knocked on the door.

"Yeah?"

"Can I come in?"

"Dad?"

"Yeah."

"Whatever." Kevin could hear the boy coming across the floor. He unlocked the door and opened it. "Come on in."

Kevin hesitated. He could hear Cindy downstairs in the kitchen getting dinner ready. Satisfied that she was busy enough, he crossed the threshold into his son's room. Andy pushed the door shut behind him. Kevin looked around. Every flat surface was covered in clothes and papers. No clear spots, no obvious drug paraphernalia. He picked up a pile, moved it off the chair by the computer, and sat down. Andy sat on the bed, feet up, back against the headboard.

"I think you know why I'm here." Kevin spoke without looking at the boy, focusing instead on the screen saver—a mass of swirling lines.

"I'll pay you back."

"Of course you will. The question is how."

"I don't know; I'll get a part-time job or something. There's still a couple of weeks left before school." The boy hesitated. "You didn't tell Mom, did you?"

"I haven't discussed this with your mother, no." He looked at the boy. "I'd like to know what you used the money for."

"I'd rather not say."

"Of course." Kevin nodded. He wondered why he wasn't angrier with the kid. He'd reached some kind of numbness with all of this. The boy was going to do drugs, and there wasn't much he could do about it. He got up. "I'll tell you what. You touch any of my money again, and I'll turn you in. Not to your mother... to the cops. You'll go to prison." He stared at Andy, letting it sink in. Then he walked to the door.

"Yeah, sure you will," the kid sneered. "I go down, *you* go down."

Kevin stopped and swallowed hard. He turned. "It's not quite that simple."

"Sure it is. I'll flip faster than you can blink. I got no loyalty to you. Just blood. Nothing important."

Kevin wasn't sure he was hearing this. "What are you talking about?"

Andy snorted. "I know, Dad. I know everything. I know why you didn't want to talk to that cop—why you couldn't get caught with a gun on you. Why you have cash stashed in a million different hiding places."

Kevin continued to the door. "Yeah, sure. You know everything. Sixteen, right? Comes with the territory." He had dim memories of being sixteen... drinking, stealing cars.

"I know your real name. All I have to do is pick up the phone. Who should I call first? FBI? Maybe that US marshal. . .what was her name again? Sally somebody? I think there's even a reward."

Kevin closed his eyes. He wouldn't take this from anyone. Why was he taking it from the kid? His mind ran over the gamut of possibilities. Let the kid go down; see how he liked prison. Or play the blackmail game; let the kid think he was in charge here, but keep him under tighter surveillance. Kevin was too tired to think right now. Was there a third choice?

In his mind he turned away from the door and crossed the room in a hurry. Grabbed his son by the neck and pulled him off the bed into a standing position, fought with him, and scared him back to his senses. But he couldn't allow himself to hurt the boy, no matter how angry he was.

Instead he gave the kid a weak grin. "Works both ways, doesn't it?"

Andy drew his eyebrows down, staring at his father.

"I turn you in, you turn me in. Maybe I don't care anymore. Maybe I wouldn't have a problem with that. Maybe I think prison would be the best thing for you."

Then he turned and stalked out of the room. He shut the door and leaned against it for a moment. "Maybe I think prison would be the best thing for me." He shook his head and limped back downstairs.

He lay awake in bed for the night, staring at the ceiling, and wondering what he was going to do with this kid. He needed a plan, a way to keep an eye on the boy without the kid knowing he was doing it. He remembered the drug issues earlier in the year and wondered if Andy was doing that again. If he was, it would have to be further away from home. That would mean big chunks of time. It took most of what was left of the night to figure out what he was going to do.

Kevin sat in a rented car in Lawrence, Massachusetts, and watched his son buy drugs. He'd followed the boy after he left work early. He'd talked to the manager of the movie theater where Andy worked, and found out the boy had been working shorter hours. He had also been cutting out early on a regular basis, but not coming home. That gave him the chunk of time he needed. Kevin realized that things were a lot worse than he had thought. It was his fault; he was sure of that. His fault for not being a better father. His kid was driving his Miata, buying drugs in a vacant lot in a neighborhood where Kevin wouldn't walk around without a piece. This was nuts. He pulled over at the same corner.

The twenty-something kid eyed him, but walked over to the vehicle.

"You a cop?" He showed a set of yellow teeth in something resembling a smile, but it ended up looking more like a wolf baring its teeth.

"No."

"You look like a cop."

"Nobody's ever accused me of that before." He let one corner of his mouth drift up. "Did you just sell those kids some weed?"

"No, girl. You want some?"

"Girl?"

"Yeah. I got nose candy... cocaine, gringo. You buying or not?"

"No." He got out of the car. "That's my kid."

The man stared up at him. "So?"

Kevin took his Colt out of the small of his back, grabbed the creep by the arm, and stuck the weapon under the man's chin. "Have you sold this shit to him before?"

"Yeah." The man was cool.

"You know which kid I'm talking about?"

The man shrugged, trying to back up.

"The blonde-haired kid driving the car... his name is Andy. He's my son. You're not going to sell to him anymore, you understand?"

"Sure man, anything you say." Then he was slashing with a switchblade that appeared out of nowhere.

Kevin jumped back and leveled the gun at the man's chest, squeezed the trigger, and watched him fall. He stepped back, studied him, breathing a little too fast, and trying to think calm thoughts. He did a quick scan of the area, but it was late and cold, and there weren't any people in sight. He put one more shot in the guy's head; then he was in the rental car with the gun tucked under the seat, and out of there within minutes. He threw the gun in the Merrimack River—much as he hated to do that—turned in the rental car, and drove his own car home.

He confronted Andy again, sold the Miata, and told the kid he would have to stick close to home for the rest of his life. The boy actually seemed to take it well—seemed to be keeping his nose clean.

He was sitting at the kitchen table when Cindy came in. "Hey," she said.

"Hey."

"Moved my mother into the Odd Fellows home."

Kevin just nodded.

"She said that guy Bill Hannaford called her up and threatened her. He said he wanted to know where you were, and he could have her arrested."

"That asshole has no right bugging an old lady. For God's sake, she's not even related to me." He got out of his chair and paced the room. "Let me make a couple of phone calls, see what I can do to call him off. You know he's not even a cop?" He paused. "Your mother doesn't know where we are, does she?"

"No."

"Would she tell him anything?"

"I don't know."

"Does she hate me that much?"

"I don't know, Kevin. I'm hoping that moving her will make a difference; he might not be able to find her."

"He's lucky he can find his own dick. The guy's an idiot. Let me know if anything else happens."

One more complication. One more loose end wandering around. Kevin was beginning to regret not killing the loser when he had a chance.

———

Kevin started by asking Michael to show him how to use a computer. He sat in front of the machine with his kid by his side and considered killing himself. It would be so much easier than this.

"Okay, see, this connects you to the Internet. It uses our phone line to dial up. Once it's connected, you can open the browser."

"So then what?"

"What are you looking for?" Michael asked.

"A person."

"Well, then type the guy's name into a search engine."

"What's a search engine?"

"Okay, there're a couple of different ones. I like Google; it's new, but it works. Or you can use Big Yellow. What's the guy's name?"

Kevin hesitated. "I can take it from here."

"There's one more thing you should know, though."

"What?"

"Anything you type into this computer will be saved on the computer in hidden files." Michael hesitated. "You might want to think about it before you use this one for anything that might come back to bite you." Kevin turned to look at the boy, who shrugged. "There are public access computers at the library. You could do your search there."

After he found Bill Hannaford's address, he tried to figure out how he was going to do this. The more he thought about it... planting himself in the woods and shooting the guy in the head, or maybe doing something that would look like an accident... the more he realized that he just didn't want to do this in the first place.

His cell phone rang as he sat staring into space in the office. "Yeah."

"Hey, Boss."

"Hey, Justin."

"Tony Masiello flipped."

"Seriously? I thought he would."

"Yeah, and he's not afraid to tell everyone he knows that it's all your fault. He's gunning for you."

"Justin, I have an idea. Do you have a phone number for Tony? One that doesn't have a tap on it?"

"Yeah. What do you have in mind?"

"I want Tony to come up here and try to take me out."

"I think we can make that work. Tony's crew has abandoned him, so he's on his own. He's not really supposed to leave the area, but if we make it worth his while..."

Kevin could almost hear Justin smiling through the phone. "I think I can make it worth his while."

It actually made the television news—just the New Hampshire station, but it impressed Kevin just the same. Tony Masiello, reputed mobster from Queens, traveled to New Hampshire and gunned down a police dispatcher in Pittsburg. Nobody could figure a connection.

There was no motive, although witnesses said the elderly mobster appeared to lose his temper when he met Bill Hannaford. Supposedly Hannaford drew a weapon, which resulted in a shootout. The dispatcher was killed and Masiello was then arrested by Hannaford's colleagues.

Perfect.

CHAPTER 28

He watched from the window as Michael charged out of the house, yelling. A dog was in the horse pasture, chasing the horses. Kevin didn't understand why the horses would run from something that small when they were so big. The dog was some sort of terrier cross, and it couldn't have weighed more than twenty pounds; yet it was chasing these 1,200-pound horses. He watched as his son threw rocks at the dog, finally chasing it off. He remained in the window as the boy came back towards the house, panting.

Ten minutes later there was a knock at the door of his office. "Yeah." He was leaning back in his chair, feet up on the desk, chewing on a plastic drinking straw.

Cindy came in. "Hi."

Kevin nodded in reply.

"We're having a little problem," she said.

"Yeah?"

"The neighbors let their dog run loose all the time; it's over here chasing the horses. Michael is worried about the horses getting hurt."

"Yeah?"

"Well, you know how much the horse cost."

"Yeah." He agreed with that. He *did* know how much the horse cost. Seventy-five hundred dollars of his money. "That little rat dog is going to hurt a horse?"

"Sure. He could run through the fence, or step in a hole. Break a leg." She sat on the couch, leaning back into the cushions. She took a deep breath through her nose. "Have you been smoking in here?"

"Once in a while."

"I'd rather you didn't."

"I know. I'm trying to quit."

"So anyway, I called the dog officer for, like, the tenth time. He won't even come out here anymore. He warned the neighbors once; we filed a complaint once. That's it."

"What does he suggest now?"

"You want to know what he suggests?" She got up and began pacing. "He told me to shoot the thing. He said, 'You take a .22, go out there, and shoot the dog. You have that right; it's chasing your livestock. You just go shoot it.'"

Kevin actually smiled at that, picturing his wife with a rifle in her hands, trying to shoot a dog.

"It's not funny, Kevin."

"What do you want me to do?"

"What do you think I want you to do?"

"You want me to shoot the dog?" She shrugged her shoulders. "Let me know the next time the animal comes around." He sighed. "You know this is not going to endear us to the neighbors, right?"

"What can we do? Should we let these redneck idiots push us around? Let them hurt our horses?"

"You want me to take the body over and put it in their mailbox or what?" She stopped and stared at him. "Call the dog officer again, tell him what we're going to do, and tell him he needs to come and get the creature's body and take it to the neighbors, okay?"

"So you'll do it?"

"Hell, Cindy—I won't like it, but I'll do it. If it makes you and the kid happy, I'll do it."

———

It wasn't more than a week later that he stood in the window, listening to the dog bark, and knew it was in the horse pasture. He was on his way down the stairs, and met Michael coming up. He saw the look in the boy's eyes, and knew in that instant that if he had handed him a rifle, the kid would have shot the dog himself. Kevin didn't want that.

"Keep it in the pasture, and keep an eye on the horses."

He headed for the pantry, pulling out his keys as he went. He opened the locked cupboard, and opened up the case that held his sniper's rifle. He loaded it, shaking his head as he considered what would happen to the little mutt when the .308 hollow point bullet hit it.

As he walked out of the windowless room Cindy was there.

"Be careful."

"This is what you want, right?"

She shrugged, digging her her hands into her pockets.

"Call the dog officer, okay? Tell him it's going down now; tell him to get his ass over here."

"You want him to see you?"

"Not really. But hopefully, by the time he arrives, I'll be finished."

She picked up the phone as he walked out the door. He went over the law in his head as he worked the bolt, chambering a round. Can't fire within what, two hundred feet of the house? Of course, that was nothing compared to all the laws he was breaking just by carrying the weapon. He stopped at the fence. Michael was standing there, watching the mutt as it ran across the field, chasing his precious horses. The boy turned to him, his eyes still showing the wild anger that had worried his father in the house.

"You sure you want to watch this?"

"I'd like to do it."

"This rifle would knock you flat on your ass, and you'd probably hit one of the horses."

He knew the scope was zeroed at three hundred yards, so he did an estimate on the distance, and then raised the rifle to his shoulder, resting the stock on the wooden fence. He sighted down the scope, leading the animal just enough. *Take a breath; let it out, squeeze the trigger.* He saw Michael jump out of the corner of his eye; saw the dog explode. The horses panicked, running off in the other direction, kicking and bucking.

"How do you do that?"

"Lots of practice." When he turned around there was a beat-up yellow van in the driveway. He let the rifle point at the ground as he headed for the house, looking for Cindy. A balding man with a large belly got out of the van. Michael was still out in the pasture, trying to calm the horses. "Dog's in the pasture." Kevin hooked a thumb in that direction and continued towards the house, feeling the stare on the back of his neck.

Summer was running out fast; school started right before Labor Day. Michael and Jen were spending most of their spare time together now. He still thought of her as a friend, nothing more. He didn't want it to be anything more. He liked Jen; that was enough.

They planned a long trail ride before hunting season, before school really got going. As they rode down the driveway Michael saw Jen look up at the house and shiver. Michael's father stood in one of the upstairs windows, watching.

They headed out on a trail they knew; they both had a good sense of direction. They brought along halters and lead ropes as well as a backpack of lunch for themselves. After riding all morning, they stopped near an old abandoned farm deep in the woods. The barn had a hole in the roof. The glass was long gone from the windows of the house, the paint faded to a soft gray. The roof on the house was sagging; it would probably have holes in it soon, but there was something about the place that Michael liked.

They ate the sandwiches, and then Jen walked over in the direction of the old buildings as Michael put the bridles back on the horses. He backed away from the clearing as he heard a car driving in. They had been to this place before, but had never seen anyone here.

"Jen," he called, "let's go." He led the horses farther into the woods. "Jen, I've got a bad feeling about this."

He watched as she froze in the clearing, like a deer caught in headlights. The car doors opened and two young men with guns jumped out and immediately headed towards Jen. Her mouth fell open, and Michael was sure she was going to scream, but she didn't. Michael jumped on Hammy and, pulling Sox towards him, backed into the narrow trail through the dense pine woods. He needed to see what was going on, but he didn't want to be spotted. He watched as the two guys reached Jen and wrestled with her as they dragged her to the house. She resisted the whole way, kicking and fighting, but they were stronger than she was.

That was enough for him. He turned Hammy and rode as fast as he could, his heart pounding. Jen was just an innocent kid. He knew those guns were real, and it scared him. He also knew he needed his father. He hated the thought, but he knew his father would know what to do. Didn't that stupid TV show say "armed and dangerous?" That was what he needed now. Somebody more dangerous than those guys in the woods.

He galloped into the yard. No sign of anybody. He hated to do it, but he threw the hot horses into their stalls, whipped off their tack, and yanked out their water buckets. They'd be okay as long as they didn't eat or drink; he hoped. Then he ran into the house. He burst into his father's study, without even thinking, much less knocking. He knew he shouldn't do that, because it was against the rules. But at this moment the rules didn't matter.

"Dad... help... Jen!" he gasped.

Kevin had been sitting behind his desk when Michael burst in. He was on his feet in a matter of seconds, with a gun in his hand.

"Help Jen what?" He set the gun down.

Michael was still out of breath. He finally managed, "Some men with guns grabbed her."

He looked at his father, appealing for help. He saw the look on the man's face change from curiosity to determination.

"Call the police."

"No Dad. These guys look like they'll hurt her if they see cops." He swallowed hard.

"You have to call her father."

"Seriously, Dad, we can't."

Kevin picked the handgun up off his desk, tucking it into the small of his back. He put on a pair of thin leather gloves, scooped his keys off the desk and headed downstairs. He strode into the pantry with Michael close on his heels. Unlocking a cupboard, he reached past a number of small metal boxes and took out a long plastic case. Michael watched as his father took out the rifle with the scope, the same one he'd used on the dog. He then grabbed a box of ammunition for the long gun.

"All right then," he said as he closed and locked the cupboard, "let's rock and roll."

Kevin picked up a camouflage jacket from a peg on the wall and grabbed a baseball cap while heading out the door.

Michael climbed into the truck. His dad set the gun on the seat, slipped into the jacket, and climbed into the vehicle himself.

His father sat for a minute, his gloved hands clenching the steering wheel. Then he grimaced and started the engine, backing the big SUV out of the garage.

Michael directed his father to the narrow dirt road that led to the old farm.

"Why would they grab her?"

"I don't know; I guess she was in the wrong place at the wrong time."

"How many guys?"

"I saw two guys. Turn here." He directed his dad into the abandoned driveway. "Slow down; we're almost there."

"Okay." He eased the vehicle to a stop. He put it in park and said, "You're going to drive."

"What?" Michael knew how to drive, had tooled around in the driveway, but it surprised him to be asked.

"You heard me." His father was pushing long brass cartridges into the bottom of the rifle now. He pulled the handgun out of his belt and laid it on the seat as he got out of the truck.

"Use it if you have to. Eight shots. See the safety?"

Michael nodded.

"Just don't shoot me; be sure of your target." He paused. "If you see me go down, or I don't come out in three minutes, you clear out and call the cops, right?" He handed Michael his cell phone, and then grabbed the rifle off the seat.

Michael nodded and slid into the driver's seat. His father climbed onto the running board on the opposite side of the vehicle, and motioned for Michael to proceed.

"Pull in slow; stop in a clear area. If you see anyone, talk to them; keep them talking. Don't shut the truck off."

CHAPTER 29

His father jumped off the running board and ran towards the woods as the truck rolled into the clearing. Michael stopped. He picked up the gun, barely holding it. A man stepped out of the house. He wasn't obviously armed, but he had a hand in his coat pocket.

"What do you want?" he hollered. Up close he looked a lot younger. No more than nineteen years old, with super short hair and the start of a scruffy beard.

"Hi, there. Maybe you can help me; I think I'm lost," said Michael.

"You sure are, kid." The teenager approached the truck, pulling a gun out of his coat. Michael heard a shot, and the youngster sagged to the ground, blood spreading from his chest. A second kid burst out of the door, holding a shotgun, and yelling.

"Chris!" He took three strides across the yard. Another shot rang out, and he crumpled to the ground, gurgling. Michael sat frozen.

A third person—younger even than the other two—came out the door now, holding Jen by the arm. He held a tiny automatic, aiming in the general direction of her head.

"You shoot me, the kid dies. You hear me?" He was looking around, frantic.

Michael stared. He recognized Andy, but he was convinced this was some kind of weird mistake. This must be someone else. Andy's gaze settled on the SUV, and even from this distance, Michael could see the understanding on his face. He watched as Andy lowered the gun.

"Hey." Their father stepped into the clearing. He carried the rifle pointed at the ground.

"You don't want that kid. She hasn't done anything. You want me. I'm the one that shot your buddies." He set the rifle down and held his hands out while he walked towards his son, whose eyes were moving from his friends, to his brother sitting in the truck, to his father.

Andy let go of the girl and raised the handgun. He pointed it at his father, holding it sideways, as if he wasn't really aiming.

"Back off, man, I don't want to get into this with you."

"Jen, run to the truck." Kevin didn't take his eyes off the boy. "Drop the gun, Andy."

Michael wanted to just go, and leave this whole mess behind. "Just drop the gun, Andy. It's over." He wanted to shout it, but it came out in a whisper.

"What are you going to do, Dad? You gonna let me walk away from this?" Andy's voice cracked.

"I don't know, Andy. You gonna shoot me?" Andy looked at the gun shaking in his hand, lowered it, and looked at the two guys on the ground. "You gotta drop it, Andy. You need to drop the gun."

Michael could hear the tension in his father's voice. Yet it still carried authority. Still demanded obedience. Andy cast one more glance at his two buddies, then dropped the little semi-auto into the dirt of the driveway.

Kevin stepped forward and picked up the weapon. He then turned and used it to fire a shot into the heads of each body lying on the ground, causing Michael to jump each time. He walked back to the truck, opened the driver's side door, and motioned Michael over. Jen was sobbing in the passenger seat.

"Andy. Get in the truck."

The boy looked at his father, then over at the two bodies on the ground. Michael thought for a moment that he was going to refuse. Then he walked to the truck and climbed in, settling in the back. Michael climbed into the back, and Kevin tossed the guns onto the front seat. He got in, turned the vehicle around, and then drove out of the clearing.

The ride home was quiet. When they got there, Kevin turned off the engine. "Okay, kids, we don't talk about this," he said, looking straight ahead through the windshield. His hands were shaking as he rested them on the steering wheel.

"We have to call the police," Jen said, sniffling a little, and wiping her nose on her shirt.

"Why?"

"Well..."

"I just killed two men, and you want to call the fucking police?" Kevin turned to glare at her. She shrank back in the seat and didn't answer.

"You just don't get it, do you? You are not going to lead the cops right to my house. You make something up if you feel the need to report this. But leave *me* the hell out of it." He climbed out of the truck, bent over by the side of the driveway, and vomited. He came back to the vehicle and gathered the guns, dropping them in various pockets.

He opened the rear passenger side door. "You. Come with me." Andy made no move to get out of the car. "Did you hear me?" Andy still didn't move; he just sat, staring. Kevin reached into the car, grabbed the boy by the arm, and dragged him out of the vehicle.

When his son fell, he drew back a foot to kick him but stopped. "Get up," he hissed through gritted teeth. "Get the hell up and into that fucking house before I do something I might regret."

Andy got to his feet and went with his father without saying a word.

"Michael," Jen said after a long silence. "What does your dad do for a living?"

"I don't know."

"He saved my life, didn't he?"

"Yeah... probably. I don't know."

"And I can't tell anyone?"

"Right."

"Why?"

"You heard him; he killed those guys. Do you want my dad to go to jail?" He paused. "Back to jail."

She stared at him. "What did you just say?"

"Nothing. Forget it. Please forget it. He'll kill me."

More silence. "So what do we do now?"

"I guess we just go on with our lives."

"I don't know if I can do that, Michael. Does this sort of thing happen all the time in your family? Are you used to this, is that it?"

"My dad has done some strange stuff before, but this takes the cake."

"And why can't we talk to the police? Does he think nobody is going to find out about this? Your brother held a gun to my head. I thought I was dead, Michael." She sat with her legs drawn up, arms wrapped around them, shivering. "I have to tell my dad. I mean, come on. How am I going to explain it?"

"It's my brother, Jen. My older brother. We can't tell the cops; you've got to let my dad handle this." He bit his lip, wondering what to do. He wanted to reach out to her but wasn't confident enough to do it. "I'm really sorry, Jen. It's over now." He started to get out of the car, then turned to her again. "Jen, we need to come up with a story. We need to agree on a story, especially if you're going to talk to your father." He paused. "How much are you going to have to tell your father? Can you just tell him we saw these guys, maybe from a distance, and we rode off before anything happened? Maybe we saw them getting out of the car? We've been out there before, and there's never been anyone there. Maybe you can just tell your dad that it worried you to see people with guns out there in the woods. I mean, it's not like it's hunting season yet. It has to be something bad, right?" He didn't know why he was even asking. Why would she care about protecting his family?

But to his relief, Jen nodded. "I could do that. Then he'll go out there and find it, see what happened."

"But you have to wait. You have to let my dad clean it up first. If you tell your dad now, he'll see those guys, and who knows, maybe there's fingerprints or something. You know, Andy's fingerprints. Let me get my dad to go clean it up first, then you can tell your dad, okay? Is he at work today?"

She shook her head. "I think he's on call for stuff like this, but he doesn't work on weekends."

"Okay, then. We should be good." Jen nodded again, bobbing her head like one of those dogs in the back of people's cars. Michael headed for the house while Jen got her bike and headed for home.

When Michael came into the house he could hear his father yelling—at his brother, he assumed. He couldn't hear any response. He wondered if his father was going to hurt Andy; he sounded that angry. As he approached the office it sounded like maybe he was calming down. He waited just outside the door, not really listening, but still catching bits of conversation. He could hear his dad walking back and forth as he talked.

"Do you have any idea what something like this could do to me, to us, to the family? This is supposed to be a safe place. You understand that; I know you do. What right do you have to bring people like that in here?"

Michael took the silence as an opportunity and knocked on the door.

"Who is it?"

"Michael."

"Come on in."

Kevin settled back in his chair, chewing on a plastic drinking straw, his latest way of avoiding smoking. There were guns on the floor—the long gun, the little gun that Andy had been carrying, the pistol Michael had held while his father was off in the woods, the little revolver from the first kid, and the shotgun from the second kid. Andy was on the couch, all the way down on one end, feet up on the cushions, hugging his knees. Michael sat down at the other end, giving his brother a quick glance.

"What do you want, Michael?" asked his father.

"Do you have any idea what this was about?"

Kevin took a deep breath. "I'll know more later, but I assume you kids stumbled into a drug operation. They were probably cooking heroin in the barn or something equally stupid. I guess they panicked when they saw Jen and grabbed her." The man was looking straight at Andy as he talked.

"Banano," whispered Andy.

"Say what?"

"Banano. We were making bananos."

"What the hell is a banano?"

"It's a joint with coke in it."

Michael glanced at him, then directed a question to his father. "What happens now?"

"Don't know." His dad was still staring at Andy. "Guess I have to clean it up."

"There's one more thing I wanted an explanation of, Dad." Michael stood up, looked out the window, then down at the guns on the floor.

"What?"

"How could you just shoot those kids?" Michael looked at his father. "In cold blood like that."

"I can't talk about it, Michael."

"I need to believe in you, Dad. I need to know you're telling me the truth." He was almost ready to beg. "Tell me the truth for once. Tell me you'll fix everything. Tell me everything will be all right. Tell me you didn't just murder those two kids."

The man looked down at the desk and shook his head. Then he met the boy's eyes. "You have to trust me, Michael. I'll take care of it."

"Why, Dad? Why?"

His father looked at him. "It was self-defense. They were armed."

Michael sat down again. The TV show was in the front of his mind—the mug shots, the long list of crimes including the murder of a young police officer.

His dad continued, "And they are scum—drug dealers, riffraff."

"Dad, that doesn't give you the right to kill people." He paused, thinking hard. "Are you, like, working under cover or something? You some kind of agent?"

Kevin looked down at his desk. "You want the truth, Michael?"

"I don't know."

"I shot those guys because I was afraid for you. You and Andy. I didn't want you to get hurt. I should have never gone there with you. I should have gone alone. I just fu... I just panicked." He started pawing through his desk drawer. He pulled out a pack of cigarettes and lit one. "Don't you tell your mother I'm smoking in the house."

Michael considered smoking in the house small potatoes compared to killing those two kids, but he wasn't about to point that out to his father. He looked over at his brother again.

"Are you done, Michael?"

"Yes, sir."

"I need to talk to Andy some more."

Michael looked at his father, trying to pick up on his current mood. The anger seemed to be done. That was pretty much the way it went with his old man; his rage was hot, but it burned out quick. Michael decided that Andy was probably safe with his dad, and he got up to leave.

"One more thing, Dad. Jen is going to talk to her father. You should clean it up, make sure there's nothing that can lead back to Andy." Michael stared at the floor while he said this, not wanting to look at his father. He couldn't believe he was saying this—that he would even have to think like this. How could he feel like he needed to help his father evade the police... or be willing to help his father evade the police?

"Thanks, Michael."

───────────

Michael was out in the barn when he heard a car door slam. His father was putting a plastic tarp into the SUV along with a red gas can. He met Michael's eyes, nodded at him, and then walked around and got into the vehicle. Andy was already in the car. He shuddered, thinking about what the tarp could be for. Michael walked to the porch as he watched him go.

When his mom drove in more than an hour later, Michael walked out to meet her. She came out of the garage with a shopping bag in her hand. "You don't look good. What's going on, Michael?"

He wasn't sure he could tell her. His dad didn't want him to talk to anyone. Michael shrugged. "I guess you'll have to talk to Dad."

She frowned. "Is he here?"

"No."

"When do you expect him back?"

"He didn't say."

She frowned and walked into the house.

When the Yukon came back, Michael stayed on the porch, swatting mosquitoes. His father approached, Andy lagging behind. Michael heard footsteps behind him and knew his mother was there. Kevin stopped and looked at her, taking off his sunglasses. Michael was surprised by the look on his father's face. He could have sworn the man looked embarrassed or guilty.

"What did you do?" she asked.

"Let's not talk about it here." He stepped up onto the porch and tried to go past her.

"Yeah, Kevin, we're going to talk about it here. I'm sick of not talking, sick of hiding things all the time."

He stepped back off the porch again. "I had to take care of some business."

"Around here? Are you nuts?"

"It wasn't my choice." The man's eyes wandered towards Michael and Andy.

Cindy followed his gaze. "My boys?" She looked at her husband again. "You got the kids involved with this?"

"Actually, Mom, I got Dad involved." Michael looked down.

She sat down on one of the chairs.

Michael met his dad's gaze and was surprised by the humanity in the man's eyes. He sat down next to his mom and related the whole story, leaving out Andy's involvement. If his dad wanted to keep it quiet, he wasn't going to interfere.

CHAPTER 30

Michael looked at his mother, who was shaking her head in disbelief. "What are you going to do when Jen starts talking? She's a thirteen-year-old kid. How long do you think she's going to be able to keep this quiet? My God, her father's the police chief."

Michael looked at his father, who was looking at the ground. "I just went back to clean up."

"You mean bury the bodies."

He shrugged. "I cleaned it up," he said. "The guys are gone." He paused, then looked up at her. "I *had* to keep the kids safe, Cindy. *My* kids." He turned away. "It wasn't my choice."

"It never is, is it? Just like it wasn't your choice to get stuck in the car with that idiot Carlos, or your choice to break out and run. Whose choice was it? Your whole life is one big non-choice after another."

"This was *my* choice, Mom. I got Dad involved. I asked him to help." Michael had never in his life imagined that he would be sticking up for his old man. He looked over at Andy, who was staring off in the other direction, his mouth shut tight.

"I've had enough, Kevin."

Michael looked from one to the other. His father looked stricken.

"What the hell did you want me to do?"

"I don't know. How about call the police?"

"I wanted to. Michael wouldn't let me."

"That's true, Mom. I was afraid Jen would get killed or something. You know, a hostage situation; it would just be a circus." Michael looked at the ground. "Besides, suppose they wanted to come here and talk to me; suppose they started asking questions? Dad's got more guns in that freaking closet than the whole police force in this town. Isn't that a federal offense?"

His father raised an eyebrow, looking sideways at him.

Cindy just stared. "Don't tell me you're taking his side?"

Michael shrugged.

"I've got some cleaning up to do in the house, okay?" Kevin said and walked through the kitchen door. He reappeared a few minutes later, looking down the driveway. A police car was coming in. Michael looked at his father, who muttered an obscenity and ducked back into the house. He then looked at the car. It was Ned McKenzie. The car stopped in the driveway. Michael could hear the activity inside the house and could imagine his father locking guns in the pantry.

Michael looked at his mother now. She was standing up, looking first at the house, then at the police chief, who was getting out of his car. Andy was shuffling towards the kitchen door, trying not to attract too much attention.

McKenzie approached the porch, hat in hand. "Hello, Cindy."

"Hello, Ned."

"I need to talk to Michael."

At least he didn't say he needed to talk to Dad, thought Michael as he moved towards the police chief.

"Michael, I just talked to Jen. She told me about the little adventure you two had this afternoon."

Stick to the story; stick to the story as we discussed it. Michael turned his head as he heard the screen door slam. He tried not to stare as his father came towards him, hat pulled low over his face, dark glasses back in place.

"Hey, Ned." Kevin's voice was quiet, without the edge Michael would have expected. His dad was cool, calm. McKenzie nodded, not even looking at him. "What's the problem?" Kevin asked.

"I need to talk to Michael." McKenzie turned his head to look at Kevin now.

"I'll talk to you," said Michael, hoping to distract him.

"Why don't you tell me what happened?" McKenzie put his hat on his head and took out a notepad and pen.

"We were riding, and we decided to go to this abandoned farm we know about. You know, just to explore. These guys drove in; we saw that they had guns, and we left in a hurry." Michael shrugged.

"Did you see any drugs?"

"No. I didn't get that close to the house." *Don't make assumptions about what Jen has already told him; just stick to your story.*

"How many did you see?"

"Two."

Michael saw something cross the man's face. What had he said wrong? Could he cover it up, distract the man?

"Have you been out there?" *Had Jen said three?*

"No, I called the State Police. I just talked to them on the radio. They said it looked like a war zone." McKenzie looked at Kevin, raising his eyes to look up at the taller man standing on the porch.

"Somebody went in there before they got there, apparently shot the guys and took the bodies. There was blood all over the ground. The house was on fire as though there was some kind of explosion. There were no people there at all unless they find the bodies after they get the fire put out." McKenzie shrugged his shoulders. "Nothing like this has *ever* happened around here."

Michael looked to his mother, who was staring at his father.

"Well, I guess you won't have to worry about them anymore," Kevin said.

McKenzie frowned. "My kid came home with this story and scared me half to death." He turned his head to look at Cindy, who was covering her face with her hands.

"I don't know what I would do if I was a civilian and my kid came to me with that kind of tale."

"I'd call the police; that's what I'd do." Kevin shifted from one foot to the other.

"But you didn't, did you?"

Kevin shrugged. "Nope."

"Why not?"

"I didn't want him to," Michael put in. "Nobody got hurt, and I was afraid that if we called the police, and those guys found out who called the cops, they'd come after us."

"From prison?"

"Oh, come on." Michael was on a roll. "They'd get out on bail, or they'd come after us when they were done with their sentences, or who knows, maybe they'd escape."

"Escape?" said McKenzie. "That only happens in the movies." Kevin wrinkled his nose; McKenzie continued his questioning. "So you were afraid of these guys?"

"Well, yeah. I mean they had guns."

"What about you, Kevin, did you let Michael make the decision, or were you afraid of these guys, too?"

"I didn't want my kids to get hurt. I recommended to Michael that we call the police. He chose to ignore my advice."

Michael heard what his dad said. He said my kids. Not my kid. My kids. More than one. Michael wondered why his dad would make that kind of mistake. Nobody had mentioned Andy yet.

"Weren't you afraid that if you didn't call the police those guys would come after the kids?"

Michael was beginning to see a trap. He looked at his father. The man pursed his lips, thinking.

McKenzie looked at the ground, rubbing the toe of his shoe back and forth.

"State Police said there were some pretty clear tire prints on the scene... tires that didn't belong to the car that was there."

"You investigating a crime that you don't even know happened?"

The officer continued to stare at the ground. "Big tires, you know, with deep treads." He raised his eyes now and looked at the Yukon parked in front of the garage.

"What's your point?"

McKenzie looked at Kevin. "I think somebody took care of these guys. Cleaned it up good, but still..."

Michael looked at his father, who cleared his throat and spoke up. "Well, if something did happen, what are the chances it would happen again? I'm just saying that if somebody did do something like that—killed these guys and took away the bodies, or set the place on fire—how would you know whether it was a rival gang, or some vigilante, or just some private citizen trying to keep his kids safe? Don't you think it's pretty unlikely that it will happen again?"

Michael thought he would faint. His dad was giving way more detail than necessary.

Kevin paused. "What do you really have for evidence anyway? No bodies, no weapons, no shell casings, and no fingerprints, I assume."

McKenzie shook his head.

"I don't think you're going to get a confession."

McKenzie sighed and rubbed the back of his neck.

"So you haven't got much of a case, have you? And I don't think you want to pursue it anyway, do you?"

Michael watched as his father walked down the steps and off the porch. He had learned an awful lot about his dad today, and he wasn't sure he liked all of it.

McKenzie took off his hat. "Sorry to take up your time." The police chief turned and walked back to his car.

Michael noticed that his father had allowed himself a slight smile. He met his father's gaze; he'd taken off his sunglasses. Michael realized that as he looked at him, the look in his father's eyes changed. He turned around; Michael thought it was so that he wouldn't have to meet his eyes.

"Dad?"

"Yeah, Michael?"

"Look at me." Michael heard his mother snicker. He knew that was one of her favorite lines. Kevin turned around, facing him. Michael studied his father's eyes. "Dad, did you use my friendship with Jen to get an in with her father?"

He saw the emotion in his dad's eyes just for a second. Then the eyes became ice again. He thought for a moment his dad was going to deny it.

"Clever, isn't it?" He turned and walked towards the house. "God, I need a drink." His shoulders slumped as he walked away.

Michael looked at his mother, but she was looking at her husband. She followed him into the house.

Michael didn't feel like going in. So his father wasn't such a nice guy. He had used his own son to establish a relationship with a police officer—a relationship that he could use to protect his own hide.

He thought back over what McKenzie had said. Where were the bodies? And what on earth did Andy have to do with any of this? He looked around. Andy had vanished. No telling where he was.

CHAPTER 31

He was lying flat on the ground, looking down at a road. More of a trail really. His rifle was propped on a log, his spotter Marty by his side. They were both silent. Waiting. Watching. A man came into view. The sniper focused his attention. *Definitely wearing the right clothes. Loose-fitting black trousers, black tunic, large, conical hat.* His scout poked him.

"Looks armed to me."

The man in the cross hairs had a .50 caliber machine gun slung over his shoulder. Kevin was waiting to see if he was alone. Two other people came into view behind him, a woman and a young girl. Neither one of them was armed.

"What's with the civilians?" Kevin hissed.

"Who gives a shit; just shoot him."

This trail was known to be heavily traveled by Viet Cong guerrillas; still, he wasn't sure. He finally decided to go on instinct, and he sighted down the scope. Took a deep breath, let it out, and fired. The man fell. The woman dropped to the ground beside him, screaming. The girl stood, looking around, stunned. Kevin fired another shot, at the ground, trying to scare the two of them off. The woman tried to drag the man's body back the way they had come. Kevin fired another shot.

"Leave him," he hissed through clenched teeth.

"It's just the two of them; let's go down there."

Kevin fired another shot at the ground in front of the woman. This finally got them moving into the jungle.

Kevin and Marty walked the several hundred yards down to the body. They kept an eye open for anybody else nearby as they approached the corpse. Kevin bent and started searching for papers. He noted the man's condition in his notebook, and placed one of his bullets on the man's chest. Marty picked up the man's weapon.

"This is one of ours."

Kevin nodded.

They started off the trail. At that moment, the woman charged out of a clump of bushes. Kevin pulled his pistol, but didn't fire. She came at him, screaming, and started pummeling him with her fists.

"Hell, Duke, just shoot the bitch."

Kevin shook his head and backed away. Her head only came up to his chest. He pushed her away, waving the handgun at her. She was still screaming when the two men walked back into the bush.

———

Kevin sat up, panting, and staring into the black.

"Talk to me," Cindy said. "Please, Kevin. Tell me what's going on in your head. We've been married twenty-four years now and I still don't know. I want you to tell me what you've been living with. Let me help you."

She reached for him, touched his arm. He was all the way over on his side of the bed, on the edge of the mattress. He took a deep breath. He had no idea why that picture was in his head, unless it was because of the way he had fired those shots this afternoon. He had killed two kids, and now his head was playing games with him again. He didn't like it, and now she was after him to talk. There were bits and pieces here and there he had talked about, but not everything. Some stuff he kept buried, and wanted to keep buried. Like that memory of the girl and the woman, who were obviously traveling with the soldier. He'd killed a man who was a father and a husband.

"I killed a man in front of his wife and his kid. His wife started hitting me— screaming at me. I can't get her face out of my mind."

"When?"

"1971."

"And it's still haunting you."

"Yeah. They all are; they all do. I can't get any of this stuff out of my head." He flinched when she put a hand on his arm. "You don't know what it's like, what I live with every day."

"Talk to me. Tell me what it's like. That's the only way it's ever going to get any better."

He shook his head in the dark, then realized she couldn't see it. "I can't."

"I used to think the same way. I thought I couldn't talk to anyone. But I've never felt better about myself and my life since I started talking to a therapist." She moved closer to him, draped an arm across his chest.

"I don't need a fucking therapist. I can deal with it." He slid sideways out of bed and headed to the bathroom.

"Then talk to me."

He hesitated in the doorway, flicked on the light, and looked over at her. "We'll see." He shrugged, turned, and walked into the bathroom.

Michael spent the week in a haze, unsure of what to do with himself. Andy seemed to spend most of his time sitting on the couch, staring out the window. School was in full swing, and Michael felt as if his world was going to crash down around him at any moment. He couldn't concentrate on his work, couldn't face Jen in the hallway. Whenever he closed his eyes, he could see his father shooting those kids.

How did he know they were bad guys? Maybe they were just in the wrong place. How could his dad just shoot them like that? And Andy. Michael didn't even want to think about why Andy would have been there. He didn't like the picture that popped into his head every time he closed his eyes. His own brother holding a gun to Jen's head. How could he ever trust Andy again?

He didn't know what to do with the knowledge that his dad might not be such a good guy after all. He thought again about the television show, about the US Marshals looking for his father. Thought about turning him in.

Kevin picked up the phone on the first ring without checking the caller ID.

"Yeah."

"Kevin? Ned McKenzie here."

"What can I do for you?"

"I need you to come with me to a school board meeting. Your kids are playing sports, right?"

"Yeah, I think."

"They're talking about cutting all extracurricular activities out of the budget. They're going to eliminate basketball from the middle and high school. I need people there to fight this."

"I don't know, Ned, I'm not the kind of person to stand up in a crowd."

"There won't be a crowd there, not in this town. There might be ten people there to fight this. You're a bright guy. I need your help."

"Okay, Ned. When's the meeting?"

"Tonight at seven. Town hall."

"I'll be there."

He sat in the back of the room, next to Ned, watching and listening. He let his mind wander, but brought it back when they started talking about how unimportant sports were, which astounded him. In this town, where the basketball team had been to the championship game just the year before, and the kids spent their free time shooting hoops, how could anyone possibly say that the sports program wasn't important? He stayed quiet, even as Ned got to his feet to protest. The room was more crowded than he expected, maybe close to thirty people there.

"You can't take the game away from the kids. They need this." Ned went on, talking about drugs and booze. "We can raise money privately, but we can't lose the sports."

When the meeting was over, Ned dragged him up to meet some of the school board members. The man who had proposed cutting sports had resigned and walked out. The others were clapping Ned on the back.

"This is Kevin Winterling; he's got two boys playing basketball."

"Oh, yeah? Nice to meet you. I'm John Everly, Chairman of the school board." He held out a soft, pudgy hand. Kevin shook it. "What do you do, Mr. Winterling?"

"Call me Kevin. I, uh, I'm retired. I do some consulting."

"So you've got lots of spare time, right?"

"I guess."

Everly looked at Ned, who was grinning and nodding. "Well, the police chief will vouch for you. He told me about you how you're helping him out with the Tuesday night basketball. You ought to be on the school board."

Kevin was flabbergasted. He backed up a step, shaking his head. "I can't do that."

"Sure you can," said Ned, clapping him on the back, close to where the gun would be, if Kevin hadn't thought to leave it at home. "You'd be perfect."

It wasn't until he got home that he really thought about what it meant. He lay in bed, staring at the ceiling, nauseous with the terror. Somebody would recognize him. He couldn't do this. He didn't understand how he could let himself get into this.

It was a couple of weeks later, just into October, when the ringing phone woke him out of a sound sleep at one-thirty in the morning. He rolled across the half-empty bed to Cindy's side and grabbed the handset off her nightstand. "Yeah?"

"Kevin?"

He couldn't place the voice. "Yeah, who's this?"

"This is Ned... Ned McKenzie."

"Hey, Ned. You know what time it is?" He glared at the clock.

"I need you to come down to the Police Station. Down to Town Hall."

Kevin didn't care for the feeling in the pit of his stomach that accompanied that statement. "Why?"

"We had to arrest your son."

He stood up now, wide awake. "Andy?"

"Yes, sir."

"What'd he do?"

"He was at a party; it got out of hand. The neighbors called us... bunch of teenagers drinking. There was nothing I could do but bring them all in."

"I'll be right there."

His first impulse was to call Harvey Longwood, his lawyer in the city, but he figured he'd wait and see. He pulled on his jeans, threw on a turtleneck, stuffed his feet into his boots, and then trotted down the stairs. He started to go to the pantry, but decided it was better not to carry a weapon into the police station and went without it.

There were two boys and two girls sitting on a long bench just outside Ned's office in the Town Hall. Andy looked bored, leaning back in his black wind pants and black turtleneck. He had his arms up on the back of the bench, feet stretched out in front of him; his huge untied yellow work boots blocked the hallway. Kevin could see a big man he didn't recognize through the open door of Ned's office, yelling at the police chief.

"It obviously wasn't my kid. I mean, come on, he's only fifteen. How could he buy booze?"

Ned was sitting in his chair, quietly looking at the guy. Kevin could see another cop in there, too. Jerry somebody—he couldn't remember the young guy's last name. He was on his feet, looking like he was ready to dive between the irate father and the object of the man's rage—the chief.

"I'm not charging your boy with anything, Mr. Johnson." Ned's eyes slid towards Kevin now, who was hanging back, staying out of the way. He focused back on Johnson. "We brought all the kids down here to make sure we talked to the parents, that's all. I wanted to sober them up a little, give them reason to think about what they did."

A vision of a holding cell flashed through Kevin's brain at that moment, his angry father standing outside the bars, telling the cops to keep his son for all he cared. He blinked and looked over at Andy. He couldn't understand how this was happening. How did his kid end up like him?

Another father stepped through the front doors. Kevin moved aside as the man marched straight to his daughter, grabbed her by the arm, and stood her up.

The girl wobbled. Her father started in on her. "What do you think you were doing? Do you know what you've done to your mother and me? Do you know how embarrassing this is?"

Mr. Johnson walked out of Ned's office with his freckle-faced boy on his heels. Ned came to the door behind them. He nodded at Kevin, but before he could say anything the girl's father turned on him.

"How dare you arrest my daughter? She's never done anything wrong in her life. This is ridiculous. She was just in the wrong place at the wrong time."

"Would you come into my office, Mr. Cleary?" He looked at the girl. "You too, Vanessa."

The young cop stepped closer to the office door without leaving it and gave Kevin a long look that made him uncomfortable. It was a cop look, that running up and down of the eyes, as if the man suspected him of something. Kevin could see his nametag now. Rivers, Jerry Rivers. Kevin met the man's eyes, and he looked away, studying the kids still sitting on the bench.

Kevin's leg was starting to ache, so he walked over and motioned for Andy to scoot down, then sat beside him.

"Hey, Dad."

"You drunk, Andy?"

"Probably."

"How much did you have?"

"I don't really know; it was punch."

"Punch? Damn, boy. If you're gonna drink, you ought to at least drink like a man. What was in the punch?"

"Orange juice, vodka, Mountain Dew, Piña Colada mix, grape Kool-Aid and rum."

"Dear God, how could you even drink that?"

The boy shrugged his bony shoulders. "Lots of kids threw up."

"Lots? How many kids were there?"

"Must have been fifteen."

"Did all of them end up here?"

"Some of them left before it got out of hand."

He sighed. "I'd really prefer that you not drink; you know that."

The other boy on the bench snickered. Andy turned and glared at him, and the boy went white and shut his mouth. Kevin wondered what his son was doing to people that they would be this afraid of him.

Andy tucked his feet in and sat up now, staring at the floor. "You gonna tell Mom?"

"Guess we'll have to."

"I think I'm going to be sick."

"Bathroom's that way." Kevin grabbed his son's arm and headed him in the right direction as yet another irate father came into the hall.

CHAPTER 32

There was only one other kid on the bench when Ned came out and motioned to Kevin. "Come on in, Kevin." He looked at Andy. "You, too."

Kevin walked into the office and sat in the visitor's chair. He glanced at his watch. Three in the morning. Yikes. He focused on the man on the other side of the desk. McKenzie looked like he was going to fall asleep at any minute. The chief glanced over at the younger officer, still standing by the door.

"Jerry, would you get me a cup of coffee, please?"

"Sure."

"Kevin, you want any?"

"No, thanks."

Ned sighed. "I don't know where to begin. The story at this point is that one of the kids was home alone for the weekend. His parents were away, and he decided to have a party. They're all around the same age—fifteen, sixteen years old. The booze was in the house, I guess." He looked down at his desk.

"You going to charge the parents?"

"It's not a crime to leave your sixteen-year-old home alone."

"Endangering the welfare of a minor?"

"I don't know, Kevin. Anyway. Your boy was there, that's why you're here." He took the mug of coffee from his associate.

"So, you charging my boy with anything?"

McKenzie shook his head. "I just wanted to bring them in; scare them a little. Let them see how angry their parents would get."

He met Kevin's eyes. "You won't do anything you'll regret when you get the boy home, right?"

Kevin resented the implication. "No, sir."

McKenzie turned to Andy. "Would you mind if I talked to your dad alone for a minute?" Something flashed through Andy's eyes. He got up and left the room. McKenzie leaned back in his chair, fiddling with a pen, and looking at something behind Kevin, rather than at him.

"Kevin, I want you to know your son tried to trade you for his freedom. He thought he was going to be in deep enough trouble that he'd need a get-out-of-jail-free card."

Kevin swallowed. "What do you mean, trade me?"

"He said you're wanted on a fugitive warrant from New York. Said you escaped from prison in January."

"Did you believe him?"

"I've never seen anything that would lead me to believe him. And he was pretty drunk." He paused, looking down at the desk. "So, no, I guess I don't believe him."

"Thanks for letting me know."

McKenzie got to his feet. "Thanks for coming in."

Kevin faced down Cindy in the morning, sitting at the table, sucking on a cup of coffee.

"So what do we do now? I mean, you've already taken away his car, and he's lost all his other privileges. What else is there to take away?"

"I'll handle it."

"You'll handle it? Are you kidding? You can't force him to quit."

"I have no intention of forcing him to quit."

"I don't know, Kevin."

"I'll figure something out."

"Give it a try." She got up and went upstairs.

Kevin was washing his car on what promised to be the last warm day of the year, with November approaching. His head came up when he saw the police car coming up the driveway. No lights. No siren. It bothered him just the same. He kept his hands resting on the cloth roof of his car, remembering his cop etiquette, and waited.

Ned McKenzie climbed out, pulled on his cap, and started towards the garage.

"Hey, Ned." Kevin kept his hands where they were, holding them still, ignoring the urge to reach for the new .45 stuck in the waistband at the small of his back. With his shirt off, the gun was going to be obvious if he didn't keep his body turned to the cop. He was only carrying it because he had just taken it out and sighted it in. He was wishing he had put it away before starting the next project.

McKenzie stopped. "Did I ever tell you how much I like this car?" He walked over to it. "What is it, a seventy-four?"

"Yep."

"XKE, right? V12?" He shook his head. "You know how much this thing is worth?"

"Probably about what my wife paid for her Yukon."

"It's a beauty." He walked around to the front. "Funny rubber bumpers, though. What are they for?"

"I think they had to put those on to meet some sort of bumper crash standard."

"You know I read somewhere that Enzo Ferrari called this the most beautiful car ever made."

Kevin shrugged. "What can I do for you, Ned?"

"I just wanted to let you know about some information I picked up from the State Police." He moved his right hand closer to his holstered Glock, just enough to make Kevin's pulse jump.

"Those guys that caused so much trouble with your kid last summer turned up. The bodies were in the house. It took a while to identify them; they were pretty well charred. Two guys from New York. The two of them had what looked like wounds from high caliber rifle rounds, and they both had smaller rounds in the head."

He took off his hat and scratched his head. "The information is only just getting back to me because it's really not my investigation, you know?"

Kevin nodded. He didn't move, didn't know if there was a point to any of this.

"Dog officer told me you have a high-caliber rifle with a scope on it. Said you shot a dog that was chasing your horses. Little tiny dog—moving target—like a pro." Ned put his hat back on and brought his hands together. He rubbed them, made a fist with his right hand, and started hitting the flat of his left palm. "You know the kind of gun I mean? A sniper rifle?"

"I told you I was a sniper in 'Nam."

The cop snapped his fingers. "That's right; I knew I had heard that somewhere."

Kevin started to move his hands off the car.

"I'd be obliged, Kevin, if you would just keep your hands right there."

God, it was starting. "You come out for a purpose, Ned?"

"Just wanted to tell you about the puzzle pieces. Wanted to let you know I'm working it out."

"Is there a reason why you felt compelled to tell me all this?"

"I have a lot of respect for you, Kevin. You're good with kids. You're doing great things on the school board. You've got more people volunteering than have ever come out for anything in this town. People like you. Hell, I like you." Ned paused and looked down at the ground for a moment, then back up. "That's why I felt compelled to tell you."

"This investigation going anywhere?"

Ned shrugged. "Some people are talking about ties to New York, to drugs and gangsters down there. I don't know if I believe it."

"You know I'm retired, right, Ned?"

Ned frowned.

"You know I don't go down to New York anymore, right?"

Ned kind of shrugged his jaw, moving it around as though he had a piece of taffy stuck in his teeth.

"Kevin, I'm just telling you what they said. I'm not jumping to conclusions." He paused. "'Course there was the whole thing with your kid saying you were wanted down in New York, too."

"Do I need a lawyer, Ned?"

"Kevin." The word came out in a sigh.

"Would you just tell me if I need a lawyer? 'Cause I'm standing here in my own driveway, keeping my fucking hands where you can see them, and you're telling me you're just making small talk. Now do I need a lawyer or not?"

"Kevin, we've been friends for a while now." Ned took a deep breath and let it out in a long sigh. "No, you don't need a lawyer."

"Well, I appreciate your telling me all this, Ned. Do you have anything else to say?"

"No, sir. Just watch your six." Ned took off his hat and climbed back into the car, leaving the door open for a second. He leaned out. "You ever consider a long vacation? Maybe go someplace warm?"

Kevin dropped his head to the roof of his car as the cop started the cruiser, turned it around, and rolled down the driveway again.

Cindy was just heading out the door to work when he came out of the pantry with his long gun, scope removed.

"What are you doing?"

"Nothing."

"What do you mean, nothing? What's with the gun?"

He didn't want to go into detailed explanations concerning ballistic evidence, so he repeated himself. "Nothing." No sense making her an accessory. He wondered if he needed to go out to the sandpit and try to dig out all the fired rounds embedded in the bank. But getting rid of the gun was a start. He walked out to the car and set it in the trunk. The handgun had gone into the house before he set it on fire, so that was taken care of.

He looked back to the house to see her frowning at him. A movement in the barn caught his eye then, and he saw Michael standing in the doorway, watching him. He started the car and drove out of the driveway.

He'd gone over every possible alternative. He considered burying it on the property, but they'd find it if he did that. He'd considered dropping it down one of the sewer vent pipes, but he wasn't sure the pipes were big enough. There was no way to trace the purchase of this weapon to him, he'd bought it out of the back seat of someone's car last winter, but the injuries would show at the very least that there was a chance it had been used to kill those two creeps at the drug house, and if it was found in his possession, it would come back to haunt him. He drove his little car to an abandoned quarry in Milford and tossed the rifle out into the greenish water, watched it sink, and walked away.

When he came back he went up to the office to take a look at his paperwork, mulling over the possibilities. South America could be nice this time of year.

Michael was sitting at the computer, staring at something on the screen, his right hand resting on the phone. When Kevin stepped that way, the boy let go of the phone and clicked the mouse in a hurry.

"What're you looking at?" Kevin asked.

"Nothing. Just a web site."

Kevin nodded and went to the closet where his safe was. "Okay."

"Dad?"

"What?"

"What were you doing with that gun this morning?"

Kevin blinked. "I took it to a gun shop to get some work done on it."

"Oh."

"Were you gonna call someone?"

"No, uh, it's not important." Michael stood up and walked out.

Kevin walked over to the computer and looked at it. It wasn't telling him anything. He shrugged and went back to the safe.

When Kevin saw the picture he nearly panicked. He couldn't remember any reporters taking that picture. Hillary's husband had taken it. So how the hell did it end up in the paper?

Cindy walked into the living room. He looked up at her.

"Goddamn," he said. He handed her the paper and went up to his office, wanting a cigarette. He was still rummaging through the desk, looking for one, when she came in.

"It's not that bad, is it?" Her face was white.

"Yeah, it is. You know how many people are going to see that fucking picture?" He looked at her, wondering if he should hand her a quarter. "Sorry." No cigarettes. He had been serious this time when he said he was quitting.

"It's a small paper."

"It's not that small. It comes out of Concord. It has a pretty big circulation. How the hell did they get that picture?" There's another twenty-five cents. He picked up the phone and put it down. He headed out of the office and down the stairs, started opening cupboards, looking for the phone book. Michael walked into the kitchen while he was searching. Kevin turned towards him, desperate. "Do you know where the fucking phone book is?"

Michael backed up.

Kevin opened another cupboard, and a cascade of plastic containers fell on his head. "Goddamn it, it's booby trapped. It's like fucking Vietnam. Oh, hell." He sat down at the kitchen table and put his head in his hands.

Cindy walked into the room and opened the drawer by the phone, pulled out the phone book, and handed it to Kevin.

He dialed the phone. "Hillary?"

"Yes."

"It's Kevin, Kevin Winterling."

"Did you see the picture in the paper?"

"Yes, I did. You didn't tell me it was going to be in the paper. You said it was just for the town, remember?"

"Well, when I talked to the reporter who was doing the story, she wanted a picture, and I remembered that one and thought it was perfect. Is there a problem?"

"Not yet. It's okay. Sorry to bother you." He hung up the phone and let his head hit the desk hard.

"Why don't you take a vacation?" Cindy asked as she walked in to the office. He knew she meant go on the run again.

He looked up. "Can't. Basketball season is just getting off the ground. My kids have a shot at the State championship this year. I don't want to let them down."

"Kevin." She walked around the big desk and put a hand on his shoulder.

He looked up at her.

"If something comes of this, I want you to make me a promise."

"What?"

"You won't fight. You won't get hurt. I don't want you to end up like that Diallo guy. I don't want a gunfight here." She paused as a tear ran down her cheek. "You'll take your punishment, you'll serve your time, and you'll come home to me. In one piece."

He closed his eyes and turned his head. He loved her, loved her more than anything else in the world, but he didn't know if he could promise this. He felt her hand on his chin. She turned his head back towards her.

"Look at me and promise me this one thing, Kevin. I've never asked you for anything this important before, but I need this from you."

He opened his eyes and looked into hers, her deep green eyes, with the tears welling in them. Oh, hell. How did he get to this point, how did he allow himself to get so attached to another human being? "All right. I promise."

Michael sat in front of the computer in what had become his father's office and stared at the web site. Not much had changed since he had last looked at it. One of the guys in the top fifteen had been captured. Michael clicked on the one he cared about, the one listed under major cases, and reread the poster. "Markinson is wanted by the Northern District of New York, based on an arrest warrant issued by the Clinton County sheriff's office ..."

He stopped reading to stare at the photo again. His eyes were burning, and he had to swallow hard. He didn't know if he really wanted to do what he needed to do. Every time he closed his eyes, he could see his father firing that little pistol into the heads of those kids. They were just kids, not much older than Andy. What was to stop his father from doing the same thing to Andy if he felt threatened by him?

There was an 800 number at the bottom of the poster, right after the warning in bold capital letters, "Do not attempt to apprehend this person yourself. He should be considered armed and dangerous. Report any information to the nearest USMS District Office or call…"

Michael picked up the phone and punched in the numbers.

CHAPTER 33

Sally punched in the numbers and waited, then worked her way through the levels until she got to the man she wanted to talk to.

"This is Ned McKenzie. What can I do for you?"

"This is Sally Barnard. I'm a deputy US Marshal down in New York. I'm on the New York State joint fugitive task force, and I have reason to believe there might be a fugitive living up there that I've been looking for."

"In my town?"

"Yes, sir."

"What's his name?"

"Kevin Markinson."

Silence. "Chief McKenzie? You still there?"

"Yeah, I'm here."

"He's in his late forties, six and a half feet tall. Got two sons, they'd be teenagers. He killed a cop."

Silence again. She prodded. "Does it sound familiar?"

"Maybe."

"What do you mean, 'maybe?'"

"I guess it's possible."

"I'm going to make arrangements to get up there myself. Don't say anything to Markinson that might scare him away, okay?"

"You don't want me to arrest him?"

"Chief McKenzie, this man is dangerous. He killed a cop; he's assaulted two corrections officers during escapes. You don't need to be going up against him alone."

"Yes, ma'am."

"I'll be there as soon as I can, okay?"

"Yes ma'am."

———————

Sally sat in her boss's office, making the case for a trip to New Hampshire. "You remember a guy I brought in last summer? Kevin Markinson?"

"Tall guy, real thin, eyes like ice? Quiet type, the kind that'd blow your head off without thinking about it?"

"Yeah, that's the guy."

"What about him?"

"We got a tip. Somebody called the New Hampshire office, claims to have seen him. Recognized him off a poster I sent up there or something. The New Hampshire office called me, because they knew I was looking for him. Knew I had history with him."

"Oh, come on, people are always calling with these kinds of tips. Ninety-five percent of them are crackpots." He picked up a spongy ball and started squeezing it.

"I did some follow-up on this, sir. The tipster told them the town where he lives. We traced the tip, and it came from the same town. The police chief in that very same town believes that Markinson may indeed be living there."

"Why hasn't this constable turned him in before now?"

"He said he wasn't sure."

"And you want to fly all the way up there and check this out?"

"I want a shot at this collar."

"All right, Sally, but if this is a wild goose chase you owe me. Understand?"

"Yes, sir."

"Be careful."

"I know this guy's history."

"I know. But you have to remember that he's probably looking at life without possibility of parole. He may not want to come in."

"Yeah."

"Don't take any unnecessary chances."

She stood up. "Don't worry about me; I can take care of myself. I'm a big girl now."

She was back on the phone with McKenzie that afternoon. "I want to do this in the middle of the night; it's the best way. Two in the morning, we go in with a battering ram, and we take him down. No shots fired."

"I don't think that's a good idea. He's got a wife and two kids. At the very least you're going to scare the hell out of them. At worst, they can get in the way, and get hurt. Do it during the day when the kids are at school."

Sally paused. "Do I need a team for this guy?"

"No, ma'am, I don't think you do. I could walk in there now and get him to come in."

"You think so, huh?"

"Yes. He's going to be here Tuesday night for a school board meeting. You could take him down then, except that it would embarrass the hell out of everyone."

"All right. We'll do it your way, nice and quiet. I'm bringing backup though."

"Okay."

"I'll see you Wednesday then."

"Right."

It was cold. Winter had come overnight somehow. The ground was pretty well frozen, but the pond wasn't safe enough to walk on yet. Kevin dragged the maul and the sledgehammer out of the garage. He was wearing a denim barn coat over a heavy flannel shirt, flannel-lined jeans, leather gloves, and steel-toed boots. All brand new clothes that made him look like some sort of country bumpkin. He was determined to make this work, though, to fit in here.

The boys were both at school. They should be getting home soon; it was an early release day. Cindy was in the kitchen, doing dishes. She'd let the housekeeper go now that Kevin was here full time.

He liked to split wood. This was a new skill for him, but he enjoyed it. It was quiet, and it was no-brain work. He could think. Thinking had never been one of his favorite things, but lately he felt he needed the time. It was hard to talk to his two boys, and he needed to work it out.

The basketball thing was good; it helped. At least Andy was talking to him now, even if it was only about basketball. The drug stuff was over; at least he assumed it was. He was keeping a close eye on Andy, watching for the signs, and keeping him under his thumb. He set up a log, raised the maul, and brought it down with a grunt. He picked up the pieces, tossed them aside, and grabbed another log. It was hard physical work, and he was sweating in a few minutes. He pulled off the coat and tossed it aside.

His birthday was coming in a couple of weeks. God. Forty-seven years old. He didn't know how he'd managed to get so old. Thanksgiving was coming, too, just a few days after his birthday. Cindy wanted to invite her mother. He could picture how well that would go.

He set up another log and brought the maul down hard on it. If he had to, he'd run soon. After things settled. After the holidays. Maybe go to South America. Europe would be good; it was easy to lose himself there. He thought about the logistics. He already had the passport. The hard part would be leaving the family again. He knew Cindy wouldn't want to go with him. There was no way the kids could go. He raised the maul again, and brought it down on another log.

Maybe he could just move somewhere else in the country. He wasn't sure the family would put up with that either. Michael was happy where he was; Andy only had one more year of high school after this year. He wouldn't want to leave. He continued thinking as he fell into the rhythm of wood chopping. Set up a log, raise the maul, bring it down, and toss the pieces. Set up a log, raise the maul, bring it down, and toss the pieces.

He raised his head as a flock of Canada geese flew over in a lopsided vee. *Heading south. Smart birds.* A domestic run might not work out. There was always the chance that some idiot who wanted to be a hero would recognize him from that stupid TV show, or even, Christ, off the FBI web site. Why did they bother with him? Almost a whole year now he'd been out, hadn't bothered anybody. Well, maybe a couple of drug dealers. But still, there had to be other, more violent criminals out there for them to spend their time chasing.

Set up a log, raise the maul, bring it down, and toss the pieces. He paused for a moment, looking at the pile of split wood. Have to pick those up and take them over to the house. Every part of his body he had ever injured was hurting. He gritted his teeth, bent over, and grabbed a chunk of wood.

He heard cars in the driveway and turned to see who it was. The first car was the police chief. The second was a black police package SUV with government plates. He felt his stomach flip and considered the options. He wasn't sure there were any. He let the piece of firewood drop, and it hit his foot. *Fuck.* Ned McKenzie got out of his car in front of the house, about ten yards from where Kevin was standing. Between him and the house. The other car stopped behind McKenzie's.

"Hey, Ned." Kevin's voice rasped as he spoke. He took off his cap and scratched his head, then pulled the hat back on. He twisted his head around, scanning for an escape route. The guns were in the house. He could run for the woods, if he could run at all, which was doubtful.

"Hey, Kevin." McKenzie's hand was on his holstered pistol. He unsnapped the strap, and Kevin's pulse jumped.

Two people got out of the car behind the police chief. The first one looked familiar. Short, with red hair, wearing blue jeans and a blazer. Kevin recognized her right away. The coat was open, and her hand was on her holstered semi-auto—looked like a Glock—worn strong side, on the left. He remembered she was left-handed and wondered why he remembered things like that. She wore a big silver star on her belt. The man wore a blue windbreaker with the word "Police" in yellow letters on the sleeves. He was stockier, with a military short haircut.

"What are you doing, Ned?" Cindy's voice came from the porch. She was wiping her hands on her pants as she moved to the steps.

"Go inside, Cindy." Kevin's voice was firm. His eyes never left the three cops in the driveway.

"No."

"I need you to come with me, Kevin," Ned said.

"You and your kids were here for dinner a couple of weeks ago, man. What are you doing?" Kevin took the splitting maul with both hands, letting it stay on the ground, but wishing it was something with a little more bang. Wishing he had thought to carry something. *How the hell had he let himself get so lazy?*

Ned set his jaw and walked towards Kevin.

"Watch yourself, officer," warned Barnard.

The man in the windbreaker turned to the Suburban, produced a shotgun from inside the SUV, and leveled it at Kevin.

"Kevin." Cindy was pleading now.

Ned shook his head. "Don't make it worse than it already is. You got a gun on you, Kevin?"

I wish to hell I did, he thought. "Do I need a gun when I'm splitting wood in my own front yard?" Kevin let go of the maul. "I know almost everybody in this town. I've been here for nearly a year." *Member of the fucking school board, for chrissake.* "Never had anything to fear until now."

He backed away from the splitting tools, tensing his muscles. He turned to the woods, his hands well away from his body, and really wished he could still run like he had when he was seventeen. *Worth a try, wasn't it? Run a pattern; dodge the bullets; it's not far to the woods.* But he had made that stupid promise to Cindy. He moved his hands towards his pockets, suddenly cold in just his shirtsleeves.

"US Marshals, get your hands up now!" Sally barked, pulling out her gun. The deputy in the windbreaker racked the shotgun, and Cindy gasped.

"You run, and I'll shoot you. You know that," the familiar deputy continued.

Kevin looked at the police chief without raising his hands, but keeping them clear of his body.

"You call these guys?"

Ned didn't meet his eyes. "I didn't call them, Kevin. They came to me. Somebody called them, but it wasn't me."

"Chief McKenzie, I think we can handle it from here," Sally said.

"Okay, Deputy Barnard." The police chief backed away with a shrug.

"Get your hands up, Markinson!" Sally Barnard continued to approach her fugitive, two hands on her Glock, arms out in front, sighting down the barrel.

"We can do this the easy way, or we can get out the Taser."

Kevin raised his hands above his head.

"You led them here?" he asked McKenzie, his eyes hard on the police chief's face.

"Get your hands behind your head, Markinson." Barnard kept coming, still holding the pistol in both hands.

Kevin shifted his gaze from Chief McKenzie to the Deputy Marshal and back. Then he clasped his hands behind his head.

"On the ground," Barnard growled. "On your face. Spread your arms and legs."

The Marshal with the shotgun came towards him now, aiming at him.

"Do you really have to do that?" McKenzie asked. "I don't think he's that dangerous."

"I'm not armed." Kevin was starting to shiver and wanted nothing more than to curl into a ball.

"I've been chasing this man for more than a year, Chief McKenzie; I think I can tell whether or not he's dangerous." She pulled out a pair of handcuffs with her right hand while holding the gun with her left.

Kevin got stiffly to his knees. He was getting too old for this.

"You have to get on your face, Markinson. I mean it."

Kevin was trying to figure out how to get down from his knees onto his face without moving his hands from behind his head. He put an elbow out and let himself down onto it, then brought the other elbow down, and started to lower himself to the ground. He twisted his head to watch as Deputy Barnard stepped up to him, tucking away her weapon. She pushed him down flat on the ground and his face met the driveway.

"Fuck you," Kevin snarled as he spat gravel out of his mouth, tasting blood. He twisted his head around, trying to catch a glimpse of Cindy, wanting to make sure she was still all right. He wished she wasn't here at all. He didn't want her to see this, didn't ever want her to see him like this.

Barnard handcuffed Kevin, did a quick search, and tugged him to his feet. "You have any weapons I should know about?" He shook his head, and she motioned to the other deputy. "Marco, you want to pat him down?"

Kevin looked at Cindy while the deputy searched him. He was shivering hard now, barely able to stand, adrenaline coursing through his system. She met his eyes, looking at him so that he could read her lips.

"You remember your promise. You stay safe."

He nodded and turned away, tripping over a chunk of wood in the driveway, almost falling. Somebody needed to clean this stuff up. Who was going to split wood if he wasn't here?

The second deputy pulled him up, yanking hard on his left arm, which caused Kevin to grunt in pain.

Cindy stepped closer.

"Where's he going?" she asked.

"Back to New York."

"I'll find out what I can, Cindy," McKenzie said as he opened the door to his car. "I'm really sorry about this."

"Follow us back to the station," Barnard said as her partner threw the shotgun back in the Suburban. She stretched up to put her hand on top of Kevin's head and helped him into the rear seat of the police car, buckled the seat belt around him, and climbed into the front.

Kevin stared out the window. His stomach was churning. The violent shivering continued, and he was sure he was going to throw up. From the smell of the car, somebody else had done that in here already. He took a deep breath and let it out in a long sigh as the cruiser started to creep down the driveway. Then he saw Andy and Michael. The boys were standing next to the driveway, jaws slack. Oh, God, how much of this circus had they seen? They must have just gotten home from school. Michael dropped his backpack, and Kevin closed his eyes as the car slid past his kids, not wanting to look at them. Almost a whole year of normal... shot to hell.

CHAPTER 34

The deputy marshal turned around in the seat to look at him. "We've done this before, haven't we?"

Kevin stared out the window. "You could have left me alone. I wasn't hurting anyone."

"I'm just doing my job," she said.

"Calling it your job doesn't make it right."

"Quoting movies now?"

Kevin shrugged.

"I am so glad you didn't put up a fight."

Kevin set his jaw and opened his eyes to stare out the window. "No point in wasting energy."

"That's a new attitude for you." She paused. "You're a hard man to track down, you know that?"

"That's what I wanted."

"Sorry to have to haul you away in front of your wife and kids. Those boys were supposed to be in school."

"It doesn't matter." He watched the dark pine trees roll away on either side of the car. He could feel blood running down his chin. "So, you on the fugitive task force or what?"

"Yeah. I asked to be on the task force."

"You're obsessed."

She laughed. "Maybe, but it's not *all* about you. I head up the Marshals service side of the New York joint fugitive task force."

Kevin nodded, trying to wipe his chin on his shoulder. "So where are we going?"

"We go back to the town hall first. Then you're going to the state prison for the night. You'll have a hearing in the morning."

McKenzie glanced at the deputy, frowning.

They pulled up in front of the town hall and Kevin was surprised to see satellite trucks and newspaper vans parked in the street.

"You're news, eh?" Sally said.

"You guys call them?" Kevin asked.

"Not me. My boss maybe or the New Hampshire office. Catching someone like you is a big accomplishment for us." She sighed. "I hate dealing with these sharks though." The cars stopped, and the reporters converged on them. The deputy in the windbreaker got out first and came up to their car, then Sally and McKenzie got out. They shouldered the crowd away and dragged Kevin out of the car.

"Excuse us, please!" shouted Sally, pulling herself up to all of her five-foot-two-inch height.

"Can you answer some questions for us?" asked one reporter, pushing her microphone at the deputy.

Kevin straightened up and glared at her. The two Marshals tugged on him now, one on each arm. Chief McKenzie elbowed his way through the crowd ahead of them, clearing a path.

"Is this Kevin Markinson?" asked one reporter.

"Is it true he's been living here peacefully for years?" asked another.

"We need to get this prisoner inside; then we'll answer some of your questions, okay?" Sally responded.

Kevin felt a twinge of panic as the crowd started to close in around them. He pulled back against the marshals, testing the handcuffs, and wondering if he could slip them. He used to be able to do that, slip cuffs and disappear.

"Don't blow it, Markinson; just keep moving," Sally hissed in his ear. "You try that Houdini shit with me, and I'll shoot you. You know that."

Kevin scanned the crowd, and saw faces he knew, people drawn by the news trucks. There were kids just getting out of school—kids he had coached in basketball—with their eyes as big as saucers. He let his shoulders slump and walked into the little town hall.

"You got a holding cell in this place, McKenzie?" asked Sally.

The town clerk poked her head out of her office. Her jaw dropped when she saw Kevin. "Mr. Winterling?" she asked, staring.

Kevin nodded at her. "Mrs. Lewis." He stopped for a second. "Guess I'll be missing the school board meeting next week."

"It's probably best to just stay in your office, ma'am," said Sally as she pushed Kevin forward.

"Keep moving," muttered the man in the windbreaker.

McKenzie motioned to the basement. "We've got a cell down here. Haven't used it in a while."

"He's officially in your custody. You need to run his prints, just to make sure we've got the right guy. Then lock him up." Sally handed Kevin off to Ned, who started to lead him into his office.

"Chief McKenzie, can I have my cuffs back?"

"Yes, ma'am." Ned removed the cuffs and handed them off.

Kevin rubbed his wrists and touched his lip. His finger came away bloody, so he used his sleeve to dab at it.

Ned spoke to his officer. "Jerry, can you get this man's prints for me while I get him some medical attention?"

Jerry nodded, slapped his own cuffs on Kevin, and directed him into the front office, while the two deputy marshals headed out the front door.

———

Kevin was sitting on a lumpy mattress on a metal cot, his feet up, and back against the concrete block wall. He was drumming his fingers on his leg, as he stared at the cop sitting outside the cell. The officer sat tipped back in an ancient wooden chair, staring at something on the wall above Kevin's head. Kevin dabbed his sleeve at his mouth again, trying to get his lip to stop bleeding.

His brain was in overdrive. He didn't know how she was going to get along without him. She couldn't split wood, could she? And the boys. He would never have wanted them to see him like that, in the back of a cop car. He wondered how badly it would scar a kid to see his father hauled away in chains.

This place smelled funny, all mold and damp, with just a touch of heating oil. It took him a minute to notice the other two people standing out in the hallway. One of them was Cindy. He stood up and shuffled to the door, trying to keep his unlaced boots on his feet.

"Come to get me out?" he asked, knowing that was a stupid question.

She shook her head. "No. I talked to Harvey Longwood."

"Any good news?"

She looked at the floor. "No. Harvey said something about a persistent felony offender."

"What does that mean?"

"He thinks they'll throw the book at you. This was your third felony escape."

"Felony, eh?" He wondered when she had become so comfortable with that kind of language. He sighed, walked back over to the cot, and sat down. "Life, then."

She nodded. "That's what Harvey thinks. Life without parole. He says he can try to talk them down, looking at your age and all." She paused. "He did say you're not exactly nonviolent."

"They'll probably send me someplace bad."

"Harvey said probably Attica at this point."

"Attica. Dear God." He looked up at her now. "I don't know if I can do that, Cindy, if I can do that kind of time anymore." He'd heard about the special housing unit up there. Twenty-three hours a day alone in a tiny cell.

"You can do it. You do it just the way you do anything else. One day at a time. You take it in small doses."

He shook his head.

"You can do it for me."

"I can't. I can't spend the rest of my life like this."

She dropped her voice. "I need you alive, Kevin."

"I can fight extradition."

She shook her head. "It's not worth it. You know they'll just ship you out anyway. Harvey said you'll have an extradition hearing in the morning. He said not to fight it; it'll look better to the New York District Attorney if you don't."

He looked down at the floor. "Didn't work out quite the way we planned it, did it?"

"We had a little time, Kevin."

"Guess I should have taken that vacation after all."

"I wouldn't have asked for that promise if I had known."

"I know. It doesn't matter."

"You want me to take your stuff?"

"Yeah." He nodded at Jerry. "He took my watch, my belt, my shoelaces, and my cash."

Jerry nodded. "No problem." He got to his feet and spoke to McKenzie. "I'm gonna go see if the EMTs are here yet, okay?"

Ned nodded. "Good idea."

Kevin sighed, and then looked at Ned. "Did you know? Know who I was?"

"No." He cleared his throat. "Can you just answer one question for me?"

Kevin got to his feet and came back over to the door.

"Did you kill those kids at that old farm? Those drug dealers? Was that your work?"

"No." No hesitation, no blinking, no turning away. Meet the man's eyes and lie to him.

Ned lowered his eyes. "Okay."

Jerry came back and handed Kevin an ice pack wrapped in brown paper towels. "Here. Put that on your lip. The EMTs are on their way."

McKenzie turned to the stairs. "We better go now, Cindy."

She looked at Kevin. He turned away, not wanting to look at her. "I'm going, Kev."

"Take care of yourself. And the boys."

"I love you."

"I know."

"Kevin." Her voice was imploring.

He nodded, holding the ice on his lip. "Love you, too." He shuffled back to the cot and flopped down. No sense wasting energy on an impossible situation.

KEVIN MARKINSON WILL RETURN IN

- STRESS FRACTURES -

ALSO FROM J.E. SEYMOUR

Blackbird and Other Stories: A Kevin Markinson Anthology

"Mickey Takes a Dive," short story in *Live Free or Die, Die, Die,*
an anthology of New Hampshire noir

"Lights Out," short story in *Quarry,*
an anthology of crime fiction by New England writers

"The Big Bash," short story in *Deadfall,*
an anthology of crime fiction by New England writers

"Life's a Beach," story story in *Windchill,*
an anthology of crime fiction by New England writers

COMING SOON FROM J.E. SEYMOUR

Stress Fractures
(Kevin Markinson Series, Book 2)

Frostbite
(Kevin Markinson Series, Book 3)

WWW.JESEYMOUR.COM

J.E. SEYMOUR

J.E. Seymour lives in a small town in seacoast New Hampshire. Her first novel, *Lead Poisoning* was originally released in November 2010 and reissued in May 2014 by Barking Rain Press. Ms. Seymour has also had a number of short stories published in anthologies—*Live Free or Die, Die, Die, Windchill, Deadfall*, and *Quarry*, as well as *Thriller UK* magazine, and in numerous ezines including *Shots, Mouth Full of Bullets, Mysterical-E, A Twist of Noir, Beat to a Pulp, Yellow Mama* and *Shred of Evidence*. The markets coordinator for the Short Mystery Fiction Society, Ms. Seymour is also a member of Sisters in Crime and Mystery Writers of America. Find out more about J.E. Seymour at her website, Facebook page or on Twitter.

WWW.JESEYMOUR.COM

ABOUT
BARKING RAIN PRESS

Did you know that five media conglomerates publish eighty percent of the books in the United States? As the publishing industry continues to contract, opportunities for emerging and mid-career authors are drying up. Who will write the literature of the twenty-first century if just a handful of profit-focused corporations are left to decide who—and what—is worthy of publication?

Barking Rain Press is dedicated to the creation and promotion of thoughtful and imaginative contemporary literature, which we believe is essential to a vital and diverse culture. As a nonprofit organization, Barking Rain Press is an independent publisher that seeks to cultivate relationships with new and mid-career writers over time, to be thorough in the editorial process, and to make the publishing process an experience that will add to an author's development—and ultimately enhance our literary heritage.

In selecting new titles for publication, Barking Rain Press considers authors at all points in their careers. Our goal is to support the development of emerging and mid-career authors—not just single books—as we know from experience that a writer's audience is cultivated over the course of several books.

Support for these efforts comes primarily from the sale of our publications; we also hope to attract grant funding and private donations. Whether you are a reader or a writer, we invite you to take a stand for independent publishing and become more involved with Barking Rain Press. With your support, we can make sure that talented writers thrive, and that their books reach the hands of spirited, curious readers. Find out more at our website.

WWW.BARKINGRAINPRESS.ORG

Barking Rain Press

ALSO FROM BARKING RAIN PRESS

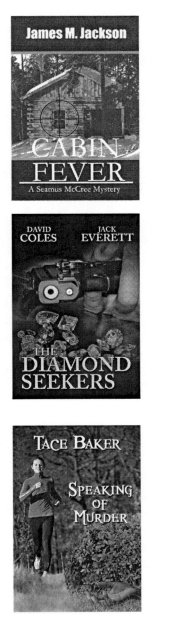

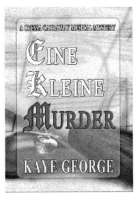

VIEW OUR COMPLETE CATALOG ONLINE:

WWW.BARKINGRAINPRESS.ORG